Tonight the Streets Are Ours

Leila Sales

Farrar Straus Giroux · New York

Farrar Straus Giroux Books for Young Readers
175 Fifth Avenue, New York 10010

Copyright © 2015 by Leila Sales
Printed in the United States of America
Designed by Elizabeth H. Clark
First edition, 2015
1 3 5 7 9 10 8 6 4 2

macteenbooks.com

Library of Congress Cataloging-in-Publication Data
Sales, Leila.
    Tonight the streets are ours / Leila Sales.
        pages cm
    Summary: Seventeen-year-old Arden finds solace in the blog of an aspiring
writer who lives in New York City, but when she goes to meet him, she discovers
that he is a very different person than she believes him to be.
    ISBN 978-0-374-37665-9 (hardback)
    ISBN 978-0-374-37666-6 (e-book)
    [1. Interpersonal relations—Fiction.   2. Conduct of life—Fiction.   3. Family
problems—Fiction.   4. High schools—Fiction.   5. Schools—Fiction.
6. Authors—Fiction.   7. Blogs—Fiction.   8. New York (N.Y.)—Fiction.]
    I. Title.

PZ7.S15215Ton 2015
[Fic]—dc23

                                                        2015003571

Our books may be purchased in bulk for promotional, educational,
or business use. Please contact your local bookseller or the Macmillan Corporate
and Premium Sales Department at (800) 221-7945 ext. 5442 or by e-mail at
MacmillanSpecialMarkets@macmillan.com.

Dedicated to Kendra Levin,
for everything we share

Leila S. Sales | has middle initial that is the same as first letter of last name | Kendra L. Levin

"Sometimes one can realize that a person is unworthy of love and love them anyway; one can form an unexplainable attachment that cannot be broken even when the object of one's affection breaks the confidences with which you entrusted them. Sometimes the one you love is blind to your feelings and for all your conversation you cannot find the words to explain it."

—from *The Thief of Time*, by John Boyne

"Yes, there's love if you want it, don't sound like no sonnet, my lord."

—from "Sonnet," by the Verve

Part One

Welcome

Like all stories, the one you are about to read is a love story.

If it wasn't, what would be the point?

Everything falls apart

*Y*ou can find your own way home," Arden says to Lindsey, her voice shaking with rage.

"Home . . . to Maryland?" Lindsey asks.

The three strangers sitting on mildewing couches beside Lindsey look on impassively. The mannequin's head, which hangs from a noose in the center of the room, sways gently back and forth, like it's making eye contact with Arden, then Lindsey, then back again.

Arden hesitates. "I mean, if you need my help . . ." she begins, but it's too late. Lindsey shakes her head. *No.* "Okay, then," Arden says. "You're on your own. Just how you wanted it."

"What's her *problem*?" the girl with a ring pierced through the center of her nose asks Lindsey, sneering at Arden.

Arden has almost never heard anybody speak about her in that tone of voice. Her stomach twists, and she swallows hard, looking to the boy by her side for support. He nods, and that gives her the courage she needs.

"I'm over this," Arden says to Lindsey. "Good luck finding your way out of here."

She turns and walks away, her legs trembling with every step. She focuses directly in front of her, navigating through the press of bodies and random sculptures of fairies and trees.

"Arden, wait!" she hears Lindsey call behind her, and she turns. But that must have just been her imagination crying out, because Lindsey is still sitting on the couch, talking to the pierced-nose girl, as if everything is normal. As if she doesn't even care that Arden is leaving her.

So Arden squares her shoulders. And she keeps walking away.

Let's go back in time

*T*wo months before that night, back when Arden and Lindsey were still inseparable, when the only septum piercing Arden had ever seen was on punk rockers on TV and the only mannequins she'd encountered had been modeling clothes in store windows, shortly before the end of the school day on a Friday in February, Arden was summoned to the principal's office.

A runner showed up at her Spanish class and briefly consulted with Senor Stephanolpoulos, and Arden paid no attention because when the principal needed someone, it never had anything to do with her. Instead she took this break in the class to try to make sense of her notes, which were supposed to illuminate the future tense, but which in practice just said things like *Irregular verbs . . . something* and *Add "i" or "e" to end of words FIRST PERSON ONLY (??).*

Spanish was not Arden's strong suit.

"Arden." Senor Stephanolpoulos beckoned her. "You're needed in Principal Vanderpool's office."

There were a few "Ooohs" from her classmates, but half-hearted ones; none of them actually believed that Arden Huntley, of all people, would be in trouble serious enough that it would warrant a visit to the principal.

"I'll take notes for you," whispered Arden's friend Naomi. Arden smiled her thanks. Naomi's notes tended to be word-for-word transcripts of teachers' lectures in stunningly legible purple-penned handwriting.

Arden lifted her bag and followed the runner out of the class-room, through a series of halls, and downstairs. Cumberland was one of those towns where land was at the opposite of a pre-mium. It was in northwestern Maryland, so far west it was al-most West Virginia, so far north it was almost Pennsylvania, a solid two-hour drive from the nearest big city (which was Pitts-burgh), in a corner of the world that should have been called something like MaryVirgiPenn, but wasn't. All Cumberland *had* was land. As a result, the high school was sprawling, mega-mall-size—and the principal's office was at the other end of it.

Maybe Arden should have been nervous on that long walk to the principal, but she wasn't. She suspected this had some-thing to do with her mother, and as such, she flat-out refused to care.

Eventually they reached Vanderpool's office, and the runner left her under the watchful eye of Mr. Winchell, the principal's geriatric secretary. Arden waited on a too-small plastic chair that seemed better suited to an elementary school than to Allegany High.

When she thought Mr. Winchell wasn't watching, Arden slid

her cell phone out of her bag and texted Lindsey. GOT CALLED INTO VAN'S OFFICE. WTF.

A minute later, Lindsey texted back. Arden knew that Lindsey should be in Earth Studies right now, so either she was cutting or she was texting in the middle of class, both of which seemed like plausible Lindsey behaviors.

OH SHIT was Lindsey's reply, and that gave Arden her first inkling that perhaps her best friend knew more than she herself did about why the principal wanted her. But before Arden could ask what, exactly, "oh shit" meant, Mr. Winchell snapped, "No telephones!" in the triumphant fashion of a man who has missed his true calling as a prison warden.

After another ten minutes of waiting, Arden was brought in to see the principal. Mr. Vanderpool was a preposterously tall human—so tall that it was easy not to notice how bald he was unless he was seated—who seemed awkward whenever confronted with actual teenagers rather than school board members or faculty. He rarely wandered the hallways and never showed his face in the cafeteria; his one interaction with the student body as a whole was during assembly, when he would stand on the stage and address them en masse from afar. He had a seemingly endless collection of novelty neckties, which was either the one area of his life where he gave himself permission to entertain whimsy or was his sad attempt at appearing kid-friendly. Arden wasn't totally sure that Mr. Vanderpool knew who she was, as this was their first proper conversation in her nearly three years at his school.

"Arden Huntley," he said once she was seated in his office,

on the other side of his desk. "Do you want to tell me why you're here?"

Arden blinked at him. "You called me here, Principal Vanderpool."

He looked pained. "I am aware of that. Do you want to tell me *why* I called you here?"

Arden really wished that Lindsey had said something a little more useful than "oh shit."

"Um, I don't know," Arden told the principal.

He cleared his throat and reached into a drawer in his desk. What he pulled out was a small plastic bag filled with some brownish flakes. "Does this look familiar?" he asked Arden.

"No?"

He sighed. "Arden, we found this bag of drugs in your locker today."

"What were you doing in my locker?" Arden blurted out, even though that was, perhaps, not her most pressing question.

"Routine random locker checks," Mr. Vanderpool replied. "But what I'd like to know is, what was *this*"—here he shook the baggie—"doing in your locker?"

Now Arden knew exactly what Lindsey's text message had meant, and she knew the answer to the principal's question, as well.

She and Lindsey shared lockers, as they shared pretty much everything. Thanks to stupid school bureaucracy and geography, they had been assigned lockers on opposite ends of the building from each other, and from where most of their classes and activities were. So Lindsey usually used the one that was officially Arden's, because it was closer to the gym, while Arden usually stored her stuff in Lindsey's, which was right by the theater and library. They had always known each other's combinations, to school lockers and to everything else, and Arden had seen nothing but benefits to this sort of sharing.

But that was before Lindsey, apparently, stashed a bag of pot in her locker.

Arden knew that Lindsey got high sometimes: weekends, parties, whatever. People did that—not *Arden*, but people, fine. But how could Lindsey have been so dumb, so thoughtless and foolhardy, as to bring it into school? Their school had a zero tolerance policy, a minimum three-day suspension for any student found in possession of any sort of drugs, no matter what kind, no matter what the quantity—though if they were worse drugs, in higher quantities, you risked a longer suspension or even expulsion. Everybody knew this.

But the worst part, for Lindsey, was that getting caught with drugs meant you were immediately kicked off all sports teams for the rest of the year. No way around it. And Lindsey *lived* for the school track team. She loved running roughly as much as Arden hated it. Not only that, but being recruited for track was basically Lindsey's only hope for getting accepted into a good college. She didn't have a whole lot else going for her. This was not, by the way, Arden's opinion. This was the opinion of countless guidance counselors, teachers, and Lindsey's own parents.

Arden knew what would happen if she explained how that bag of marijuana wound up in her locker. Lindsey would lose it all. Over one casual, stupid decision, and one massive helping of bad luck. That sounded about par for the course for Lindsey.

But fortunately, Arden didn't play any sports.

Let's go even further.
Let's go way, way back

When she was nine years old, Arden Huntley was turned into a doll.

It's a very competitive process, to be a doll.

Only one girl gets this honor each year, and there are a lot of rules. She must be between the ages of eight and twelve. She must be a United States citizen. She must write an essay explaining why she thinks she has what it takes to be the Doll of the Year, and she must submit this essay to the Just Like Me Dolls Company by July 1, and if her application is chosen above all the other thousands and thousands of girls who are vying for this honor, then she and only she will have a Just Like Me Doll modeled after her that goes on sale six months later.

When she turned eight, Arden's grandparents gave her the Just Like Me Doll of that year, whose name was Tabitha. Tabitha had brown skin, brown eyes, and brown hair. Tabitha was a ballerina. That was her "thing." They could have given her Tabitha's barre and Tabitha's performance tutu and Tabitha's pointe shoes as well. Instead they just gave her Tabitha herself, in her normal, everyday leotard, and the four illustrated books that told the story of Tabitha's life. Arden would have preferred the pointe shoes to the books, but she dutifully wrote a thank-you note anyway.

Tabitha's first story was called *Tabitha on Stage*, and it was about Tabitha's performing in *The Nutcracker* and how she took a leadership role to get all the mouse dancers to work together. The next one was called *Break a Leg, Tabitha!* and was about how Tabitha helped teach ballet at an underprivileged elementary school. Maybe you are starting to get a sense of what the Just Like Me Dolls' books are like.

Arden didn't know anything about the real-life Tabitha, not even where in the country she lived, but she was fascinated by her. Whenever Arden saw a black girl around her own age (which didn't happen all that often, since Cumberland was overwhelmingly white), she would stare at her, trying to figure out if maybe *this* was the real Tabitha. Then her mother told her this behavior was rude and borderline racist and asked her to please stop.

Arden dreamed of becoming a Just Like Me Doll, but she didn't see how to make that happen, since she, unlike Tabitha, did not have a "thing." She didn't do ballet, or gymnastics, or figure skating (all of which would lead to excellent doll accoutrements). She played soccer but badly, she took swimming lessons but only so she wouldn't drown, she hadn't quite yet gotten the hang of riding a bike without training wheels. She drew pictures that her mother called "abstract" and wrote stories that never got gold stars and got cast as fish number two in her class's production of *The Little Mermaid*. One time she tried to cook something, and she exploded a glass mixing bowl on the stove. After that, her mother banned her from the kitchen.

What Arden did superlatively was this:

She was nice.

She absolutely *killed* at reading buddies—all the kindergartners fought to be paired up with her. She was the first to volunteer to collaborate on group projects with the kids who got bad grades. She was never without a hair elastic or tissues, just in case somebody needed to use them. One time she paid the library twenty dollars because her friend Maya had borrowed a book and lost it somewhere in the park, and that was enough to make Arden feel responsible.

Arden came by her niceness honestly. Her grandmother was nice. Her mother was nice. Her house was filled with wall art and embroidered pillows with quotations like *If you don't have anything nice to say, don't say anything at all* and *Practice random kindness and senseless acts of beauty* and *You become responsible forever for what you've tamed. You're responsible for your rose*—this last one being a quote that her mother loved from Antoine de Saint-Exupéry's *The Little Prince*.

The height of Arden's kindness career came near the end of third grade, though she didn't know it at the time. Her dad had been representing someone who worked for the Disney corporation, and when the case was over, this client had, in gratitude, given Arden's dad family tickets for an all-expenses-paid trip to Disney World. This was easily the best thing ever to happen to Arden, or possibly to anyone.

And then she met Lindsey.

It was a Sunday in May. Arden's brother, Roman, who was three at the time, was throwing a temper tantrum, as he did every single day, sometimes more than once. This particular tantrum was about how their cat, Mouser, was maliciously hiding under the couch instead of playing with him.

Arden escaped to the woods just behind her house so she wouldn't have to listen to the screaming. She brought her Just Like Me Doll with her, even though her parents repeatedly asked her not to do this, since Tabitha had cost more than a hundred dollars and was already, after about five months, looking decidedly worse for the wear.

And it was there, in the woods, that Arden first encountered Lindsey.

She saw a tall, skinny, dark-haired girl in between the trees, focusing on a long metal device in her hands.

"Hi," Arden said to the girl she did not recognize.

The girl looked up from the metal thing.

"I'm Arden," said Arden. "You're in my woods." As soon as she heard the words come out, Arden realized they sounded selfish, and she hastened to add, "It's okay that you're in my woods. There's enough woods to go around. I just thought you should know."

The girl gave Arden a weird look, and Arden wondered about the sentence *There's enough woods to go around*. That was what her mother always said, like when she and Roman got grabby over a pint of ice cream. *There's enough ice cream to go around.* Maybe it didn't make as much sense when it came to woods.

"These are my woods, too," the girl said in a low, uncertain voice.

"I don't think so. But like I said, it's okay. You can play in my woods."

"We just moved in there." The girl pointed to the house behind Arden's. Its backyard abutted the small section of woods, like a mirror image of the Huntleys' own home. "So I think these are both of our woods."

"You're right," Arden said. "We're neighbors!"

Arden learned that the girl's name was Lindsey Matson, and that she was finishing up third grade, too, and that she and her parents had just moved to town from a farm.

"You had your own farm?" Arden demanded. "Did you have sheep?"

"Yup."

"Did you have horses?"

"Two of them!"

"Did you have zebras?" Arden had a particular yen for zebras.

"Um, no."

"That's okay." Arden hadn't really expected Lindsey's personal farm to house zebras. She just thought it couldn't hurt to ask.

Lindsey told Arden that her dad had gotten very sick. He couldn't work on the farm anymore, and they couldn't afford to pay anyone else to do it. So the Matsons sold the farm, they sold the sheep and the horses and everything else, and they moved here.

"It's very expensive to treat cancer. Especially the kind my dad has," Lindsey told Arden, sounding somber but also a tiny bit proud, like her dad was special for having a special kind of cancer. "That's what this is for." She gestured at the long metal object in her hands.

"What does it do?" Arden asked, wondering if the answer was somehow "cure cancer."

"It's a metal detector," Lindsey explained. "I'm looking for coins. Preferably gold. That would help pay for my dad's hospital bills."

"How much have you found so far?" Arden asked.

"Nothing. But I just started looking."

Arden thought if there was gold buried in her backyard, she would probably know about it. She changed the subject. "Are you going to start at Northeast tomorrow?" Northeast Elementary was where she went to school.

"I guess." Lindsey scuffed at the dirt. "I don't really want to make new friends."

Arden didn't quite know what to think of this. She'd never considered whether she wanted or didn't want to make new friends. It was just something that happened. In fact, she was pretty sure it was happening right at this moment. "Everyone at Northeast is really nice," Arden reassured Lindsey. "I'll introduce you to them all tomorrow."

Lindsey looked cheered by this. "Anyway," she said, "it's just for another few weeks, and then it's summer break."

"Yeah!" Arden enthused. "Are you going to camp this summer? I'm going to Disney World for the first time, and then day camp at the Y, and then we're visiting my grandparents in Atlantic Beach in August. They live right on the ocean." Arden was excited for all of this, even visiting her mother's parents, which usually was boring, but now she had hope that they might give her Tabitha's barre and pointe shoes.

Lindsey shook her head. "I wish I could do something like that," she said, "but we can't anymore. We have to save all our money for Dad. That's what my parents say." She shrugged, like *What can you do?*

Arden nodded. She felt bad about her expensive Just Like Me Doll still in her arms, and bad about her secret wish for Tabitha's performance tutu. Probably Lindsey didn't have any Just Like Me Dolls. "I hope you find some gold," Arden said.

Arden thought about Lindsey all the rest of that afternoon, all through dinner and her TV time and her nightly bath. She liked her new neighbor. But she sensed Lindsey's powerlessness, the odds stacked against her like a pile of bricks, and it made Arden sad. If there was one thing Arden never felt, it was powerless. Her mother had always drilled into her, from the time she was a baby, that her power was something that came from inside of her. Her strength was her kindness, her generosity, her positive spirit. "And no matter how bad circumstances get," her mother would sometimes say, "no matter how bleak things might seem, never lose that part of you. If you only have ten cents to your name, give it away to charity.

Being a charitable person will do more for you than ten cents ever could."

Her mother had this idea that some people were like flowers and some people were like gardeners: each needed the other. She prided herself on being a gardener, and though she hadn't much considered it before meeting Lindsey, Arden supposed that she was the same.

By the time her parents came to tuck her into bed that night, Arden knew what she wanted to do. "Can we give the Disney trip to Lindsey?" she asked.

Her parents, sitting on the edge of her bed, exchanged a look. "Who's Lindsey?" her mother asked.

"Her family just moved into the house behind ours, on the other side of the woods," Arden explained. "Her dad is sick, so they can't afford to go on vacation. She can't even go to camp. And she told me she doesn't have any brothers or sisters to play with at home. And she's new to town so she doesn't have any friends. And . . ." Arden shook her head and sat up. She didn't need to explain this to her parents. She knew what she wanted. "I want to give the Disney trip to Lindsey."

She worried that maybe her parents would say no because maybe they had really wanted to go to Disney World. It was her dad's trip, after all. He'd said that Space Mountain seemed like a blast. But when she looked at them now, they were both smiling at her, and her mother's eyes were moist with happiness.

"Okay," said Arden's mom, and, "Okay," said Arden's dad.

That was only the first day of a million days of Arden and Lindsey's friendship, but it established how it would be: Lindsey would need, and Arden would deliver.

After Arden gave away the Disney trip, she wrote an essay about it, and she sent the essay in to the Just Like Me Dolls Company. She didn't really think they would choose her to be the Doll of the Year when they had so many gymnasts and figure skaters and ceramicists and budding chefs to choose from. But she wanted somebody to know what she had done. Plus, she really wanted to be a doll.

A couple months later, her mom got the call. Out of all the thousands of girls between the ages of eight and twelve who had sent in their essays, Just Like Me Dolls had chosen Arden as their winner.

Because Arden was Girl of the Year, she got free copies of her books, with titles like *Arden in Charge* and *Arden's New Friend*. She got a free doll, designed with peach-colored skin and light brown hair and hazel eyes, just like her. She got every single one of the Arden Doll's accessories for free, too: a doll-size tire swing and doll-size metal detector, a doll-size cat and doll-size dog to mimic her own pets. They made it out to seem like Arden spent a lot more time in the woods than she actually did, like she was some kind of budding naturalist when actually she just went out there occasionally, and less so now that Roman's tantrums were less frequent. But the slight inaccuracies didn't bother Arden whatsoever.

She also got a free trip to New York City with her mother to visit the Just Like Me Dolls flagship store once the Arden Doll had gone on sale. It was the first—and wound up being the only—trip that was "just us girls," as Arden's mom put it. Going on this trip without her father or Roman made Arden feel delightfully grown-up.

She had never been to New York before, and she didn't like it at all. The neon lights outside her twenty-first-floor hotel room windows kept her awake at night, and it seemed like every taxi driver was hell-bent on running over not just anybody, but *her* specifically.

But she loved the Just Like Me Dolls Store.

It was right on Fifth Avenue, nestled among the fancy department stores and jewelers, like Tiffany, which Arden recognized from her mother's favorite movie. Much like the streets outside, it was a madhouse inside Just Like Me Dolls. The difference was that this madhouse was caused by hundreds of girls striding purposefully through the store, each trailed by at least one adult, sometimes by a full family, toting coats and bags and matching doll-and-girl clothing and tea party sets. Arden's mother described it as the stock exchange floor of elementary school girls, since they were all marching around shouting, "Buy! Buy!" at their minions.

The Arden Doll was in a Plexiglas display, lined up with the dolls based on real girls of past years. Arden pressed her nose to the glass, as if trying to get closer to her doll. But even there in person, at the Just Like Me Dolls Store itself, nobody looked at the doll and the girl and put two and two together. Not one of the other children or their parents said, "Hey, you both have peach-colored skin and light brown hair and hazel eyes! You must be the real Arden!"

But that was okay, too. Arden didn't need any of these strangers to know that doll was her. *She* knew.

She looked at all the past years' dolls. Each one had a little placard that summed up her identity in a short phrase. There was Tabitha, of course, though without the dirt stains of Arden's version. Tabitha's placard said she was "graceful and inspiring." The Jenny Doll was "brave and committed." Katelyn was "quick-witted and fun-loving." But the Arden Doll's placard described her in this way:

"Arden is recklessly loyal."

Arden looked into her doll's eyes and knew without a doubt that her identity was the best one of all.

For a while there was talk of making a Lindsey friend doll, too, since Lindsey's character was such a big hit in the Arden stories. But within a few months, the idea was dropped, and the Just Like Me Dolls Company moved on to picking the girl of the next year. Lindsey didn't seem to mind. Arden had given her a free vacation to Disney World. And Lindsey had given Arden the opportunity to be a doll.

To both girls, this trade-off seemed more than fair.

Arden gets more than she bargained for

our hours had passed since Arden had been called into Principal Vanderpool's office. Four hours since the principal asked her to explain the baggie of marijuana in her locker. Four hours since she looked him square in the eyes and admitted it: yes, those drugs were hers. Yes, she was guilty.

Now they were both waiting for Arden's father to show up and escort her home. A principal can't just release a known drug user into the world, of course. It can't be done. There are protocols.

When the school day ended, Lindsey came flying into the reception area outside Vanderpool's office, where Arden was sitting, reading a book under Mr. Winchell's watchful eye.

"Oh my God," Lindsey said, flinging herself onto a plastic chair beside Arden's. "I am so, so, so—"

"I'll be okay," Arden cut in, casting an eye toward the eavesdropping secretary. "It's my fault. I'm the *total idiot* who decided to bring drugs into school. I'll bear the consequences."

Lindsey paused. "Are you kidding?" she asked.

Arden shook her head. That was what she had told their principal. Whether he believed her, given her squeaky-clean record, was beside the point. All the evidence pointed toward her. He had a crime, he had a confession, justice would be done.

Besides, why *wouldn't* he believe her? Who would lie about such a thing?

"Wow," Lindsey said, and suddenly she laughed, the carefree laugh of someone who has just been caught by an unanticipated parachute when she thought she was plummeting out of the sky to her death.

But it was Arden's parachute Lindsey was using, so Arden didn't laugh. "Why the *hell* did you bring pot to school?" Arden whispered, so quietly that Mr. Winchell's hearing aid would never make out her words.

"To smoke it?" Lindsey replied in a small voice.

Arden rolled her eyes. "Linds," she said, "go home. Honestly, I've got this."

So Lindsey hugged her, and she went home.

But the longer Arden sat waiting for her father, the school emptying out around her, the less confident she became. The thing was, she didn't *want* to miss three days or more of school; she'd fall behind in everything (especially Spanish). She didn't play any sports, that was true, but she did stage crew—would she be forced to quit that? And what would her classmates think of her after this? Naomi, Kirsten, all of her other friends—not to mention Chris.

But this was selfish thinking. Arden knew she could live

without the spring musical. She could live if she never figured out how to conjugate a single verb in a foreign language. The one thing she couldn't live with was Lindsey's misery.

What had become abundantly clear to Arden over the past month was this: There were people in this world who didn't know how to take care of others. There were people who walked away even when they'd made a promise to stand by you. There were people who threw around the word *love* but only acted on it when it was convenient for them.

And Arden was not one of those people.

It was nearly six p.m. by the time her father finally showed up to collect her. The custodian had already come through the office to take out the recycling and trash, and Mr. Winchell kept shooting Arden death glares, as if it were all her fault that he was still at work at a time when he would have otherwise been already chowing down on the early bird special at Mamma Luciana's Pasta Shack.

When her father arrived, he was wearing his business suit and carrying his briefcase, and he looked annoyed. "What's going on here? Arden, I got two messages at work saying you're in trouble and they're going to be taking 'disciplinary action.' I had to call Roman's after-school teacher and beg her to let him stay late. What on God's green earth is this about?"

He probably got those messages four hours ago, but whatever; Arden was actually impressed he'd made it there before midnight. This may have been the earliest he'd left the office in a month. She felt simultaneously accomplished and ashamed to be the cause of her father's abbreviated workday.

Arden's father was a lawyer. Not a TV-style lawyer, with custom-made suits and luxury cars and multimillion-dollar cases argued in front of the Supreme Court. Arden's dad was the other kind of lawyer, the kind with a small office downtown and his name on a plaque on the door, the kind who sometimes argued in front of the judge at the district courthouse, but who mostly settled out of court. Being that kind of a lawyer wasn't fancy. Still, it was a good job in a town without many good jobs on offer, and it was important. He didn't like for it to be interrupted. So it almost never was.

Mr. Vanderpool ushered them into his office and closed the door. Arden could see Mr. Winchell craning his neck from his desk in reception, trying to keep his eye on the drama.

"Mr. Huntley," the principal began, "I appreciate your taking time to address this situation. As I indicated in my message to you earlier, your daughter has admitted to bringing contraband substances to school and storing them in her locker."

"Can you define contraband substances?" Arden's father asked.

"Drugs."

Arden's father showed no obvious reaction. He didn't sigh, or put his head in his hands, or yell at her. Only a daughter would notice the slight droop in his shoulders, the minor widening of his eyes.

"What classification and quantity of drugs are we talking about here?" he asked in a measured tone, a lawyerly tone.

"An eighth of an ounce of marijuana," Mr. Vanderpool replied.

Arden's father sighed impatiently. It was an on-purpose impatient; Arden recognized that. "That's hardly a criminal quantity. Clearly it's not enough for you to peg my daughter with intent to deal."

Mr. Vanderpool fussed with his flamingo-print tie and rearranged the impressive metal pens on his impressive oak desk. Arden could not understand why he had so many pens. Surely he, like everyone else in modern-day America, did most of his work on the computer.

"I never accused your daughter of planning to sell drugs, Mr. Huntley. But as I'm sure you're aware, we have a zero tolerance policy here at Allegany High. That means no type of controlled substances, of any sort, in any quantity, on school property."

Arden doubted that her father was aware of this particular detail about the rules of her school—he wasn't the sort of parent who sat around at night and read through the school handbook—but he nodded like he was. "Arden"—he turned to her—"is this true? Did you actually bring *drugs* to school?"

Lying to her father was harder than lying to the principal, but both were important. Arden would need to lie to everyone about this, she realized in that moment, and she would do it without breaking. This would be a secret between her and Lindsey and no one else.

"I wasn't thinking," she admitted to her father, lowering her eyes. "I'm sorry."

"This isn't like you," her father said. But his confidence in that statement served only to annoy her, because for all he knew, maybe this *was* like her. Maybe she'd been doing this for years and had just never been caught before today. Arden imagined that was probably what Marie Baker's parents said when she told them she was pregnant two months into junior year, or what Dean Goddard's parents said when he broke a team-mate's nose in the locker room after football practice. *This isn't like you.* As if parents know what their kids are like, day in and day out.

Arden's father turned back to the principal and said, "Look, I agree with you that Arden should be disciplined. And she will be. But I can take that over from here. This is an issue for her parents, not for the school. As I'm sure you're aware, Arden is a responsible student, with a 3.4 GPA, and she is an asset to the Allegany school community with her contributions to the theater program."

Arden twisted in her seat to look at her father. Her GPA was actually 3.5, but he got close, and that alone was surprising. She didn't know he ever looked at her report cards, and he hadn't attended a play she'd worked on in years.

"Furthermore," her father continued, "Arden has difficult ex-tenuating circumstances, which I'm sure are causing her to act out right now."

Principal Vanderpool looked blank and fiddled with his pens. Arden immediately felt bad for him, this man with his sad, trying-too-hard necktie. Somehow he had not been briefed on her extenuating circumstances. Somehow this news had not made it into her file, or whatever Vanderpool had refer-enced before calling her in here, and now he was going to look like he didn't know what was going on with his own students.

Arden spoke up just to spare him the embarrassment. "My mother left," she explained. "Four weeks ago."

The principal's eyes widened. "I'm so sorry to hear that."

Arden could tell he was dying to ask where she went, and why she left, and whether she was ever coming back. The same sort of questions that Arden herself was wondering about, really. He didn't ask, though, maybe because he didn't want to be rude, or maybe because he didn't actually care about the answers as much as he cared about leaving his office and diving headfirst into his weekend. She wondered if he had a special place in his closet for weekend neckties, and, if so, she wondered just how wild they got.

"As you can see," Arden's father said, "this is not Arden's typical behavior. But it hasn't been a typical month for our family."

That was an understatement.

"I hear what you're saying completely, and you're right that this is Arden's first offense," Mr. Vanderpool agreed, going on as though Arden herself weren't actually present in the room with him. "Nonetheless," Vanderpool continued, "a zero tolerance policy means that the school is obligated to respond to her actions with disciplinary action, no matter what her background and circumstances. I've already decided against expulsion—"

"Expulsion!" Arden cried.

Both men looked at her.

"You would actually expel somebody just for having a teeny tiny bit of marijuana in her locker?" Arden demanded. She was starting to get the very bad feeling that when she stepped in to save Lindsey, she had gotten way more than she'd bargained for.

"You would really consider such a severe retribution against a little girl who made a small mistake?" her dad added.

Arden was hardly little, but she shrank down in the big winged wood chair to try to appear like she was.

"As I said, we decided against expulsion. But of course, we must take some action."

And here's what the action was:

Arden would be suspended for three days.

She would no longer be allowed to tutor the underclassmen, lest she expose them to her drug-addled ways.

She *would* be allowed to keep doing theater, provided that she stuck to stage crew and other backstage responsibilities— nothing where she showed her marijuana-owning face on stage.

All of this would go on her permanent record, and when she applied to colleges next year, Allegany High would inform every school that she had a history of drug possession.

"Mr. Vanderpool," Arden appealed to him, feeling her breathing grow shallow, "please don't. I could actually not get into college because of this."

"You know how competitive the college admission game is these days," her father agreed. "Those admissions officers are looking for any reason not to accept a student."

Mr. Vanderpool spread his hands helplessly, as if to indicate *It's out of my control*, which was stupid—of *course* it was in his control, it was *his* decision—and he said, "Arden has always been aware of the school rules. She should have considered the consequences before she decided to break them."

"I can't *believe* you, Arden!" her dad yelled, slamming his

31

palm down on the desk. "You really didn't think this one through, kid."

He was right. She really hadn't. *It's for Lindsey, it's for Lindsey,* she reminded herself, knotting her fingers together in her lap. Her permanent record could take it, probably. Lindsey was going to have a hard enough time getting into college even without this mark against her. Her father could deal with it, probably. Lindsey's parents would have most likely sent her to military school. *It's for Lindsey, it's for Lindsey.*

Arden had just never imagined that when she threw Lindsey a life jacket, she would be drowning herself.

Arden and Lindsey see how the other half lives

"She called again today," Arden told Lindsey. *She* meant Arden's mom. Lindsey, of course, knew this without it being spelled out.

It was ten o'clock on a Friday night, two weeks after the baggie of pot had been found in Arden's locker, and now she and Lindsey were sitting on a futon in Matt Washington's family room, watching an assortment of boys playing Grand Theft Auto.

Arden's suspension had come and gone. After watching every Internet video that looked like it might be interesting, reading two books, and painting her toenails in rainbow stripes, she had spent her remaining prison sentence cleaning the house, which seemed not to have been swept, mopped, vacuumed, dusted, or treated in any other positive way since her mother left. When Roman and her dad came home, she expected them to laud her cleaning skills. She had literally gotten on her knees on the floor and *scrubbed a toilet*. She was essentially a scullery maid. But they did not seem to notice, or, if they did, they kept their noticing very well concealed. And by bedtime, someone had left pee on the toilet seat again.

She had expected her father to have a stronger reaction to her suspension. She'd thought that he might stay home from work for those three days, monitoring her in person to make sure she wasn't running off with her pothead friends or whatever. She'd thought that he might try to talk to her about what issues were plaguing her that might drive her to drugs, that he'd force her into therapy or Narcotics Anonymous. She'd been prepared for all kinds of overreaction, but instead all her dad did was yell at her for a while, search her room for a hidden drug stash, and then pay their neighbor to stop by the house randomly throughout the day to make sure Arden was still there.

Now she felt ridiculous for thinking that she might get anything more out of her father, for thinking that he'd be so easily derailed. She'd even thought her mother might come home to deal with her. That was silly.

Arden had returned to school, where she'd missed basically nothing in her classes—except for Spanish, which seemed to have morphed into an entirely different language in those three days. But her brief suspension had not gone unnoticed, and now gossip was swirling around school that Arden Huntley was actually, under her demure exterior, a badass drug dealer. That rumor was what had led to this unusual party invitation for her and Lindsey.

Actually, the invitation had just been for Arden. Lindsey

rarely got invited anywhere on her own. But where Arden went, Lindsey went, too, an arrangement that everyone seemed to accept without question.

In a different world—a world where Arden's mother was around—there was no way Arden would have been allowed out of the house tonight. Not when she'd been suspended from school two weeks ago. She'd be stuck at home, playing cards or engaging in other family-friendly activities, where her mom could keep an eye on her. But left to his own devices, that was not her father's style. Left to his own devices, Arden's father may or may not have even noticed that she'd gone out tonight.

"I am *so wasted*!" shrieked Beth Page in delight as she crashed into an unforeseen coffee table.

Arden and Lindsey exchanged a glance. They did not usually go to parties where people were *so wasted*. They did not usually go to parties with Beth Page.

"So did you talk to your mom when she called this time?" Lindsey asked.

"Barely."

"What did she say?"

"She said, 'I'm sure you want an explanation for why I left.'"

"And what was her explanation?"

"I don't know. I just told her I wasn't actually curious to hear it, and I gave the phone back to Roman."

"And that was it."

"Yeah." Arden gulped some cranberry juice from her plastic cup. "It's fine. My dad and Roman talked to her. They told her I'm a drug addict. She told them she's subletting an apartment

35

in New York City. We don't need to speak directly to cover any of that."

"New York? Whoa." Arden watched Lindsey process the three hundred eleven miles between Cumberland, Maryland, and New York City. Arden knew it was three hundred eleven miles because when her father had given her her mother's address—133 Eldridge Street, New York, New York—written down on a slip of paper, as if she might want to tack it to her bulletin board or something—she'd looked it up.

As far as she was concerned, when your mother walked out of your life and moved three hundred eleven miles away, you owed her nothing. Not a phone conversation, not an e-mail, not even a spare thought. For Roman to act otherwise was fool-hardy. It was self-destructive. It was ignoring the mom that they had for the mom that they wished she would be.

"I swear," Arden went on, "my brother is like an excitable dog. His neglectful owner walks back through the door and he jumps all over her and drools."

The Huntley family used to have an actual dog, too, until about three weeks after their mother left, at which point Spot died. Roman didn't seem to have figured out that their father had taken their needy old dalmatian to the vet and had him put down because it was too hard to take care of him without Mom there. "Two kids and a cat is quite enough," her dad calmly told her when she confronted him about it. Now they were left with elderly, emaciated Mouser, who quaked with fear when-ever anyone went near her—particularly Mr. Huntley.

Arden wasn't telling Roman that their father was the one who issued the death sentence for their Spot, lest he worry that he was next in line. The argument could be made that no pets *or* kids would be quite enough for someone like their father.

"It's just so weird," Lindsey reflected, "because I always really *liked* your mom. Remember when she used to drive us to school?"

Arden did remember. In sixth and seventh grades, kids on their school bus—some of the same kids who were here at this party tonight, in fact—kept teasing Lindsey. They made fun of her for unexciting, stupid middle school reasons—because she was too tall and gangly, because she didn't know what to wear and didn't seem to realize she was supposed to care. Lindsey was upset, but Arden was miserable: the character of her best friend was under attack, and she felt powerless to protect her.

Arden poured out her heart to her mother, who decided that from then on, she would drive the girls to school. Simple. This didn't mean that all of their classmates suddenly treated Lindsey with respect, but it did mean that she didn't have to start every morning with soda cans getting accidentally-on-purpose spilled on her.

That was just how Arden's mother *was*. She came to the rescue. If Arden was having a problem with a teacher, she solved it. If Roman had a nightmare, she'd curl up in bed right next to him and stay there until morning. If Arden forgot her homework, she would drive it into school for her in the middle of the day. If Roman was trick-or-treating, she handmade him three options for Halloween costumes and let him pick among them. If Arden was having a birthday party, she decorated the entire house. If Roman was doing a book report, she read the book right alongside him and helped him collect materials so that, while his classmates were handing in one-sheet essays, he was handing in a diorama with moving parts.

Arden understood what Lindsey was saying, because she had also liked her mother, at the time.

She couldn't imagine her mother now, renting an apartment in a big city, apparently taking some graduate-level class at an extension school, as her dad had reported. Even though she knew, rationally, that her mom would look the same today as she had six weeks ago, Arden would not have been altogether surprised to discover that her mother had gotten a face trans-plant. She just didn't sound like the same person at all—she sounded like a stranger.

"I don't want to talk about this anymore," Arden said to Lindsey. "We're at a cool high school party, for once. Let's just be cool high schoolers, you know?"

Lindsey snickered and nodded. They both watched as Dillon Rammstein lit up a joint and Matt Washington shouted at him to "Take that shit outside, man." Dillon shoved past the girls' couch to go onto the patio. It was reassuring to know that Matt was such a conscientious host.

"Arden, I love you for not ratting me out to Vanderpool," Lindsey said as they watched Dillon go. "You are the most amaz-ing friend, you know that, right?"

Arden had not told Lindsey how severe the punishment for that decision had actually wound up being, and she was never going to. Of course Lindsey knew that Arden had been suspended for three days—it seemed like every single person in Cumberland knew that. But Lindsey didn't need to know that all of this would be reported to colleges in the fall. What's done was done, and it would only make her feel guilty.

"It's fine," Arden told Lindsey now. "It was weeks ago. Just promise me you will never, ever touch any kind of drugs again. At *least* not until we're in college. Okay?"

"Promise," Lindsey said instantly. "I am officially scared straight. You don't have to worry about me anymore."

Arden half smiled. She would always worry about Lindsey.

A couple feet away from them, Beth Page and Bo Yang fell into a slobbery kiss. Arden watched Bo dribble spit on Beth's chin as she might watch a nature documentary. Arden sighed. "I wish I had that."

"Which part?" Lindsey asked. "A second-string soccer player's hand on your ass, a terrible dye job, or the STD they're currently swapping?"

Arden giggled. "A boyfriend who wanted to come to this party and make out with me. That part."

"At least you have a boyfriend, though," Lindsey pointed out.

"Yeah. And where is he?"

"I'm assuming that's a rhetorical question. Because it's Friday night. So I'm going to put money on Chris being at Kirsten's house, playing some elaborate game of charades right as we speak."

Lindsey was correct. That was what Chris and the rest of the theater crowd did pretty much every Friday night after rehearsal. It was what Arden and Lindsey did most Friday nights, as well, except for the occasions when they hung out with Lindsey's track teammates, who went to bed around the time the sun set so they could get up and go for ten-mile jogs the next morning.

This was a different crowd, here at Matt Washington's house. Nobody seemed particularly interested in playing charades, or any game that didn't involve killing computer-generated prostitutes. And nobody had gone to bed yet.

At rehearsal yesterday afternoon, Arden had tried to get Chris to come with her to this party. "Why would I want to do that?" he'd asked. "I don't even like Matt Washington."

"Because you could study him in his natural habitat," Arden had suggested. "And then someday if you play a character like Matt, you'd know him inside out."

"Did you just call him Matt?" Chris asked. "Are you now on a first-name basis with Matt Washington, just because he invited you to one party?"

"Jealous?" Arden asked.

Chris hadn't graced that with a response. Her boyfriend had his good qualities and his bad qualities, and the fact that he never got jealous of anything she did or any boy she knew fell somewhere in between the two.

"You should go because I'm going," Arden said, which seemed like it should be reason enough. Wasn't that the point of being in a relationship? Having someone to hang out with on Friday night? "I bet we could have some alone time there," Arden had added. She kissed him, trying to hint that "alone time" could involve more things that were similar to kissing. Supposedly boys were very horny and were more likely to do things when those things might involve making out.

Arden's boyfriend, however, seemed to be the exception to that rule. Maybe because he had already made out with her enough times and had gotten bored of it.

"Why do *you* even want to go, anyway? Since when are you friends with that group?"

Arden didn't have a particularly good answer for him. She was just curious, she guessed. Curious about what life was like outside of the bubble of her and Chris's theater friends, who were all the sort of kids who participated in class and went home in time for their eleven o'clock curfews. There was a whole other high school world that was coexisting with her own, and it seemed like that world should be thrilling and vibrant—the exact opposite of her high school world in every way.

Plus, didn't everybody want to go to cool kids' parties? Wasn't that just a generally understood rule of adolescence?

"I'll think about it," Chris had said. That was how they'd left it.

Now, Arden took a Cool Ranch Dorito from a giant wooden bowl, pulled out her phone, and texted him. UR FAVORITE CHIPS R HERE. U COMING?

He did not text back immediately. Maybe a particularly rousing round of improvisational comedy was going down.

Lindsey stood up from the couch. "I just saw Denise go into the kitchen. I'm going to go get a drink and say hi or whatever while I'm in there."

Arden stood, too. "Want me to wingman you?"

Arden and Lindsey had spent a lot of time debating whether Denise was a hundred percent straight or possibly bisexual, and, if the latter, whether Lindsey should ask her out or no. Denise's mere choice to attend this party pointed to "likes guys" with a high degree of certainty; however, Arden reminded herself, everybody could have a different reason for being here tonight.

"I'll be okay," Lindsey said.

Arden just looked at her.

"I'm going to be like twenty feet away from you. What kind of trouble could I possibly get into? Chill."

Lindsey squared her shoulders and went off to casually brush shoulders with her crush. Arden headed outside to the empty patio so she wouldn't just be sitting on the couch looking obviously alone, which was pathetic.

Arden stood with her back to Matt's house and looked out over the landscape, the two-story houses and two-car garages eventually giving way to mountains in the distance. The trees were barren, the stars stark against the sky. Arden checked her phone for a response from Chris. Nothing.

This shouldn't make her feel so sad. She didn't have to spend every weekend night with Chris. So he was busy. So what? She was busy, too. And anyway, she wasn't alone. She was here with Lindsey.

When they were in elementary school, Lindsey and Arden liked to imagine that they would live together when they got older. They planned to buy a house someday. Maybe they would run a bakery out of their shared kitchen. Maybe they would live on a farm, like Lindsey's family used to, and she would feed the chickens while Arden tended to the zebras. (Their imaginary farm obviously had zebras.) Maybe they would adopt some children. Maybe they would marry identical twins and the four of them would live in one big mansion together. One time Lindsey suggested that she and her twin husband could get a separate house, across the street from Arden and her twin husband, and Arden was like, "I don't see why that would be necessary."

Arden didn't know if it made her an idiot or a romantic that this all still sounded like a good idea. Okay, not the twin boys thing because Lindsey was gay, but she'd be down to co-marry a set of fraternal twins.

Misfortune followed Lindsey, and so Arden did, too. In the nearly eight years of their friendship, Lindsey had suffered through her father's battle with cancer, her grandpa's death, getting arrested for shoplifting, getting caught plagiarizing an essay, failing her driver's test, losing her mother's engagement ring—and that was only scratching the surface. Lindsey was dyslexic and so teachers assumed she was just stupid, she was gay in a town whose primary understanding of lesbians came from occasionally watching Ellen DeGeneres, and she had parents who fundamentally believed that both dyslexia and homosexuality were just bad choices that Lindsey had made, probably to piss them off.

Until a month and a half ago, when her own family had so spectacularly collapsed, Arden had led a stable life, compared to Lindsey. Sometimes she'd wondered how she would handle it, if she *could* handle it, if she had Lindsey's same bad luck. Maybe if she faced Lindsey's same problems, she'd make Lindsey's same mistakes.

"Hey, Arden."

She turned at the sound of her name. A guy was standing there. Ellzey. Okay, his *last* name was Ellzey, but that's what everybody called him, even the teachers. Arden's heart quickened as she wondered why he had stepped outside right now when the whole party was indoors, if he'd seen her out here, if he'd been looking for her. For a brief moment, she let herself imagine kissing Ellzey, out here under the stars. She imagined him as a prince in a fairy tale, coming to save her.

Then she kicked the thought away. She was taken. Girls who are taken shouldn't fantasize about kissing boys they barely know on Matt Washington's patio.

"Hey, Ellzey," she said. "What's up?" She wondered if he was going to mention the last time they had spoken—one of the *only* other times they had spoken—and hoped fervently that he was not. It had been an ignoble experience. She felt very glad that Lindsey was missing this conversation now. There was no way Lindsey would have been able to keep a straight face if she'd seen Ellzey talking to Arden.

"Beautiful night, huh?" he said, coming to stand next to her. Even though he didn't touch her, she felt the warmth of his skin from his arm next to hers. "So many stars," he went on.

Arden was impressed. She couldn't help but compare Ellzey to her boyfriend, who had never commented on the number of stars. Unless it was the number of Hollywood stars in a particular movie or something. Arden said to Ellzey, "My dad used to keep a telescope on our roof when I was a kid. He wanted us to learn facts about astronomy, I think, like to identify different constellations. I could never find anything other than the Big Dipper. But I loved looking at the stars." This was, hands down, the most sentences in a row Arden had ever spoken to Ellzey.

"You know what would make the stars even more beautiful?" Ellzey asked, looking into her eyes.

Arden wondered if Ellzey knew that she was taken. She and Chris Jump had been going out for more than ten months, so it seemed like everyone would know, but maybe they didn't. Why would someone from the popular crowd monitor the relationship status of every random girl at school?

"What?" Arden said.

"If we were high right now," Ellzey said.

They were both silent for a moment, as Arden expected him to produce a joint from his pocket or something. He did not.

Then Arden remembered that she had just been suspended for possession of drugs, so presumably she would be the one carrying joints in *her* pockets.

"I don't really do that," Arden said.

"Oh yeah?" He gave her a teasing smile. "You don't have to keep secrets from me, Arden Huntley."

I'm not, Arden thought. "That was just a one-time thing," she explained.

"Oh."

"Sorry."

Ellzey shrugged. "No sweat. Just thought I'd ask."

"About the stars—" Arden began, but Ellzey had already headed back indoors.

Arden's heart sank. That wasn't what she had wanted from

an interaction with Ellzey, not at all. That wasn't what she'd thought he would be like, or what she'd thought she would be like around him. It all seemed wrong.

But then what exactly *had* she wanted, anyway, from Ellzey?

Arden checked her phone again. One text message had come in from Chris while she had been letting down her end of a drug deal. I'M NOT GONNA MAKE IT THERE TONITE. HAVE FUN! LOVE U.

She shouldn't have felt so disappointed. She'd known he probably wasn't going to come anyway. But, there you have it.

Chris had understood, sort of, about Arden keeping pot in her locker because she was "acting out." He understood, he said, that it was really hard to have your mom leave you, and that this might lead someone to rash decisions. Still, Arden sensed that he was judging her. Maybe just because she knew that Chris Jump would never be so foolish as to disrupt his future plans like this, no matter how many parents or other loved ones left him behind.

Her phone buzzed again, and her heart skipped, thinking maybe Chris had changed his mind, but it was Lindsey. LET'S GET OUT OF HERE. I'M WAITING FOR YOU BY YOUR CAR.

Arden didn't argue. After that conversation with Ellzey and that text message with Chris, she was through with this night.

She walked back through Matt's house and smiled at a few people, but didn't bother to say good-bye to any of them, figuring they were either too drunk to notice her leaving or they hadn't realized she'd been there in the first place.

So, now she knew how the other half of high school lived.

As promised, Lindsey was down the road, leaning against Arden's car, a decrepit old sedan that the girls had dubbed the Heart of Gold. Lindsey didn't say anything as Arden unlocked the doors, or after they got in and Arden drove away, and that silence was how Arden knew that, despite Lindsey's earlier reassurances, something had indeed gone wrong.

Once Matt Washington's house had disappeared in the rearview mirror, Lindsey started talking. "So I asked Denise if she wanted to hang out sometime."

"Wow." Arden was impressed. In her life, she'd tried lots of tactics to get people to go out with her. Simply walking up to them and asking them, however, was one she'd never attempted.

"Denise said no. She said thanks, but she doesn't like me like that."

"Well." Arden patted Lindsey's leg. "That's disappointing, obviously, but at least you said how you really felt. Good for you."

"And then Beth and Jennie came up to me and said I should leave the party because I was creeping them out."

"*Excuse* me?" Arden stepped on the gas too hard, and both girls jerked back against their seats.

"They said it made them uncomfortable that I was hitting on Denise, because for all they knew, I might turn to either of them next. They said it's one thing to be gay and hook up with other gay people, but once a lesbian sets her sights on a straight woman, anything is possible."

"Are you *kidding* me? I am going to turn right back around and kick their asses."

"Oh my God, Arden, don't you *dare*. I tried to explain to them that I thought Denise *was* interested in girls, and that's why I asked her out. And also I told them that I'm not remotely attracted to either one of them, or frankly anyone else at Matt's house tonight, but I actually think that made it worse? Because Jennie was like, 'Are you saying I'm not pretty?' And then Beth was like, 'You're not such a prize yourself, Lindsey Flatson.'"

"Is this girl nine years old? *Flatson?* Where does she get her insults from, *Sesame Street?*"

"I know I don't have, like, *ginormous bazooms*, or whatever the cultural standard for feminine attractiveness is," Lindsey went on. "But she didn't have to say it like that, not to my face."

"Linds, that girl is an idiot."

Lindsey's body looked like it was built up and down in a straight line, a very long straight line. She was the tallest girl in school by far, and there were guys on the football team with bigger chests. But that shouldn't have mattered, because her body did exactly what she wanted it to, which was run: fast, far, and often. And wasn't that a positive thing, to be great at something?

"I know everybody says I look like a dude behind my back. Obviously they're right. But it's not my fault. It's not like I chose to look this way. If I had a choice, of course I'd be beautiful. Do you think that's why Denise doesn't like me? Because I'm ugly?"

"No," Arden said. "I think Denise doesn't like you because she doesn't like girls, or at least she doesn't like girls at this particular time in her life. You *are* beautiful."

"I don't know," Lindsey said. "Maybe Denise just likes hot

girls. Do you think I'm going to be alone forever? Tell me honestly."

"Definitely no."

Lindsey sighed and leaned her head against the back of the seat, closing her eyes. "You wouldn't know what that's like, anyway. You have Chris."

Ah, yes. Chris. The world's most secure security blanket.

"I hate living here sometimes," Lindsey said without opening her eyes. "I wonder, if I could just run fast enough and far enough, do you think I could run all the way out of here?"

"I bet you could."

Lindsey shook her head. "I just want someone to want to kiss me," she mumbled.

This had been a frequent refrain in Lindsey's life. It had reached its zenith a couple years ago, but now she rarely expressed it, as if she was embarrassed to be nearly seventeen years old without a kiss to her name and didn't want to call attention to it. But Arden knew it was still something that troubled Lindsey. There just weren't that many out lesbians at their school, and those who were didn't evoke much interest in Lindsey, or she didn't evoke much interest in them. Either way, Lindsey wanted something that seemed like it ought to be simple but had proven impossible to achieve in Cumberland.

Arden remembered when they were thirteen, asking Lindsey, "How do you know you're gay when you've never even kissed a girl?"

"How do you know you're straight when you've never even kissed a guy?" Lindsey shot back.

Arden couldn't argue with that.

Actually, a little-known and never-discussed fact was that Lindsey, technically speaking, *had* had her first kiss. It happened freshman year, with their classmate David Rappaport, at a school dance. She'd just come out to Arden and to her parents, but not yet to the world at large, and when David Rappaport asked her to dance, she'd said yes because she couldn't figure out how to say no. Afterward Lindsey slept over at Arden's, and she cried and cried. "You only get one first kiss in your whole life," she kept saying, "and I wasted mine on some dumb boy."

The answer finally came to Arden. "You don't have to count it," she told Lindsey.

"What do you mean?"

"You can just decide that your first kiss hasn't happened yet. It's going to be with some amazing girl who you probably haven't even met yet."

"Can I do that?"

"It's your life," Arden told her. "Of course you can."

That night was the last time they ever mentioned Lindsey's one make-out occurrence.

Now, Lindsey just sighed and reclined her seat all the way back. "It's fine," she said, more to herself than to Arden. "Tonight's over. Tomorrow will be better."

Arden thought about Beth and Jennie, and Chris and Ellzey, and Denise and Matt Washington, and her mother, and she didn't believe that, not any of it, not for a second. But she didn't say so to Lindsey. She just kept her eyes on the road, and she drove.

Why doesn't anybody love Arden as much as she loves them?

By the time Arden had dropped off Lindsey and driven home, it was late, but still she wasn't tired. Everything seemed rotten. She had expected something about tonight's unprecedented party invitation to transform her, yet she had come home exactly the same, and somehow, therefore, even worse. Now she prowled around the house, looking for distractions. Her father was locked in his study—she didn't go in, but she could tell he was there from the light coming through the crack under the door.

Arden's dad had always worked hard. But ever since her mother moved out, it was like something deep inside of him kept telling him that the reason she left was that he wasn't successful *enough*. And if he could just be *more successful*, then he could prove to her, or to himself, that he was worthy of her love again. He'd been working on being more successful for a month and a half now. He might be getting somewhere with that, but he'd not come any closer to bringing his wife back home.

Arden thought about her mother's words on the phone earlier that day. *I'm sure you want an explanation for why I left.* She wondered if this explanation had been offered to her father, too. She wondered if he'd listened to it. She couldn't imagine that her mother had left because her father wasn't ambitious or hardworking enough. She thought that's what he was doing to win her mom back not even because he thought it would work, but just because it was the only thing he knew how to do.

Roman had fallen asleep on the couch, Mouser catnapping on his feet, the overhead lights still on, the paused video game on the TV awaiting his next command. Arden watched him for a moment, the rise and fall of his little chest. In moments like this (when he was unconscious, basically), Arden's love for her brother overwhelmed her, almost like a physical pain. His feet were resting against the pillow with the *Little Prince* quotation on it, and, without thinking about it, Arden pulled it out from under him and threw it in the trash.

That pillow was bullshit. Her mother did not know the first thing about being responsible for her rose.

Arden carried Roman up to his room and laid him down on his bed, something that he never *ever* would have let her do if he were awake, but as it was, he just drooled a little on her shoulder.

Arden felt a pang of guilt for going to Matt Washington's house; she should have known Roman never would have gotten his act together to put *himself* to bed. There was no way he had brushed his teeth tonight before passing out. She wasn't going to wake him up to make him do it now, and if her family continued on like this, Roman was probably going to contract gum disease before he made it out of middle school.

Arden left Roman's door open because, even though he was eleven, he still freaked out if he woke up and the door was closed and the room was too dark. Then she went to her own room and curled up on her bed. She'd left a pile of rejected Matt Washington party outfits on top of her comforter, and now she kicked them to the floor. She'd eventually settled on her tightest, most revealing top and jeans, but all that had really accomplished was making her unnecessarily cold when she stood out on the patio with Ellzey.

She narrowed her eyes across the room at her Arden Doll, who lived in a glass case on the wall. Since her mother had seen the way Arden treated Tabitha, she'd built this case for the Arden Doll to protect her. "You're going to want to show your doll to your children and your grandchildren," Arden's mother had said. "You're not going to want her to be filthy and falling apart."

Arden's mother was correct, but on this particular night, Arden didn't feel like being watched over by some pristine doll.

Arden is recklessly loyal.

It was a description she'd thought about a million times since it had been handed down by the Just Like Me Dolls Company. In school earlier this year, she had learned about a pivotal historical event called "the blank check." This was in 1914, and the heir to the throne of the Austro-Hungarian Empire had just been assassinated in Serbia. Obviously the Austro-Hungarian government was furious at the Serbs because, hello, they had murdered the emperor-to-be.

Then Germany showed up on the scene. The German emperor wrote a letter promising Austria-Hungary his nation's faithful support in whatever Austria-Hungary decided to do to punish Serbia. That promise of blind support, no matter what—that's what historians called "the blank check."

When Arden read this in her history textbook, she felt breathless. She thought it was the most romantic thing she'd ever heard, this hundred-year-old political letter from the German chancellor to the Austro-Hungarian ambassador. Because in that moment, she realized that was exactly what she had done for Lindsey, for Chris, for Roman—she had written them each a blank check, a silent promise to stand by them through good times and bad, whether she agreed with their actions or not, to give them whatever help they needed, even though none of them could know yet what help that might be.

The first blank check, by the way? The original one, the letter that Germany wrote to Austria-Hungary? They honored that to a T. This decision ultimately led to World War I, which completely decimated the German economy and populace. Maybe not the smartest move the German government ever made. Maybe if they'd known what it would someday come to, they wouldn't have signed the blank check in the first place. But that's the thing: when you swear to take somebody's side no matter what, sometimes you have to go to war for them.

Now, Arden pulled her quilt around her and got up and walked to her desk, where she wouldn't be under such direct scrutiny from her Arden Doll. She pulled up an Internet window and, still thinking about her reckless loyalty, she typed in her question for the universe. It was a really straightforward question, and Arden thought she was a pretty smart girl, so it seemed absurd that she couldn't just figure out the answer.

Why doesn't anybody love me as much as I love them?

She didn't expect the Internet to have a particularly wise answer to her question. At best there might be a humorous video clip on the subject. Like anyone else, Arden sometimes went to the Internet for answers—like how to get a chocolate stain out of white pants, or how many countries there are in Latin America—but usually she went to the Internet to reassure herself that there was a whole world of people out there, living their lives just as she was living hers. Sometimes they had experiences like her own, and sometimes they had experiences that seemed completely bizarre, but either way, their mere existence made Arden feel less alone. No matter what time of day or night you go online, there are always countless other people there, too, announcing the recipes they're cooking and the sights they're seeing and the songs they're recording. She'd discussed this with Lindsey before, and it made Lindsey frantic that all these things were going on and she couldn't keep up with them all. But Arden found it comforting.

The first result that came up when she typed in that question was from a website called Tonight the Streets Are Ours. It used that exact phrase: *Why doesn't anybody love me as much as I love them?* And that jolted her, that some random website had expressed this idea in the very same way as Arden, like someone else had seen inside her brain. So she clicked on the link.

The page was written like somebody's journal. It was dated

October, five months ago. She could tell this post was letting her in midstory, but she didn't know when the story began, so she just started reading.

October 10

I called Bianca three times before she finally texted to ask what I wanted. "I want my stuff back," I replied. Come on, Bianca. Cut me a break.

She insisted on meeting at the bookstore because she didn't want me to come over to her house, and she refused to come over to mine. The bookstore, where it all began. What cruel bookends. She got there five minutes after I finished my shift.

"I can't believe you're already back at work," she said.

"Life goes on," I told her. "It has to."

"*Yours* does, maybe."

"What did you think was going to happen if we met at your house?" I asked. "Did you think I was going to throw you down on your bed and start ravishing you?"

"No," she said. "But I thought you would have wanted to."

"I still want to," I said. "And we're not anywhere close to a bed. We're at a bookstore."

"Ha," she said, handing me a tote bag of my stuff. There wasn't a lot in there. I never left much at book-shopping world. Peter could be a fifty-year-old physical therapist in Akron, Ohio, with a fondness for Cheetos. But she felt like he probably wasn't.

She read on to the next post.

October 12

Why do I lose everyone who matters? First my brother. Now Bianca. I don't really know which of those losses hurts worse: my brother, because he has always been a part of my life, or Bianca, because I *chose* her into my life, and I thought she chose me, too—but I thought wrong. I will walk down every street and avenue knowing that she might be walking right in front of me, but she will never again be mine.

I hate that this is how life has to be. The progressive loss of everyone who matters to you. That's all there is to it, you know: if you live long enough, your reward is that you get to watch everyone you love die or leave you behind.

Oh, but I am being ridiculous. I know. I know. Death and a broken heart are not the same.

Now Arden didn't just want to know what happened with Bianca, why they broke up. She wanted to know what had

Bianca's house, for obvious reasons. I knew that already, but I wanted it back anyway. Because I wanted a reason to see her. So sue me. The bag contained just a T-shirt, two books, and an opened bag of Cheetos.

"Really?" I said, looking up. "Some half-eaten snack food, Bianca? You couldn't have just thrown that away?"

She shrugged. "You said you wanted your stuff."

Why can't you love me as much as I love you? I wanted to ask in that moment. I thought about the events of these past few weeks, and I just felt so defeated and indignant. The world has cracked open over my head, like a smelly egg. *Why doesn't anybody love me as much as I love them?*

"You'll find another girl," Bianca said as we stood across from each other. At a bookstore. Like strangers. "You're Peter. Girls love you."

As if all of my feelings for her come down to the fact that she's a girl and I'm a guy. Substitute in any other guy and any other girl, they'll fit those empty spaces just as well.

"I don't want another girl," I said. "I want you."

I didn't get her, though. I got my Cheetos. Then I threw them away.

Who were these people, Peter and Bianca? Arden wondered. They could be any age, living anywhere in the English-speaking, happened to Peter's brother, too. She wanted to know everything. She never had been able to manage a calm, reserved interest in other people.

Maybe she needed to start at the beginning. That would make this whole story become clear, if it unfolded in chronological order.

Peter's very first post was from nearly a full year ago, but it said nothing about Bianca or a brother, or love or loss at all.

March 21

Hi, my name is Peter, and this is Tonight the Streets Are Ours. (What do you think? I needed a URL, and it turned out basically everything else was taken. Plus I'm really into that song, and I figured, hey, if it works for Richard Hawley, it'll work for me, too. Tonight the streets *are* mine, you know.)

If you're here, then congratulations! You've found my blog. Welcome! Stick around awhile.

I want to be a writer when I grow up. Actually, I want to be a writer *right now*, and also when I grow up. Today is my seventeenth birthday, so I have made a new year's resolution. (Yeah, it's not the new year for everybody, but it's a new year for ME, so, good enough.) I'm going to post here every day, and that will be good writing practice, and also when it's time for

me to write my memoirs, I will already have these collected notes on my teen years. You're welcome, Future
Peter.

My dad says that I don't want to pursue a career as
a writer because writers are—what did he say? Something like "congenitally miserable alcoholics." If he's
right, then I guess I'll fit right in! Haha, kidding.

Also, my dad is a congenitally miserable alcoholic,
too, and he doesn't even produce any writing or whatever to show for it. You can be a congenitally miserable
alcoholic even if all you do is manage hedge funds,
apparently. Seems like a waste. If you're going to have
the tortured soul of an artist, then you might as well
create some art while you're at it.

Arden smiled a little at Peter's description of his father. It was
nice to know that her mother wasn't the only screwed-up parent around. And now that she knew Peter was just a year older
than she was, she felt even more intrigued by him and his miserable dad and the girl who broke his heart and the mysteriously
disappeared brother.

She wanted to read whatever came next, but more than
that, she wanted to know where Peter's brother went. So she
skipped forward a few months. At last she found an explanation, in a post dated just a couple weeks before Bianca and Peter's breakup.

September 24

I know I haven't written here for a while, and I'm sorry. I'm sorry for a lot of things, in fact.

I don't really know where to start. That's the problem with updating a website every day: once you miss a week, you'll be behind forever.

So, basically, my brother ran away. He's been gone for a week now, and he's left no trace. He'd only been at college for a month, and from all we heard from him, he seemed to be fitting in well, making friends, going to classes, learning stuff, I don't know, whatever it is people do at college.

And then he took off.

None of his new college friends know where he went. None of his old high school friends have heard from him. The cops say they can't be much help because he's eighteen, he's a legal adult, he can go where he wants. There's no sign of him; it's as if he never existed in the first place.

My dad is hiring a private investigator. He's livid. He says, "I will spend every penny, if that's what it takes to find that boy." My mom keeps crying. It's like they know it's their fault. If they weren't like this, maybe he wouldn't have left.

Everyone's asked me if he told me anything, if I have any ideas. Because we're just a year apart, we're supposed to be so close. We're supposed to share things. From the time we were little kids, we shared toys, we shared clothes, we shared friends. But I'm as clueless as everyone else right now—how do you think that makes me feel?

I stayed home from school almost all last week. My parents stayed home from work. It's as if he died. For all I know, maybe he *is* dead.

Can't say *that* to my parents.

I remember when I was eight years old, when I finally really understood where babies come from—or at least, where my brother really came from. I asked him, "But what if Mommy and Daddy *hadn't* adopted you? What if your birth parents had kept you? Or what if somebody *else* adopted you instead? What if Mommy and Daddy got the call about some other little boy two weeks before they got the call about you, and then by the time you were available, they weren't looking for you anymore?"

"That was never going to happen," he answered with the confidence of a nine-year-old who's got it all figured out. "I always belonged to our family, even before Mom and Dad knew it, even before you were born. We didn't have to come together exactly the way we did. But one way or another, it was going to happen."

I always liked this explanation because it meant that if he and I ever lost each other along the way, we would always find each other again. That's how it seemed to me, as a stupid little kid.

I don't know what else to say. Why is it that I can find a million words to write about a party, and I can't think of a single word to explain how I feel right now?

Arden turned away from the computer and hugged her quilt around herself, chilled to the bone. Because this, Peter's story—this was why you needed to love people while you could, while they were right there in front of you. Because if you waited, it might be too late.

And that, of course, made her think of her mother.

When Arden's mom left

Arden's mom did not leave *because* of the dress. But if the dress had never existed, maybe she would still be here now.

Arden had seen the dress in a photo of the movie star Paige Townsen, featured in an issue of *Us Weekly* a few months ago, which Arden had borrowed from her friend Naomi. Naomi was on stage crew and was a celebrity gossip junkie. Deep down, Naomi really did believe that stars—they're just like us!

Although Arden didn't think she was anything like a star, she wished that she were when she saw this dress. It was maroon, with cap sleeves and a belt at the waist that could create the illusion of a well-defined waist even though Arden did not exactly have one for real. The dress was classy and stately and seemed like it belonged in a movie from the 1940s, along with a veiled hat and elbow-length gloves. Arden clipped the image from Naomi's magazine and taped it to her mirror.

"Wouldn't it be great to have a dress like that?" Arden asked her mother one night as her mom quizzed her on the elements of the periodic table.

Her mother stood to inspect the picture more closely. "I don't know where you could buy such a thing."

"Oh, it's by some designer and costs a trillion dollars," Arden assured her. "You *can't* buy such a thing."

"I could sew it for you," her mother offered.

"Really?" Arden blinked. Her mother had needlepointed wall decorations and done quilting. She'd sewn dresses for Tabitha when Arden was little. But Arden didn't know that her mom could make human-size dresses, too.

"I bet I could figure it out. And then you could wear it to the Winter Wonderland dance!" Her mother smiled in the way she did whenever she solved a problem—even though this time, Arden hadn't even known that a problem existed.

"*If* Chris and I are still together then," Arden cautioned. It was hard to imagine Chris breaking up with her—they'd been a couple since last April, so another few weeks together seemed like it should be a given. But it didn't totally feel that way.

Her mother gave her a knowing look. "That boy is wild about you. Trust me, honey, you don't have anything to worry about. Don't be silly." Arden's parents were themselves high school sweethearts, so to her mother, being silly was imagining that a teenage romance might even end.

And so Arden's mother set to work on sewing the dress. She mostly worked on it while Arden was at school, so Arden didn't have much awareness about how it came together. She just knew that one day there was red fabric and then one day there was a dressmaker's dummy and one day she was getting measured and then, a few days before the dance, the dress suddenly existed and she was trying it on.

"Well?" her mother said as Arden modeled it in the living room. "What do you think?"

"I think, can I have my screen time yet?" Roman asked from his perch on the arm of the couch.

"Soon. Say something nice about how your sister looks first."

"You look red," Roman said.

"Roman," their mother said in a warning tone.

"Your dress, I mean," he said. "Your dress looks red."

"Dennis!" their mother called toward their dad's closed study door. "Do you want to come out and see your beautiful daughter?"

There was a pause, and then he shouted back, "I'm in the middle of something right now, sweetie. I'll be out in a minute."

Arden rolled her eyes. "Out in a minute" was dad-code for "I've already forgotten that you asked me to do something." Only about two weeks remained before the Super Bowl, which meant her father was chest-deep in fantasy football. Ostensibly he was working on some important legal case right now, but it was equally likely that he just wasn't coming out of his study until he'd read every post about every game on every NFL news site that he frequented.

"What do *you* think of the dress, Arden?" her mother asked.

Honestly? Arden thought it looked slightly off in some way. It just didn't look on her like it did on the actress taped to her

66

mirror. The cap sleeves seemed too long, the neckline too high and bunchy, the waist too low, the fabric too matte. Or maybe this just wasn't the dress for her—maybe when she saw it in that magazine and pictured it on her own body, she was picturing herself as somebody else entirely.

"I love it," her mother went on. "I can't believe it—this is the first dress I've made in years, and somehow it turned out just right. You look stunning, honey. So grown-up."

"I love it, too," said Arden.

Two days later, she was at the mall with her two closest theater friends, Kirsten and Naomi. Arden had of course invited Lindsey, who had declined; Lindsey was not a mall person. Kirsten was riffling through clothing racks at an alarming rate when she stopped and declared, "This is it, guys! This is going to be my Winter Wonderland dress!"

Arden and Naomi crowded in to inspect it. It was gauzy, pink, strapless, sheer at the top, barely ass-covering at the bottom. The sort of dress an extra in the nightclub scene of a music video might wear.

"Ughhh, it's so amazing, I want one, too," Naomi said immediately.

"Do it!" said Kirsten. "I'll get the pink one and you can get the silver one and Arden can get the gold one and we'll match."

Naomi squealed.

Arden considered saying that she already had a dress. That her mom had made. But the thing was, she didn't actually want to wear that dress. And now that she'd seen what her friends were going to be wearing, she *really* didn't want to wear that dress, to be the one frumpy, old-fashioned girl in a skirt past her knees.

So she spent some of her hard-earned tutoring money to buy the gold dress. She figured she would wear the one her mother made to some other event. Like the theater club's annual masquerade ball. Or a church service. Until then, she hung it in her closet.

The next day was Saturday, and the dance. All the theater kids were getting ready at Kirsten's house, which was always where they had big gatherings, because Kirsten's place was huge, and her dad and stepmom didn't really care what their kids' friends got up to so long as nobody set their house on fire. Arden packed her stuff to take over there: makeup, curling iron, gold dress, high heels. She grabbed her car keys and headed downstairs.

"I'm leaving," she said as she stopped by the kitchen.

Her mother and brother both ignored her. They were locked in battle across the kitchen table from each other. "You *love* macaroni," her mother was saying, staring him down.

Arden's eyes flicked to the tray of homemade macaroni and cheese sitting at Roman's place. It smelled amazing. If she hadn't known that Kirsten was ordering in pizza, she would have just eaten Roman's dinner herself.

"Not anymore," Roman said.

"Since when?" asked their mother.

He shrugged his skinny shoulders impatiently. "I don't *know*. Since sometime."

"You liked macaroni last week."

"Well, I don't anymore. Can I go watch my movie now?"

"No," their mother said. "You have to eat dinner before you can watch."

"Why?"

"Because," Arden jumped in, cuffing him on the shoulder, "Mom says so." In the years since Roman's toddler-age tantrums, he had stopped crying so often, but he had never gotten less finicky.

"Fine," he said. "I'll eat." He stood up, crossed to the cabinet, and pulled out a bag of Goldfish crackers. He stuck a handful in his mouth. "Okay?" he mumbled, his teeth gummy with orange gobs.

"Not okay," Arden said. "That's disgusting."

"Not okay," said their mom. "That's not *dinner*. Sit down, Roman Huntley, and *eat your macaroni and cheese*."

"But I don't want it!" he cried. "You said I don't have to eat anything I don't want to eat! Are you going to force-feed me macaroni? What is this, *prison*?"

"I'm not force-feeding you anything!" Their mother threw her hands up. "I worked hard on that macaroni, Roman. I made a special trip to the grocery store just to get the sort of shells you like. I made the bread crumbs from scratch. All of that, just for you, Roman. Arden isn't even joining us for dinner tonight, and I made poached salmon for us grown-ups. The macaroni exists for you. So please, at least *try* it."

Arden stole a bite off his plate. "It's delicious, Mom. You've outdone yourself."

Roman crossed his arms. "You can't psychology me into eating it."

"Dennis!" their mother called.

"One second!" their father shouted back.

"Not 'one second'—*right now*."

Arden was impressed. Her mother sounded firm. Even her father must have heard something unusual in her tone, because he emerged from his study to ask, "What's going on?"

"Your son won't eat his dinner," Arden's mother explained, pointing to the offending meal.

"Roman, eat your dinner," their dad said immediately. "It's dinnertime."

"*You're* not eating dinner," Roman retorted.

"I'm finishing up a big project. But once I'm done, I'm going to eat some of this tasty food that your mother cooked for us."

"No, you're not," Roman said. "You're going to eat poached salmon. I'm the only one who has to eat this macaroni. And I don't *like* macaroni."

"Oh." Their father scratched his head. "I didn't know you didn't like macaroni."

"None of us did," contributed Arden.

"Do you want to just eat the salmon, too?" their father offered.

And even though Roman had a strict anti-seafood policy, he said, "Yeah!"

"Well, then." Their father grinned and tousled his son's hair. "Problem solved."

"Problem *not* solved," their mother snapped. "Dennis, please. Back me up here."

"I'm leaving," Arden tried again.

"If you're leaving, then where's your dress?" Roman asked.

All attention in the room shifted to Arden. She felt the blood rush to her cheeks and mentally cursed her little brother. Roman was the only sixth-grade boy she'd ever met who would notice whether his big sister was bringing the correct outfit to a high school dance.

"Where *is* your dress?" Arden's mom asked softly.

A moment too late, it occurred to Arden to lie. To say that she'd forgotten it, and hold on a sec, she was just going to run back upstairs and grab it.

"I . . ." Arden began. But her guilt was written all over her face. She started over. "Kirsten and Naomi wanted us all to wear matching dresses, so . . ."

"You know what?" her mother said, standing up shakily. "Forget it."

"Forget what?" asked their father.

"All of it. Everything. I can't do this anymore. I've had it. It's clear that none of you need me anyway, so I'm sure you'll be just fine."

"What?" Arden asked.

Her mother didn't answer. She just grabbed her purse and walked out the front door.

The three remaining Huntleys stared at one another in stunned silence for a moment. At last, Roman said, "Nice going, Arden. You made her mad."

"*You* made her mad," Arden retorted. "You couldn't have just eaten the mac and cheese?"

"I can't think with your bickering!" their dad shouted.

They immediately shut up. Their father was much scarier than their mother when he yelled.

"She's just gone for a walk," their dad told them, pressing his fingers against his temples as if he were holding his head together. "She's just gone to get some fresh air."

"Okay," Arden said. "I am leaving, though." She checked her phone. Chris had already texted to say that he'd arrived at Kirsten's. She kissed Roman's head and kissed her dad's cheek. "I'm sorry Mom's mad," she said.

Her dad nodded. "It'll be okay, Arden."

So she drove to Kirsten's, where she met up with the rest of her friends and all the girls changed into their dresses and a couple of the guys put on suits but mostly the boys just hung out and ate as much pizza as they could before Kirsten told them to "leave some for the rest of us." Then they caravanned over to the dance, five kids in Arden's car and five in Chris's.

Once they were there, Chris and Arden danced in the center of the room, and with the music too loud for words and his arms around her, things between them felt better than they had in weeks, like a Rubik's Cube that had just been shifted into place. Though they were surrounded by people on all sides, it was one of those rare moments when Arden somehow felt like they were all alone, just the two of them.

She leaned in close, so her lips were right up against his ear, and she shouted, "I love you!"

"I love you, too!" And he kissed her, that same stage kiss that had swept her off her feet nine months prior.

Arden closed her eyes and felt like she was being sucked backward in time. At the end of the summer, right before the Huntleys' annual family trip to visit her mom's parents in Atlantic Beach, Arden was packing and thinking that she really, really didn't want to be apart from Chris for ten days. The idea of their physical separation made her heart hurt, so, just to see what it would feel like, she imagined them being apart forever. And the thought of it made her heart contract, her throat seize up, and her hand reach for her phone to call him, to hear the sound of his voice. That was how she knew that she loved him: she couldn't picture her life without him anymore.

She told him the day she got home from Atlantic Beach. As soon as she was free from the car, she went running to Chris's dad's hardware store. And Arden, unlike Lindsey, was not a runner. She was the opposite: a sitter, a lie-downer, a sedate-stroller. But she ran to see Chris, because she wanted to tell him she loved him, she wanted to tell him in person, and she didn't want to wait another minute.

She showed up at the hardware store breathless and sweaty. Chris was vaguely helping a woman choose between varieties of packing tape, a cause that he abandoned as soon as Arden walked in the door.

"You're home!" he said, his eyes lighting up.

"I love you," she blurted out.

The woman choosing the packing tape started to laugh.

"I love *you*," Chris said right back.

And they'd never stopped saying it since then.

Now, at the school dance, it felt like they were back to that, that sunniness and heat of August. Arden's mother had been right: she was silly to have any doubt about her and Chris.

When the dance ended, Arden dropped off everyone in her car, driving around Cumberland in a circuitous route until each one of them was delivered to his or her own house. And then Arden herself went home. It was late by then. Midnight.

But still her mother hadn't come back.

Arden's dad called her mom's cell phone, but she didn't pick up. He tried Arden's mom's brother, too, but Uncle George hadn't heard from her. Arden had the surprising realization that she didn't know who else her mother would go to after she stormed away from home. Unlike her father, who had his fantasy sports leagues and work buddies, her mother seemed to be friendly to everyone and close to no one outside of the family. Who *would* she go to in a moment of crisis? Where *would* she be, other than here?

The three remaining Huntleys waited up for her, sitting in the dark on the living room couch, the TV on without any of them processing what program it was showing. Roman passed out first, followed sometime thereafter by their father, until at last only Arden was left awake, watching the lights from the television screen cast flickering shadows across their faces. She waited and waited. But her mother never came home that night. When she did return, it was two days later, while the kids were at school. But that was only to pack a suitcase before heading out again.

And now weeks had passed. The Super Bowl had been played, Roman's basketball team had lost five games, Arden had been suspended from school and returned to school and attended her first supposedly cool party. Life was marching on. And still, her mother was gone.

Arden realizes that the grass is always greener

The day after Arden asked the Internet *why doesn't anybody love me as much as I love them?* and discovered Tonight the Streets Are Ours, she and Chris went shopping for props for the spring musical, *American Fairy Tale*, a nonsensical, borderline hallucinatory debut written by Mr. Lansdowne, the theater teacher, in what Arden considered to be a serious abuse of power. Chris picked her up early in his car. He didn't like to drive in Arden's car because he said it was likely to break down or explode at any minute, which was, quite frankly, a fair critique. Chris drove a three-year-old Honda Accord with automatic locks and working air bags. He liked to play it safe.

"How was last night?" Arden asked once she was settled in the passenger seat.

"So fun. We played some games and watched a movie. You'd have loved it."

This was what Arden's boyfriend and their theater friends did literally every single Friday night. Trust Chris to present it like it was the most exciting activity ever.

And—though Arden had never even hinted as much to her boyfriend—she didn't actually enjoy playing theater games. That's why she did stage crew in the first place—so she could be backstage, where if she made a fool of herself, no one would see. Chris Jump had something in him, like at the level of DNA, where he didn't care if he made a fool of himself. Or maybe he didn't even know how to look foolish. In their ten months of dating, Arden had never seen Chris do anything remotely embarrassing.

"How was the rest of Matt Washington's party?" Chris asked, turning onto the main road.

Arden shrugged. She didn't want to admit that it had been a total bust, because Chris would probably say, "I told you so," and, "I don't know why you even went in the first place when you could have come with me." So Arden just said, "Lindsey finally asked out Denise Alpert."

"Whoa. How'd that go?"

"Well, she didn't say yes. Beth and Jennie also offered some choice opinions on the matter."

Chris snorted. "I'm not surprised. What did Lindsey *think* was going to happen?"

Arden couldn't answer that question, because that was the thing about Lindsey: she *didn't* think. She wasn't doing some statistical analysis of the likelihood of Denise saying yes or no. She was just guided by hope.

"Dumb move," Chris said, with a smug knowingness that

made Arden want to strangle him. Chris had never come out and said it, but it was clear that he didn't like Lindsey very much, probably because she was constantly making "dumb moves" like asking out straight girls or oversleeping or forgetting about math tests—all of which Chris found to be illogical behavior.

In return, Lindsey did not like Chris very much, because she thought he ate up too much of Arden's time and attention. Last summer, Lindsey had said accusingly, "You're turning into one of those girls who's always, 'Blah blah *my boyfriend* says blah blah, oh I can't come because *my boyfriend* wants to blah blah, oh that's cool that you're into blah blah because *my boyfriend* is, too.'"

"I am not turning into one of those girls," Arden had defended herself. But, just in case, she tried to mention Chris to Lindsey as little as possible. And she tried not to mention Lindsey to Chris, either. And when one said something negative about the other, she simply tried not to engage. Now, for example, she pulled out her cell phone as if an important text had come in.

The first thing she saw on her phone was Peter's website. Tonight the Streets Are Ours. She'd been reading it in bed last night until almost three a.m., after she had finally heard her father leave his study and go to bed.

She'd made it through all the posts of the first two and a half months, which felt like an accomplishment. But now that late-night reading seemed like a poor decision, since Chris was a big believer in the early bird getting the worm and she'd had to wake up a full hour before he picked her up in order to get ready. She hadn't always been a daily makeup-wearing kind of girl. It was something she'd started doing a few months ago, to make Chris think she looked prettier than she actually was. He didn't seem to have much of a response to it, but she kept doing it anyway, just in case. Even if the presence of makeup on her face didn't make him think she was gorgeous, she didn't want the *absence* of makeup to make him think she was a troll.

Now, instinctively, she picked up reading where she'd left off seven hours before.

June 21

Today a customer came into the bookstore looking for a title called *The Soft and the Furry*. I spent about half an hour helping her scour the shelves in the pet care section before I was like, "Wait. Do you mean *The Sound and the Fury*? One of the most famous American novels of all time?"

She shrugged. "That's what I said, isn't it?"

Of course we had, like, ten copies of it in stock. She read the back cover. And then she didn't buy it.

June 22

This evening I rang up a customer who was buying a book called *What to Expect When You're Divorcing*.

"Oh," I said. "Are you getting a divorce?"

"No," she said, really quickly.

"It's okay if you are," I said, then added, just so she wouldn't feel like she was the only one, "I mean, *I'm* divorced."

She rolled her eyes, like she didn't believe me.

"See?" I held up my left hand. "No ring."

"How old are you?" she asked. "Seventeen?"

"Yes, actually. I got divorced when I was fourteen. So I've moved on now. Don't worry; you will, too."

It's possible that I think I'm funnier than other people do.

June 23

I was working registers today (again). It's so interminable. No matter how many customers I check out, no matter how quickly, eventually another customer will always come along. It's impossible to feel like you're making any actual progress because there is no finish line. If this is what actual full-time employment is like, I don't ever want to get a job.

I said this to Julio, and he pointed out, "Dude, you don't even need to have a *summer* job. Your family is richer than God. You have a maid come over, like, every day. If you're that bored, just quit."

But I want to be a writer. And the best way to become a writer is to surround yourself with words.

Today I checked out a man about my dad's age. He was buying a copy of *Corduroy*. I said, "I remember this book! I loved it when I was a kid. Let me guess: do you have a five-year-old son?"

The man looked at me with a combination of sadness and resignation and anger. "My son is fifteen," he said. "He's developmentally delayed. I don't need a receipt." And he walked away.

I should really stop expressing my opinions on customers' purchases, maybe.

June 24

Something amazing happened today. Or maybe not. Maybe it's nothing at all. It *felt* like something, though.

If you want something to be amazing, if you *really* want it, do you think you can somehow make it become that way? Like you somehow imbue it with amazingness, even if it doesn't have anything special inherent to it?

Let me back up.

Today I was working registers. Again. It's a beautiful day out, the sort of day we get here in NYC only a handful of times a year, when the skies are clear, and it's hot but not muggy, and the air doesn't even reek of garbage. If I were a tourist in NYC today, I'd think to myself, *Yeah, I could live in that city.* Anyway, because it was the most beautiful day of the year, the bookstore was vacant, which meant there didn't need to be three of us hanging around behind the registers. So I offered to shelve some books to kill time.

That's when I saw Her.

She was standing next to the poetry display table, thumbing through a copy of *Sonnets from the Portuguese.* She was the most beautiful thing I've ever seen in person. She put that sunshiny day to shame.

It's hard for me to pick out what the specific thing is that made her so breathtaking. It's something about the way all the parts of her body fit together, not just any one in isolation. Her hair was long and silky and the shade of red where I couldn't quite believe that it was natural, but I also couldn't ask if it was dyed because I'm sure everyone asks her that. She was wearing a bright yellow sundress that made her look like a daffodil, with thin straps accenting her delicate shoulder blades, and a little bit of lace at her, you know, *décolletage.* (Shame on the English language for not having a word for *décolletage.* This is why the French are better than we are.)

I saw her and I wanted to . . . I don't even know. I know that she inspired me to want to do something. I just don't know exactly what that something is.

I walked over to her because I couldn't stay away. She seemed engrossed in the book—I don't think she noticed me. When I was next to her, I said, "How do I love thee? Let me count the ways. I love thee to the depth and breadth and height my soul can reach, when feeling out of sight for the ends of Being and ideal Grace."

She looked up from the book, and her long eyelashes fluttered. I'd had no idea that eyelashes could be sexy.

"I'm sorry, what?" she said.

And in my head, I thought of *Romeo and Juliet*. *She speaks! O speak again, bright angel!* But I didn't say that aloud. Because maybe I had already said too much.

Instead I said, "I was quoting one of the sonnets. From there." I pointed at the book she was holding.

She smiled. She smiled *at me*. "You're an Elizabeth Barrett Browning fan?" she asked.

"I'm a poetry fan."

"I don't know very much about her work," she admitted.

"Well, if there's anything you want to know," I said, "I'm happy to teach you."

She opened her mouth to reply. And then Leo showed up.

"Hey, man!" Leo said. He seemed glad to see me. "So I guess you already met Bianca?" And he put his arm around her. Around *her*, that gorgeous girl.

So this was Bianca. Bianca, whom we'd been hearing so much about for the past six weeks, but whom we'd never seen, to the point where I'd started to wonder if maybe Leo had just made her up to sound cool. Yet here she was. In the flesh. In the smooth, tanned flesh.

Leo had mentioned some things about her before. She's my age. She lives on the Upper West Side. Stuff like that; practical stuff. He didn't mention that she was more beautiful than the sun, and I hated him for that— had he never noticed? How dare he never notice what he had in front of him?

"Bianca," I said. "Hey. I've heard so much about you."

"All good things, I hope." She looked up at me through lowered eyelashes.

I locked eyes with her. "Of course. What else could there be?"

"I thought we'd come by to surprise you," Leo said.

"You succeeded," I said, not looking away from her.

"When do you get off work?" he asked. "Maybe we could all get iced coffee or something after."

The thing I most want to do is go out for coffee with this girl. The thing I least want to do is go out for coffee with this girl and her boyfriend.

"I'm here for another few hours," I said. "Sorry."

"Bummer. We'll look around then. Maybe buy some books. You'll hook us up with your employee discount, right?" Leo asked.

"I'll hook you up with anything you want," I said. To Bianca.

I walked away and returned to my stupid cash register. Once she wasn't directly in front of me, I started berating myself. *Dude, she's Leo's girlfriend, you don't know anything about her, lay off.*

But those arguments only make sense if you don't believe in fate, or things that are meant to be. And I can't make myself not believe in that.

Twenty minutes later, she came to the cash register. Leo was hanging out a little ways behind her, doing something on his phone.

"Hi again." She set a book down on the counter in front of me.

"So you decided to buy the sonnets after all, huh?" I asked as I rang her up.

"Yeah," she said, leaning forward on the counter, like she wanted to get just a little closer to me. "Did you know it's called *Sonnets from the Portuguese*, but it has nothing to do with Portugal? Elizabeth Barrett Browning just claimed that her poems were translations of traditional Portuguese sonnets because she was too shy to claim credit for writing them." Bianca paused, then added, "I read that on the back flap."

"I always wondered why it was called that," I said. "Thanks for telling me."

While she was looking into her purse, fussing with her wallet, I quick wrote on the back of her receipt:

Let me know what you think of the book.
Call me.
—Peter

And I added my phone number. I stuck the receipt in her book, stuck the book in a paper bag, and handed it to her.

If Leo found that note, I could play it off, I think. Like, *Oh, just little old bookish Peter, looking for someone to talk about sonnets with.* Anyway, what are the odds that Leo's going to open a book of poetry?

"Thanks!" she said. "Have a good day." Then she smoothed the lace over her chest, pulled on her shades, and headed outside into the blinding sunshine.

That's what happened today. Like I said, it could be nothing at all. Or it could be the start of the rest of my life. Ball's in your court, Fate.

"Babe, are you coming in?" asked Chris.

Arden snapped back into the present, Peter's hot summer day vanishing in an instant. Chris had parked outside The Grass Is Always Greener, a junk shop in the strip mall just outside of town. He was already out of the car, his coat on, while Arden was still sitting in the passenger seat, staring at her phone.

"Coming," she said, and she opened the door.

Arden and Chris's task for today was to purchase hats for all sixteen members of *American Fairy Tale*'s chorus. Chris was not

86

in the chorus, obviously. He was Chris Jump; he was the leading man. But he still wanted to be involved in the selection of hats because it was crucial to him that everything on stage look exactly right, even down to the hats on the heads of the people swaying in the background behind him.

Inside The Grass Is Always Greener, Chris tried on every single hat. Arden's job was to rank each one on a scale from one to ten, and then he also ranked it on a scale from one to ten, and if the average score between them was higher than a five, he put it into the "maybe" category, and if its score was lower than five he returned it to the rack. Except in one instance where he overruled Arden's score of one because he said it was "wacky" and she just didn't "get" its "wackiness."

He was wrong, by the way. The hat was covered in purple and green polka dots, but that didn't make it wacky—it just made it stupid.

In between hat ratings, while Chris studied himself in the mirror, Arden clicked back to Tonight the Streets Are Ours, and she read on.

June 25

I am such an idiot. I keep checking my phone— maybe she's called, maybe she's called! A few minutes ago—this is so embarrassing to admit, but whatever, almost nobody reads this journal, so I'll say it—a few minutes ago I called *myself* from my mom's phone, just to make sure my phone was working. As if maybe the reason I haven't heard from her is some major tele-communications technology breakdown, not just be-cause *she hasn't called me*. My reception is never out. I live in New York City, and there's a cell phone tower on every street corner.

I didn't have work today, but I went back to the book-store anyway and hung around for a while, just in case she might wander in again. I would make a terrible crim-inal. I always return to the scene of the crime.

GET A GRIP, PETER. YOU ARE PATHETIC.

"Hey," Chris said. Arden looked up from her phone, blinked at him. "Which of these hats?" He modeled.

"We already did those two," Arden said. "I rated them both sevens, remember?"

"Yeah, but I'm not going to get *two* black derby hats. They're for the footmen, and Jaden and Eric already look enough alike without us putting them in the same hat. We're trying to help the audience differentiate between their characters. So?"

"Get the one with the ribbon around it," Arden said. "That one. Yeah. And give Jaden the green and purple polka dot one. That will help the audience tell them apart."

"I thought you hated that one?"

"I changed my mind."

Chris assigned the hats to their correct piles. "This would be a really fun thing to do on a date," he said.

Arden's shoulders drooped. "We are on a date," she reminded him. Was she really so unremarkable that even when she was right there beside him, doing just what he wanted, it still wasn't enough?

He glanced at her for a second. "Oh, right, I know. I just meant it'd be fun with someone you didn't know very well, you know? Like, trying on silly hats with someone. Taking funny pictures, playing different characters."

"*We* could be taking funny pictures right now, if you want," Arden suggested. "*We* could play different hat-wearing characters."

Chris shrugged. "Nah, that's okay. We still have a lot to get through."

Arden didn't argue. She hadn't really wanted to put away Tonight the Streets Are Ours, anyway. She was just offering because it seemed like what Chris wanted.

June 26

I'm sorry to keep harping on this when I know there are major events of real significance going on in the world, but—do you think Bianca might be my soul mate?

I know this is a ridiculous question. Contrary to what my father believes, I do listen to myself talk. I know ridiculous when I hear it. I know that Bianca is just a beautiful girl with great hair buying one of my favorite books on a sunny day. None of that makes someone your soul mate. If that's all it took, then Bianca would be *everybody's* soul mate. On that day she was wearing the sundress with the lace accenting her chest, maybe twenty people alone fell for her. They can't all be her soul mates.

But it makes me feel better to imagine that she might be mine. Because if we were soul mates—if this was somehow ordained on a higher plane—then I wouldn't have to worry about what the future might hold, because I'd know we were right on course.

I am worried, though. What if she never calls? What if the only time I see her is on Leo's arm—what if she's never mine? Why couldn't I have met her first?

The problem is that there are a million different New Yorks, all layered on top of one another yet never intersecting. The girl of your dreams may live down the block without your ever seeing her, until it's too late. Circumstance plays no role, and Fate turns a blind eye.

"Babe!"

Arden looked up again. Chris sounded frustrated.

"I like that one," she said, gesturing at the newsboy cap on his head.

"I know. You already said that. What is going on with you today?"

"What do you mean?" she said. "Nothing."

"You're being super spacey. You're not paying any attention to me."

"Of course I am," she snapped. "You're trying on hats, Chris. There's only so much I can contribute to that process. It's not like you're paying so much attention to *me*, either, by the way."

Why doesn't anybody love me as much as I love them?

"Well, that's because you're not *doing* anything," Chris countered. "You're just sitting there staring at your phone. On that gross old armchair. Which is probably infested with bugs, by the way."

"It's vintage," said the sales clerk, who happened to be walking by.

Bianca didn't do *anything, either,* Arden thought. *Bianca just walked in the door, and that alone was enough for Peter to pay attention to her.*

"I'm sorry," Arden said to Chris. "I'm tired, that's all. I didn't get to bed until almost three last night."

Chris shook his head and returned to his piles of hats, and Arden returned to her phone. He said, "You're so crazy sometimes, babe."

June 28

A lot of the time I don't understand what I'm doing here. In life, I mean. I'm not saying that I wish I were dead or anything. Most of the time, I'm glad for the opportunity to be alive. I'm just not sure what I'm supposed to be doing with it. I *think* my purpose is to be a writer: to craft beautiful sentences that change the way people view the world, to create something meaningful outside of myself. That's what I think a lot of the time. But then sometimes I wonder if I just made that up in order to make myself feel like I have a reason for taking up space.

Anyway, all of that is just a depressing, navel-gazing introduction to what I wanted to say here, which is that today, I had a rare day where I understood without any doubt why I'm alive.

Miranda texted me in the morning and asked what I was doing, and I said I had work at the store until two and then I was going to go to a coffee shop to write. Miranda told me to blow off work and screw writing and meet her in Prospect Park for a day of sunbathing and gossip. I said I am a professional bookseller, and professionals do not just "blow off work," and also my skin doesn't tan, but I would meet her after work anyway as long as she brought wine juice boxes. She said done. Miranda's father is a liquor distributor.

(I wonder if you can get in legal trouble for referring to your own underage drinking on the Internet? Let's assume not.)

I found Miranda in the park a bit before three. She was lying on a picnic blanket in nothing but a bikini and sunglasses.

"You're already pretty tan," I told her.

"It's an art," she replied.

This is a line from some marketing video that our school issued last year. The video showed kids painting and playing cello, and there was even a shot of Miranda pirouetting, and then various voice-overs said, "It's an art!" I don't know if this video resulted in more applications to the school or not.

"Still pining after that unavailable chick?" Miranda asked, rolling over to give me room on the picnic blanket.

"It's an art," I answered.

"That's true, actually," she said.

We hung out for a while and I drank wine through a little straw and Miranda described her summer dance program, which sounded exhausting and made me glad that my art isn't the sort of thing you have to go to summer camp for.

Then my phone rang.

It was a New York City number, and I didn't recognize it.

"It's her!" Miranda shrieked. "It's her, it's her!"

"Or maybe not," I said.

It was her.

"Hi," I said. "What are you doing right now?"

"Calling you," Bianca said. "Why?"

"Come meet me in Prospect Park."

I heard her breathy laugh through the phone. "Now?"

"Yes."

"It'll take me, like, an hour to get there."

"I'll wait."

Then I had to get rid of Miranda, which she pouted about, but I didn't need to be getting to know Bianca in front of a friend of mine who was dressed like a model out of *Sports Illustrated*'s swimsuit edition.

About twenty minutes after Miranda had taken off, Bianca showed up—alone, fortunately. I had wondered a little, what would I do if she showed up with Leo? But deep down, I'd known she would come alone. I'd known she wouldn't tell him what we were doing. Not that we were doing anything, but . . .

We sat in the park for hours. I don't know how, but we just kept finding things to talk about. Either we'd agree on things, which felt amazing, like she somehow *got* me, or we'd disagree on something, which felt equally amazing, like she was opening my eyes to a way of looking at the world that had never occurred to me before.

Here are some things I learned about Bianca today:

1) Her mother is from England, so she's spent most vacations in Bath, and she can fake a flawless British accent.

2) She's lived in New York her entire life, but as far as she's aware, she's never seen a movie star.

3) She daydreams a lot, so she admits that it's possible she's seen lots of movie stars and just didn't notice them because she wasn't looking.

4) She's trying to read her way through the Modern Library's list of the 100 best novels ever written. (Then we pulled up the list on my phone and she told me which

ones she's read so far and I told her which ones I've read so far, and she's actually three ahead of me, but I'd never seen the list before today, so I'm sure I can get caught up.)

5) Her favorite place in the city is Times Square. (She's the first New Yorker I've ever met who actually *likes* Times Square. As far as I'm concerned, Times Square is tourist-land, and let them have it. But Bianca swears that she loves it there. "Do you even go to watch the ball drop on New Year's?" I teased her, and she answered—totally honestly—"I used to go every year! Now I just watch the whole thing on TV. It's my weird little obsession.")

6) She hates romantic comedies. ("Because you hate romance, or because you hate comedy?" I asked her. "Neither," she said.)

7) She wants to get a job in international politics when she grows up, like work for the UN or be a diplomat or something else where she travels a lot and wields influence.

8) Her biggest phobia is fire, which she says is a "rational fear," since fire can kill you. She laughed at me when she found out that my biggest phobia is public speaking, because according to Bianca, public speaking cannot actually result in death.

9) She's the most incredible girl I've ever met.

When the field started filling up with the after-work crowd, we left our spot and walked around for a while.

I bought us lemon Popsicles from a pushcart. We were talking so much that we barely made the time between sentences to eat, so her Popsicle melted all over her hand. She was laughing at the sticky mess, and I wanted so badly to lick every last drop of lemon off her fingers—but I didn't, I didn't touch her fingers with my tongue or any other part of her with any part of me.

We wound up at the carousel, so I bought tickets for both of us and we rode horses next to each other. Afterward, I walked her to the subway, all the way down to the turnstile, as far as I could go without actually getting on her train with her.

"I had a lot of fun this afternoon," she said.

"Me, too," I said. "Maybe we'll do it again sometime."

And neither of us said anything about Leo at all.

I wanted to kiss her. I would have traded anything for it. Watching her walk away felt like suffocating, and again I thought of *Romeo and Juliet. My lips, two blushing pilgrims, ready stand to smooth that rough touch with a tender kiss.*

See, this is why it's hard to be a writer. Some other writer has always said it all before you, and surely they have said it better.

But today I don't care, not about any of that. Life is sort of like Goldilocks and the Three Bears, if you know what I mean. Some days are too big. Some days are much too small. But today was one of those rare days that was just right.

While Chris was buying his sixteen hats, Arden poked around The Grass Is Always Greener. On one of the racks, she found a dress that didn't look too far off from what Bianca had been wearing the first day Peter saw her in the bookstore. It was bright blue, not yellow, but it had that lace trim at the top, just like what Peter had described. That style had been very en vogue last year, so it wasn't surprising to find it here.

Arden slipped into the dressing room and tried it on. The straps were a little too long, so they kept sliding down her shoulders, but maybe that was sexy? Otherwise, it fit well. She stood on tiptoe and held her hair off her face in an improvised upsweep. *I look pretty,* she thought. *I think.*

"Arden?" She heard Chris's voice from outside the dressing room.

She opened the curtain. "Hi." She looked up at him through lowered eyelashes.

"Oh, there you are," he said. "I'm ready to go. I got the last hat for free, because I'm buying so many! Anyway, I'm starving. You want to get some food?"

Arden swallowed hard. "Um," she said. "What do you think of this dress?" She pirouetted slowly, still on her toes.

When she turned around to face front, Chris seemed to have only just registered that she wasn't wearing the jacket and jeans that she'd been in all day. "It's nice," he said. "But don't you already have something like that?"

She dropped to flat feet. "No."

"Well, then you should get it if you like it. I'm going to start loading the hats into the car while you're doing that, okay? I'll meet you out there. And then food! God, I'm starving."

He galloped out of the store, and Arden returned to the dressing room. Before peeling off the dress, she looked in the mirror for a second, but she didn't see anything pretty there anymore. She just saw herself.

Back in regular clothes, she handed the dress to the sales clerk, who asked, "You buying this?"

"No, that's okay."

"It looked good on you," the sales girl said with a shrug.

Arden shook her head. "It's not really worth it." And she followed her boyfriend into the cold outside.

Things with Chris weren't always like this

Arden had nursed a dormant crush on Chris Jump through most of freshman and sophomore years. She wasn't obsessed with him in the way she'd been with some other boys—like Ellzey, for example. But Chris was tall and handsome and very much at the center of the theater crowd, even when they were freshmen. So she was vaguely interested.

And then he got cast as Abélard in the play adaptation of the love letters of Héloïse and Abélard, and she was a goner.

Arden got to watch Chris as Abélard most days after school, because she did stage crew: costuming, lighting, scenery, props, whatever else was needed backstage. She'd discovered stage crew at the beginning of freshman year, when Lindsey dragged her along to a drama club meeting. Lindsey never went back after that first time—as with so many other things, her interest flared and then disappeared within the course of a few days— but Arden was hooked. She saw it as a personal victory when a play went off with all the actors wearing exactly what they were supposed to be wearing, walking on stage at exactly the moments they were supposed to make their entrances.

This wasn't just an inflated sense of self-importance. If she weren't there with her walkie-talkie, muttering instructions, each actor would literally have no idea what was happening in the play outside of his or her own scenes. If she didn't run onstage when the lights went dark to quickly reposition the scenery into the spots that she had marked with glow-in-the-dark tape, then the scenery would not get moved, and classroom scenes would take place in monasteries, kitchen scenes in forests. It made her feel like she mattered.

Plus, she made good friends through drama club, even before there was anything romantic between her and Chris. Arden clicked quickly with Kirsten, who, as an excellent singer and a mediocre-at-best actress, got major parts in all the musicals and bit parts in all the straight plays. Arden took a little while longer to connect with Naomi, who did stage crew with her and had a classic "don't notice me" backstage personality, until she got comfortable with you. But after Arden and Naomi stayed six hours after school one time in order to rush a stage backdrop to completion, that friendship, too, was solidified.

Freshman year, Arden's parents came to her first play. Afterward her dad complimented her, and then he said, "Maybe next year you'll even make it *on* stage!" She hadn't invited him to any performances since then. He didn't get it. Arden's ultimate dream, for when she was a senior, was to be the stage manager, the one who called the entire play. Like God, basically.

Last year, sophomore spring, Arden was doing tech for *Abélard and Héloïse*. It was based on a real-life doomed romance of a couple in twelfth-century France. Héloïse was a beautiful young woman, and Abélard was her teacher . . . until they fell in love. Nobody approved of their union, so Héloïse was forced to join a nunnery and Abélard became a monk. For the last twenty years of Abélard's life, the two wrote passionate love letters back and forth, forbidden to ever see each other again. They loved each other and nobody else except for God up until the day they died. Arden thought this was one of the greatest love stories she had ever heard. She would kill for a life like that—minus the bit where she had to become a nun.

Mr. Lansdowne's decision to cast Chris as Abélard angered every theater guy in the junior and senior classes. There was a lot of indignant gossiping about it backstage, and, since Arden was always backstage, she overheard it all.

"The leads are supposed to go to the upperclassmen," Brad griped. "Everyone knows that."

"Mr. Lansdowne just cast Chris because he's cute," bitched Eric. "He's not even that good an actor."

Actually, Chris was cute *and* a good actor, but whatever.

Shortly after rehearsals for the play kicked off, Chris started dating Natalia. Natalia played one of the nuns, which, from what Arden knew of Natalia, was basically the opposite of typecasting.

Natalia and Chris went together like fire and gasoline. When they weren't on stage, or making out, they were screaming at each other. Then Natalia would stomp off to weep in the girls' room, and the rest of the nuns would run after her, and Chris would complain to Arden.

"She's just so crazy," Chris would say.

"I know," Arden would sympathize.

"It's all about the drama with her," Chris said one time, a hammer hanging idly from his hand while Arden pieced together scenery. "It's like she *wants* to fight. We just spent half an hour arguing over which side of the stage was stage right and which side was stage left."

"The left side from the audience's perspective is stage right," Arden said.

"That's what I told her! But she refused to listen. So I looked it up on my phone, which obviously confirmed that you and I are right, and then she started crying because I was being 'mean.'"

"You were not being mean," Arden said, taking the hammer from Chris's hands since he was not doing anything with it except swinging it around, which had the distinct potential to do more harm than good. "It's not like you were telling her she was wrong in order to hurt her feelings. You just wanted her to know so she wouldn't sound silly in front of anybody else."

"Exactly," Chris said. "Thank you." He followed Arden around to the other side of the backdrop she was working on. "So how do I get her to stop fighting with me? What should I do so we can have a conversation without it turning into her crying? Should I just agree with her, even when she says something totally wrong, like that stage left is to the audience's left?"

All told at that point, Arden's dating experience included two kisses at school dances, one kiss at a bar mitzvah, and one week of "dating" Benedict Swindenhausen when they were in the seventh grade. She had no idea why Chris thought she was some kind of relationship expert, but she liked the role.

"I think you have to respect where she's coming from," Arden said, thinking it over. "You can't just say, 'No, you're wrong.' Say, 'I see why you might think that stage left is to your left. That would make sense. I was also surprised when I learned that wasn't the case.' Then it seems like you're on her side, you know?"

"That's smart," Chris said. "You're smart."

"Thank you." Arden blushed a little.

"You give me hope that not all girls are total drama queens," Chris said.

"Not me," Arden said. "Not a drama queen." She held up the hammer. "Just a hammer queen, I guess."

That sounded stupid, but Chris laughed anyway.

"Why are you with her, anyway?" Arden asked. "If you make each other so unhappy, what's the point?"

Chris just shook his head. "I don't know. I can't explain it."

Arden felt envy pulsate in her chest. She wanted that: the sort of love that you can't explain. Like Héloïse and Abélard. It didn't make sense to anybody else but them—but that didn't make it any less true.

But apparently what Chris and Natalia had wasn't really love, since a couple weeks later, during intermission between the first and second acts of their final performance of *Héloïse and Abélard*, she dumped him.

It was five minutes before Chris was about to make his entrance, and he was nowhere to be seen. "Find him!" ordered the disembodied voice of the stage manager through Arden's headset.

Eventually she tracked him down behind a rack of coats in the costume closet. He was sitting on the floor in his monk outfit, his face buried in a floor-length fur cloak.

"Is everything okay?" Arden asked, crouching down beside him.

He shook his head and rubbed his eyes. Arden waited for him to speak. Finally he got out, "She broke up with me." He sucked in his breath and bit down on his knuckles.

Arden pushed her way through the coats so she was sitting on the floor next to Chris. She rubbed his arm. "I'm sorry," she said.

"Where is he?" demanded the stage manager's voice in her ear.

"This will be for the best, though," Arden said. "I know it doesn't feel like it right now. But she wasn't making you happy. You fought all the time. Everything was an argument. Remember?"

Chris nodded, slowly. Then he protested, "But sometimes we were happy," and his face crumpled again.

Arden put her arm around him. "Not often enough, Chris. And not happy enough. You deserve better. You're a great guy, and you should have a girl who appreciates you."

"Not that great, I guess." He gave a sad little laugh. "I'm sitting in some ladies' coats when I should be preparing to make my entrance. But, Arden, how can I go out there?"

"Because you're an actor," Arden said. "Because you're the real deal. You're talented, and you're driven, and you're thoughtful—"

The next thing she knew, he was kissing her.

When they pulled apart, Arden was breathing hard. *So that's what it feels like to be part of a stage kiss.*

"Chris. Why did you . . . What was that? I mean, thank you. Wow. But . . . where did that even come from?"

"From eight weeks of dating the wrong girl," he replied. He stood up and smoothed his hair. "Arden," Chris said, "will you go out with me?"

Arden stood up, too. After a lifetime of unrequited crushes and secret stalking, how did the answer turn out to be so easy?

"Yes," she said. She stood on tiptoe to kiss him again. "I'd love to go out with you."

He put his hands on her shoulders and held her back from him a little, so he could look in her eyes. "But no drama," he said. "I can't take any more drama."

"Don't worry," she said. "From here on out, all your drama will be strictly on stage. Speaking of . . ." She looked pointedly at her watch.

"All right, stage crew." He gave a little salute. "I've got it." His face broke into a grin, and she could see his dimple. Even if Mr. Lansdowne *did* cast him just because he was cute, that seemed like a good enough reason. "I'll see you after the play," Chris said, and, after one more kiss, he jogged off, just in time to make his entrance.

Arden followed after him at a more sedate pace, running her fingers over her lips, trying to make sure that this was real. She, Arden, backstage girl, nice girl, perennially single, lonely girl, had somehow snagged the leading man. And they'd stayed together ever since.

Stalking people, take one

The last guy Arden had been obsessed with, in her pre-Chris days last year, had been Ellzey. Yes, Ellzey of trying-to-smoke-pot-on-Matt-Washington's-patio fame. The thing was, Ellzey was a tremendous singer. He was in show choir and sang a solo of Billy Joel's "And So It Goes" so beautifully that it brought tears to Arden's eyes every time she heard it, which was often, since she liked to watch online videos of the choir when she was supposed to be doing her homework. She had thought Ellzey was the most romantic guy in the world, or at least in Cumberland. There was no way he could sing a song with such depths of emotion if he weren't.

Ellzey seemed to have a passing knowledge of Arden's existence, mostly that she was the girl who said "great job" after every single chorus performance. Also one time he complimented her on her Harry Potter tote bag, which she then made a point of carrying to school every day, until Lindsey told her,

"That bag is filthy. Dumbledore is rolling in his grave. Put it out to pasture, Arden."

One Saturday night last March, Arden, Lindsey, and Naomi slept over at Kirsten's house to celebrate her sixteenth birthday. At the time Naomi was going out with one of the guys in show choir, so she had insider information about choral activities. She happened to mention that a bunch of the guys in choir were also having a sleepover. That very night! She didn't know exactly who was there. The guy she was dating, Douglas, for sure. Alex, Ellzey, maybe Carter?

"We should go," Arden said.

"To the boys' slumber party?" Kirsten asked, wrapping her long blond hair around a curling iron. Kirsten's hair was her pride and joy. The rest of them called it "mermaid hair," and while Kirsten would shoot down any other compliments sent her way ("No, I swear, these pants just make me *appear* skinny"; "Honestly, I had my dad explain the reading to me— I couldn't finish it, either"; "I'm actually way worse at piano than should even be possible"), she accepted "mermaid hair" with the calm acknowledgment of one who knew this praise to be undeniable.

"Yes, to the boys' slumber party," Arden said.

"Why?" Kirsten asked.

"To say hi," Arden explained.

"Why?" Kirsten asked again, holding her hair in place. "I just mean, like, what's the point?"

"What's the point of anything? Like, what's the point of curling your hair?" Lindsey countered. Arden knew that Lindsey meant her question innocently—Lindsey genuinely did not understand the point of curling hair—but Kirsten glared at Lindsey as though this were a personal attack.

"Wouldn't you like to see your boyfriend?" Arden asked Naomi.

"Douglas isn't exactly my boyfriend," Naomi said. "I mean, we haven't had the 'are we boyfriend and girlfriend' talk or anything."

"Obviously we should crash the boys' slumber party," Lindsey volunteered. Arden threw her a grateful look, while Kirsten and Naomi both frowned. They were not exactly Lindsey Matson fans, since most of the time they wanted to gossip about boys and try on each other's jewelry, while Lindsey almost never wanted to gossip about boys, and last year she'd sold the small amount of jewelry that she owned in order to purchase absurdly expensive "performance" running shoes. She was here as a package deal with Arden, and all of them knew it—except for maybe Lindsey herself.

"What else is there to do?" Lindsey reasoned.

"We could stay here and watch a movie," Kirsten suggested.

Arden felt deep in her bones that she was not put on this earth to sit in her pajamas in Kirsten's finished basement and watch a movie.

By the time she'd convinced her three friends to go to the boys' sleepover, it was one a.m. "Whose house are they at?" she asked Naomi.

Naomi shook her head. "I don't know. Not Douglas's."

"Will you text him and ask where they are?"

Naomi scrunched up her face. "Um . . . we don't totally have that kind of relationship yet?"

They decided to try Alex's house first. Alex's house was big, and he didn't have any younger siblings who might get underfoot, so this seemed like a likely location for a sleepover. Plus he lived only a few blocks away from Kirsten's house. Kirsten scribbled a note that said, cryptically, *We'll be back,* and left it on her kitchen table as they silently snuck out of the house. At the last minute, Arden grabbed one of the helium balloons that Kirsten's stepmom had festively tied to the fridge. "When we show up, it'll be like a parade," she whispered.

But when they got to Alex's, every window was dark. Either the boys weren't there, or they were already fast asleep.

"I can't imagine they've gone to bed already," Naomi said as the girls stood in Alex's driveway, staring up at the house. "Douglas said that last time they had a sleepover, they stayed up until four in the morning singing the entirety of *Les Miz.*"

"Are you *kidding me*?" Arden shrieked.

"You just described Arden's most dearly held sexual fantasy," Lindsey explained.

"Maybe they're at Ellzey's," Kirsten suggested.

"Does anybody know where Ellzey lives?" asked Naomi.

Arden raised her hand. "I do."

"Wait, how?" Naomi asked.

"Because she's his stalker," said Lindsey.

"Should we tie the balloon to Alex's mailbox?" Arden asked before they left. "So they know that we were here?"

"Let's not," Naomi said quickly. She looked concerned.

Ellzey's house was nearly a half-hour walk away, but it was a surprisingly warm night for March, and none of them was tired. When they entered his driveway, they noticed a light still on, on the second floor of the house, and three cars parked outside.

"That's where they are," Arden whispered.

They stared reverentially at the lit window. Arden imagined that she could hear Ellzey's gentle tenor voice floating out and down to her. She felt momentarily like she was in *Romeo and Juliet*, the balcony scene. Only she would be Romeo, in this situation.

"Now what?" Kirsten asked.

"We have to get their attention," Arden said.

"Are you sure you can't just text Douglas?" Lindsey asked Naomi.

Even in the moonlight, it was clear that Naomi was blushing. "No way."

So they tried throwing rocks at the window. This had no impact. Either because they had no aim and the majority of their rocks missed their mark, or because the boys were singing so loudly they were deaf to the thumping of rocks against their house. Maybe both.

"You're an athlete," Arden said to Lindsey as she hurled another pebble from Ellzey's gravel driveway and it went flying off into the distance. "You're supposed to be good at this stuff."

"I'm on the track team," Lindsey said, her next stone falling ten feet short of its mark. "There's no throwing in track."

"Think of this as cross-training," Arden said.

When their arms grew tired, Lindsey suggested singing. "Like sirens in a Greek myth," she explained.

"I can't really carry a tune," said Naomi. "That's why I do stage crew."

"Pull it together, Naomi," snapped Lindsey.

Kirsten, of course, was already belting out her song from the fall production of *Cabaret*.

Together, the girls sang "And So It Goes," with Arden trying her hand at Ellzey's solo. It seemed like if anything would draw him to the window, that would work. But still, she saw no Ellzey.

The girls were about to admit defeat when the front door opened. The porch light turned on. *This was it.*

In the doorway stood a gray-haired woman in a bathrobe. She stared out at the four girls, who were frozen like startled deer in the sudden light. "Hello?" she said.

"Hello," the girls chorused. Then, because it seemed like somebody needed to say something, Arden added, "We're here to see Ellzey."

"Well," said the woman in the bathrobe, "I'm *Mrs.* Ellzey."

She opened the door wider, and even though it seemed like the wise course of action would be to flee the scene, the girls followed her inside like a string of dutiful ducklings.

"Bart!" Mrs. Ellzey hollered upstairs.

"Yeah, Mom?"

"Come down here. Bring your friends, young man."

So that was Ellzey's first name. *Bart.* Arden wondered if he started going by Ellzey because he didn't like that name. She wouldn't blame him. It sounded an awful lot like *fart*.

Ellzey and the rest of the guys stampeded downstairs. Their faces registered shock when they saw the four girls and the one yellow balloon still tied to Arden's wrist. Ellzey clearly had not planned to see any girls tonight. He'd replaced his contacts with wire-frame glasses. He was wearing socks but no shoes, baggy gym shorts, and a shapeless sweater. Arden had dreamed of this, seeing Ellzey in his natural habitat. But maybe these weren't the exact circumstances she had imagined.

"Did you really think you could get away with inviting girls over for a late-night rendezvous?" demanded Mrs. Ellzey, hands on hips. "You thought I wouldn't notice?"

Ellzey's friends turned pale. They furiously shook their heads. "We didn't invite anybody," Ellzey said.

"We have no idea what they are doing here," added Douglas, narrowing his eyes at Naomi.

"Then what *possibly* brought four girls over here in the middle of the night?" Mrs. Ellzey countered.

Arden thought about Kirsten's question before they'd left the house. *What's the point?* This seemed, suddenly, like a relevant inquiry.

"Mom!" Ellzey cried. "We didn't ask them to come here to, like, hook up with us or whatever gross thing it is that you're thinking!" His voice cracked and he looked mortified.

"Can I just say something?" Lindsey asked. "I'm gay. So I'm definitely not here to hook up with your son."

Mrs. Ellzey looked pained. "You girls need to go home," she said. "And as for you, Bart . . ."

Arden and her friends fled. They didn't say anything for the first four blocks on their walk back to Kirsten's. Then, finally, Lindsey spoke.

"Well, it's a good thing we didn't leave the balloon at Alex's."

And they collapsed into giggles.

On Monday, Douglas broke up with Naomi. He said he thought they were "looking for different things." Up until he approached her at Matt Washington's party, a full year later, Ellzey acted like he didn't really know who Arden was. But since that was how he'd always behaved, that felt disappointing but not dramatic. The most positive outcome was that in the year since then, Lindsey and Arden had been able to say to each other, pretty much any time they needed a laugh, "I'm *Mrs.* Ellzey," and it never failed to cheer them up. And that alone made the whole thing worthwhile.

The Parakeets vs. the Wolverines

The weekend after she and Chris went shopping for sixteen hats at The Grass Is Always Greener, Arden woke up to a pounding on her door. She rolled over, blinking the gunk out of her eyes. "What?" she croaked out.

Roman flung open the door and stood there fully dressed in a basketball jersey, mesh shorts, and sneakers. "Can you drive me to my game?" he asked.

Arden sat up, slowly coming to terms with the fact that she was, yet again, awake. Why didn't any of the boys in her life know how to sleep late? "You have a game today?" she asked. Mouser, who had been restlessly catnapping on the foot of her bed, bolted for the door, as though she, too, wanted no part in this.

"Yeah, duh," Roman said. "In like twenty minutes."

This was the first Arden had heard of it. "Can't Dad take you?"

"He was supposed to." Roman looked down at the floor and

scuffed his shoe. "Uh, he left a note. He already went into the office. So . . ."

"It's *Sunday*," Arden said. When she was little, Sunday mornings meant eating their mother's homemade pancakes in her pajamas and watching cartoons on TV. Her mother made silver dollar pancakes and laid them out on her plate like they were lily pads, with the syrup forming a river that flowed between them. Arden would take little plastic toys and place them on the pancakes like they were forest creatures who lived on these lily pads, and she would send them rafting down the syrup river. She would play like this until her pancakes were absolutely grubby, and then her mother would make her another batch, and those she would actually eat.

Arden should have woken up even earlier and made pancakes for her family today. She'd never tried to make them herself, but it couldn't be that hard. She'd figured out how to do some cooking in the past two months. Some cooking, and a lot of ordering takeout. Her father turned out to be clueless about every aspect of the kitchen except for how to make hummus and spaghetti. (Not together, thank God.) Arden had started to seriously wonder how her father had ever survived on his own before her parents got married. How had he not starved to death?

"I'm calling him." Arden reached for her phone. "He can't just forget you have a basketball game today, Roman. That's not right."

"Yeah, whatever, but can you call him from the car? I'm going to be late, and then Coach won't put me in the game. It's the rule."

There was a solid chance that Roman's coach wouldn't put him in the game anyway, since Roman was about half a foot shorter than any of the other sixth and seventh grade boys on his team, and also he was desperately nearsighted and refused to wear contacts when he played sports because he was scared of touching his eyeballs.

But Arden did not say this. She just threw on the jeans and sweatshirt closest to her bed and headed downstairs.

Roman had already gone down to the kitchen and was eating brown sugar straight out of the bag. Arden took it away from him. "One, that's disgusting. Two, are you an animal? Three, it's like eight in the morning." She stuck the bag on the uppermost shelf in the cabinet, which Roman would not be able to reach unless he climbed onto the counter, which he definitely would later.

"I need fuel," Roman explained. "For my game. Coach says it's important to eat an energizing breakfast before playing."

They stepped outside, and Roman ran down the driveway to Arden's car. March was still going through its "in like a lion" phase, and he was only wearing shorts. She should have made him put on a coat. Why did it never occur to children to dress for the weather?

"It's locked," he hollered at her.

She patted her pocket for her car key, then realized that she must have left it in her school locker. This was not the first time she'd forgotten her key—which was why she had Lindsey hold on to an extra copy for her.

"Wait here for a sec," she told Roman.

"I'm gonna be late!" Roman protested, hopping in place to warm himself against the cold.

Arden ignored him and jogged through the woods between her house and Lindsey's. The woods seemed smaller these days than they had when she first discovered Lindsey there. They were much smaller than they were described in the Arden books. No one from the Just Like Me Dolls Company had actually shown up in person to scope out the size of the woods where the drama went down. They just wrote the story.

Arden knocked on Lindsey's back door. Knocking was a stupid rule that Mr. and Mrs. Matson enforced, even though Arden and Lindsey had been constantly in and out of each other's houses for half of their lives. All things being equal, Arden's parents had way more reason to be suspicious of Lindsey than Lindsey's parents had to be suspicious of Arden. Short of that one supposed pot-ownership incident, Arden was a rule-abiding, hand-raising, crosswalk-obeying, absolute golden child, and Lindsey was . . . well, Lindsey.

Arden's father thought Lindsey was a troublemaker, which was true from an adult perspective, but irrelevant to how good a friend or person she was. He thought she was unambitious, which was decidedly *not* true; it's just that her ambitions were not the sort that Arden's father cared about. And though he would never come out and say this, and would deny it to the death if Arden had asked him point-blank, he didn't like that Lindsey was gay. Whenever he was around and Lindsey was over, he would watch her like a hawk, as if concerned that she was going to suddenly try to stick her tongue in his daughter's mouth.

But at least Arden's parents had never given a damn whether or not Lindsey knocked on their door before she came in.

"Hello!" Mrs. Matson called from the kitchen.

Arden took this as her permission to enter. All three Matsons were sitting at the kitchen table, eating oatmeal. Lindsey perked up considerably when she saw Arden. "What are you doing here?" she asked. "It's like the middle of the night for you."

"Roman needed a ride to basketball." Arden chose not to mention the bit where their father had forgotten about his son's game, because that was just guaranteeing that Lindsey's parents would gossip about and judge her dad as soon as she left the room. They didn't understand that ever since Arden's mom had left, her father was suffering, he was alone, he was lost, and he was focusing all his attention on the one part of his life where he felt like he was in control.

"Want to come to the game with me?" Arden asked Lindsey. If Lindsey came, then maybe this youth sports game would not be as tremendously boring as it was shaping up to be.

"Sorry, Arden, we have church this morning," said Mr. Matson.

"It's Sunday," Mrs. Matson added, her tone implying that the equivalence of *Sunday* and *church* should be obvious to anyone who wasn't a complete heathen.

Arden's family had never been particularly religious. According to Lindsey, her parents used to be the same—until

Mr. Matson got sick, a decade ago. To Arden this seemed backward. Wouldn't it be more logical to believe in God *until* you got cancer? But as far as Lindsey's dad was concerned, it was his newfound faith that had helped him pull through, and he'd been cancer-free for seven years now.

"I can stop by afterward," Lindsey volunteered. "The game's at Roman's school, right? How long will it go for?"

"Like a hundred hours," Arden guessed.

"Cool. See you there. Go team. Wait, what's his team's name again?"

"The Parakeets." Arden shrugged.

"Go Parakeets. Tweet, tweet, tweet."

"Can I borrow my car key?" Arden asked.

"Sure." Lindsey ran upstairs to get it, her feet pounding the steps. Her parents watched this transaction with baffled expressions. There was a lot about having Lindsey as their daughter that they did not seem to understand.

Arden grabbed her key and headed back to the car. She unlocked the door for her shivering brother. "My muscles are going to seize up," he told her once he was buckled in and the car was on. "Can't you turn up the heat?"

"The heater's working as hard as it can, kiddo. If you're not satisfied, you are totally welcome to get out and walk," Arden said, driving down their quiet street.

Roman considered this and said nothing more on the matter.

Arden watched early-morning Cumberland pass by her windshield. It was a quaint little city with lots of history, old houses that sold for cheap, and attractive church steeples that dotted the hillside. In the 1700s a vaguely important fort had been here, and in the 1800s Cumberland was a shipping junction and home to industry, facts which brought the city great pride and were commemorated by many plaques around town.

But if you were on a tour to see the Important Sites of Cumberland—a tour that every middle school student in the town had done, and almost nobody else—you would quickly realize that Cumberland's most vibrant years were well behind it. Maybe that's part of what attracted Arden's parents here in the first place, that it seemed uneventful. Eighteen years ago, they'd bought a pretty brick house and two gently used cars, and Arden's mom planted a garden out front, and it seemed like the perfect place to raise a family.

Now the garden was dead and straggly, and her mother's car was gone, replaced by Arden's junkyard heap. And it shouldn't be like this, and her dad should be home and her mom should be home and Peter's brother should be home as well, and everything seemed off-kilter.

As she drove through the empty morning streets, Arden pulled out her phone and called her father.

"Mom says you're not supposed to talk on the phone while you drive," Roman contributed.

"Mom isn't here," Arden said. And that shut him up.

"Arden?" her father answered. "What are you doing awake, honey?"

Arden wondered if everyone she knew secretly had received

some sort of Arden Handbook, containing key Arden Facts, like "Arden does not like to wake up early." Or maybe she was just really, really predictable.

"Roman has a basketball game today, Dad," she said. "You were supposed to drive him."

"No, I had that on my calendar. His game is on the fourteenth."

"Today *is* the fourteenth."

Her father paused, and she could picture him in his ergonomic desk chair that she used to spin around on when she was a kid, looking through his calendar on his computer. "Dammit," he said. "I totally screwed up. I'm so sorry, honey. I got my days completely confused. I feel terrible."

"It's okay."

"I'm coming over right now. I'll pick him up now." She could hear him shuffling around.

"We're already in the car," she said. "I'll get him there."

Her father was silent for another moment, and when he spoke, his voice was low. "You're a really good kid, Arden, do you know that? I hope I tell you that enough."

"Don't worry about it, Dad." It wasn't really *his* fault that she was in a car driving to a children's sports game in what was basically the middle of the night. He was just doing the best he could with the situation he was given.

"I love you, honey. I'm sorry it's such a hard time right now. Things will get better. I know they will."

And she wanted him to be right, if only so he didn't have to be so sad.

"It's okay," Roman said once she'd hung up, "because maybe Mom will be there."

Arden felt her muscles tighten. "What makes you think Mom will be there?"

"Because I invited her."

"What? When?"

"When I talked to her on Friday."

Arden had artfully dodged that call, as she had so many others in the past seven weeks. She heard Roman's and her dad's ends of these conversations, though. She couldn't help but over-hear them pretending like everything was great at home, prom-ising a repaired kitchen sink and an A+ science project and recordings of all Mom's favorite TV shows, as if any of those things would be worth returning for. Arden couldn't miss her father's and brother's desperate voices going on and on about what a blast they were having, what a delight it was to live here in this house with this family, and asking again and again, *Will you come home now? Will you come home now please?*

Arden didn't want any part in these negotiations. They made her sick. What she knew was that you couldn't force somebody to love you, you couldn't convince them to feel something they didn't feel, no amount of begging would work. All you could do was try, try to make yourself into somebody worth loving.

"Did Mom say she would come to your game?" Arden asked Roman.

"Not *exactly* . . ."

"What *exactly* did she say?"

"She said it was too soon," Roman mumbled.

"Too soon for what?"

"I don't know. Just that it was too soon." He stared out the window for a moment, then sat up straighter. "But I think she was just saying that. I told her my team is doing really good this year. I told her I was the point guard and if she came I'd score a basket just for her."

Arden didn't know anything about basketball, but she highly doubted that her brother's role on the team was anything so important-sounding as "point guard," and she was confident that he would not be scoring any baskets today, regardless of who was in the stands.

She hated this. The bargaining, the gambling, the promises. It was the same thing her father was trying to do by working seventy hours a week. *You should come back because I am so successful. You should come back because I'm so good at basketball. Come back come back come back.*

It was a stupid game and Arden wasn't going to play it.

"She's not going to come, Roman," Arden said. "She's three hundred miles away. She'd have to wake up at like four a.m. to make it there on time."

He shrugged his bony shoulders. "Maybe she's going to surprise me."

"It's not a surprise if you think it's going to happen. She's not coming."

Roman was the last kid to arrive at the gym, but he still made it there two minutes before Coach's cutoff, so good enough. The Parakeets were playing the Wolverines, which seemed like a recipe for a bloodbath. Arden settled into the bleachers with

124

the parents and tried to fall back asleep. But these bleachers seemed to be torture devices designed to keep the people sitting on them awake. So Arden pulled out her phone and returned to Tonight the Streets Are Ours.

Yesterday she'd read further through Peter's posts from last summer. He joked about the bookstore. He occasionally went to the Hamptons with his family. The Hamptons were a rich-person beach vacation area, so, as Peter put it, "Obviously my parents *have* to have a house there." He went to parties— countless parties, with countless friends whose names Arden could never keep track of, and often couldn't even tell if they were guys or girls.

There was no hint in any of these posts of Peter's brother's tragic disappearance, which Arden knew, from reading ahead, was barreling down on them. There was very little mention of his brother at all. Peter's summer seemed bright with possibility and hazy with freedom, and it made Arden feel nostalgic for a summertime that she had never actually experienced and likely never would. Today was cold and tomorrow would be cold, too, and even when the weather finally warmed up, what could Arden expect? Ten weeks of waking up to drive Roman to sports games and playdates while her father worked and her mother was off enjoying her big-city adventures. Keeping the house clean and getting food on the table. Trying to keep Lindsey out of trouble. For excitement, she could have a job at the hardware store with Chris—Mr. Jump had already offered.

Her summer plans weren't anything bad, nothing to complain about. But Arden felt like Tonight the Streets Are Ours had shone a spotlight on her own life and revealed that everything in it was happening in black and white, when there was a whole world of color out there. Arden never would have said that tonight the streets were hers. At best, she felt that this space on the bleachers where she sat right now was hers, at least for the next couple hours.

But for all the color and light in Peter's life that Arden enjoyed reading about, there were no entries she loved to read as much as the ones about Bianca. She never knew when Bianca was going to appear in Peter's stories, so every time she did, Arden felt a thrill.

July 15

Bianca showed up at the bookstore today. Alone.

"Oh, yoo-hoo, shop clerk," she said to me. "I'm trying to decide which of these books to buy. Any recommendations?" She set down in front of me three books of poetry. Love poetry. And she winked at me.

"Buy them all," I said. "I get paid on commission."

She did.

I swear to God, this girl is driving me crazy.

August 4

Miranda and Julio and I went to the free Probiotics show on the pier tonight. Miranda kept talking about how her mom knows somebody who knows somebody who knows the Probiotics' manager and maybe she could get us backstage afterward. She kept threatening to "make some calls," but I never actually saw her call anybody.

It was offensively hot, but there was some rainbow sprinkler set up that you could run through to cool off (like a normal sprinkler, but somehow they'd put rainbow lights over it?), and there were people giving away bottles of free Vitaminwater.

I do not understand Vitaminwater, by the way. Drink some water. Eat some vitamins. Are you so busy that you need those two tasks combined into one? I mean, I know New Yorkers have a lot going on, but chill the hell out.

We were dancing in the middle of it all, sweating up a storm, when we ran into Bianca. She was with Leo and a bunch of his asshole teammates.

Sorry. "Football teammates." That's what I meant.

I kind of froze when I saw her and Leo together, as though she and I had been doing something illicit, even though we haven't, we haven't done anything that's not completely G-rated, I haven't even held her hand. I barely ever see her. I felt guilty and then I felt mad at Leo for making me feel guilty, even though I guess that none of that is his fault.

Leo's friends were all, "Dude, this is so lame," and, "Dude, does anybody have any beer?" and, "Dude, why aren't there any chicks here?" I have met some of these guys one-on-one before and they've seemed like reasonable human beings, but somehow their intelligence gets halved every time you add one more of them to the mix, so that by the time you have five of them in a crew like today, they are basically a pack of mentally challenged terriers.

"So *you're* Bianca," Miranda said, taking her in. Miranda is not the world's greatest secret keeper, and I found myself wishing that I'd never said anything to her.

"Pleased to meet you," Bianca said, sticking out her hand for a shake. "And you are . . . ?"

Today Miranda was wearing a midriff top and shorts showing off her ass cheeks, and all Leo's friends were salivating over her, but I only had eyes for Bianca. "You look really nice," I told her. She was wearing about twice as many clothes as Miranda (which is not that hard to do), and she reminded me of an angel. If wings had sprouted from her shoulder blades, I would not have been the least bit surprised.

Leo and his friends came up with some asinine game where they had to burp as loud as they could in between the band's songs, and if any of them burped loud enough to get the band's attention, then they "won."

"What do you win?" I asked.

The dog pack looked at me blankly.

"You just *win*," explained Leo.

Okay.

"So, Leo," I asked, making sure Bianca was in ear-shot. "What's your favorite Probiotics song?"

He shrugged. "I don't know many of their songs. That one they play on the radio is pretty good. What's yours?"

Why are you doing this, Bianca? I wanted to ask her. *Why are you still with him?*

I mean, I love Leo. I love Leo more than anyone does. But she's not right for him. He's not right for her. She belongs with someone like me.

You just win.

Easy for you to say, Leo.

Arden had taken to skimming the entries that didn't involve Bianca. She was as fascinated by Bianca as Peter was. She just wanted to spend more time with her, know more about her, uncover all the secrets of being Bianca.

Arden had also started reading the comments left by other Tonight the Streets Are Ours readers. There seemed to be a whole community of them. Whereas the early entries had garnered no feedback, the further into Peter's story she got, the more commentary there was. The commenters didn't seem to be people Peter knew—none of them said anything like "Yeah, I was at that concert with you!" Presumably they were not Leo or Leo's friends, since she couldn't imagine Peter writing about his crush on Bianca if he knew that her boyfriend was reading. On this post, for example, the comments said:

I found ur blog cuz i am the biggest probiotics fan evarrr. probiotics rock!!! u r so lucky u got to see them for free!!! i have already seen them 8 timez.
—MyKingdom4AHorse

I love your writing! I've also always wondered that about Vitaminwater. You're so funny.
—Delicate485

Are you and Bianca ever going to get together??? I'm dying out here! Leo sounds like a tool. Ugh I don't know what she sees in him.
—MessyDressyBessy

Arden considered leaving a comment, too. She couldn't say, "Are you and Bianca ever going to get together?" because she was reading this now nine months in the future, so she knew that, yes, they would, and then later still, they would break up. She could add her voice to the chorus saying "I love your writing" and "You're so funny," because she did, and he was, but she didn't want to be just another unnamed voice crowing about how great he was. She wanted to be something special to him, in the way that he was becoming something special to her. So she said nothing.

She glanced up at the court. Roman was still sitting on the bench. He scanned the bleachers. She caught his eye and smiled, then remembered that he probably couldn't identify her without his glasses. The plus side was that he wouldn't notice if she kept staring at her phone rather than watching his game. So she read on, skimming, skimming—until she came to the next post with Bianca.

September 2

Mom had to go back to the city a day early for some meeting of some charity board that she's on, so last night it was just us guys out in the Hamptons. You know what that means: BBQ! I don't know why Dad is so into grilling out except that Mom never lets him do it, and I don't know why Mom is so opposed to it except that she can tell it makes him happy. Thank you both for your extremely healthy relationship model, parents.

Also I think men like grilling more than women do because it appeals to some caveman part of our brains. The part of our brains that goes, "Fire! I like fire!" Do women not have this part of their brains? Is this some biological difference between the sexes? Are women's brains like, "Fire! That's that thing that burns down my dwelling shack!"?

I don't know, guys. They don't really teach biology at art school. Shh, don't tell my dad.

I love when my father barbecues, though. It's one of the only times when he seems like a human being instead of a machine. Okay, so he still wears a designer

131

button-down shirt that some personal shopper picked out while he's grilling, but he rolls up the sleeves and doesn't freak out if he gets some grease on it. He was in a good mood this weekend, too, actually asking me some questions about my life instead of just ordering me around. Not that I told him anything, of course. The more you tell him, the more ammunition he has.

I get it bad, but you know sometimes I think my brother gets it worse. To some extent they've given up on me as a lost cause. I'm younger and I'm a day-dreamer and a screwup, and I care more about fashion and poetry than a "real man" is supposed to, and I listen to music too loud. Whenever my father looks at me it's like I'm some sort of vermin who's crawled into his house that he can't exterminate, but it's not like he *expects* much from me.

They didn't even want me, you know. They wanted a kid, but they were getting old and it wasn't happening, so they finally decided to adopt. They'd had my brother for only a couple months before they found out they were pregnant with me. Maybe they even conceived me during some celebratory "We have a baby now!" sex.

Gross.

But they never let me forget it. That my brother, they chose. Me? A mistake.

The problem for my brother, though, is that he acts

like he's everything my dad wants in a son: respectable and honest and business-minded. Which means *he* doesn't get ignored and condescended to; he gets all the attention, all that suffocating attention, because he should know better and should do better. I don't know how he stands it, but maybe he doesn't know how I stand it, either.

Anyway. Whine, whine, whine, it's all beside the point, because this weekend didn't feel like that, for once. This weekend was *good*. Mom was gone, Dad was grilling meat, everyone else was there eating it. And I do mean *everyone*. Even though obviously the Hamptons house is there year-round and we could go any time, the truth is that Hamptons *season* ends at Labor Day weekend. Coffee shops with a half-hour-long line today will have a handful of customers this time next week. So last night we were closing out the *season*, if not the house itself, in force.

Julio kept cannonballing into the pool, and Uncle Todd was there being Uncle Todd, and Trotsky had invited over some heiress he met on the beach on Friday, and there were, like, five dogs running around and playing catch and I don't know who any of them belonged to. It was chaos and I loved it and I just hope that none of the photos we were taking get seen by my mother, ever. The moment when one of the dogs stole a steak off the grill and then dropped it in the pool was priceless, and it would give my mother a heart attack, for no good reason, since nobody was hurt, except for the cow who gave its life, I guess.

Leo had brought Bianca, which is how you know things are getting serious between them, because I have never known him to invite a girl out to the Hamptons for the weekend. It made me feel sick to see them together, and to know what that signified about their relationship. He goes to college next week, and obviously she'll still be in the city, and I wonder if I'll see her more now that he's going to be physically out of the picture, or less, now that the official glue to bind us together will be out of town. Or maybe the distance will tear them apart anyway. Maybe he'll fall for some college girl and Bianca will be just a distant memory for him. That would be nice.

Not that he's going *so* far away. And he's arranged his schedule so all his classes are just Tuesdays, Wednesdays, and Thursdays. He kept chattering about how excited he was about that. So he could come back to see Bianca any time.

If I only had to go to class three days a week, I could write a novel with all my time off. I could write freaking *Don Quixote* if I had as much time as Leo has. After he bragged about it for the third time, I asked what exactly he was planning to produce with all his spare time. He told me to shut up.

It was late, late, late by the time everyone went home

or just crashed at our place. It's a big house, lots of beds, so no big deal, and some of those people were *wasted*. Probably everyone in the Hamptons was wasted last night, though. It would have been competitive for anyone to get a taxi home.

It was a beautiful night and I didn't feel like going inside, not least because the last time I checked, Julio and some famous painter's daughter were making out in my bed. I just lay out in one of the deck chairs, staring up at the stars, until the fire in the grill had been put out and the dogs had been kenneled and the beer had been finished and everyone had gone to wherever everyone goes. I think they all forgot about me. I think I fell asleep.

I woke up to the very quiet sound of waves. Our house is beachfront property, so you can always hear the ocean waves, but this was different. Quiet and different.

I opened my eyes and saw someone swimming laps through the pool. It was pretty dark, so I just saw the shape of a person moving smoothly and rhythmically through the water.

Maybe she sensed me watching her, because after she finished her next lap, she hoisted herself up the ladder and out of the pool, walking over to stand in front of me, her wet feet a quiet *slap slap slap* on the pavement.

"Bianca," I said. "What are you doing up?" She looked black and white in the moonlight, like an old photograph of someone you'll never really meet.

"Night swimming," she said. She shook droplets of water out of her hair. "What are *you* doing up?"

"Waiting for you," I said, because I wasn't, but I should have been. "Are you drunk?"

She shrugged. "A little."

"You shouldn't swim if you're drunk."

"I figured you would have rescued me if I'd needed it."

"For all you know, I'm drunk, too." I wasn't, but I thought I should say that I was, because I didn't know what was going to happen between us there in the dark, and I wanted to be able to blame something outside of my control if I needed to. If I needed to forget everything about this whole night, I wanted that excuse ready for me.

She shivered. Maybe that's why the season ends at Labor Day. Because when it's September and it's impossibly late at night and you're wearing nothing but a wet bikini, you get cold. We didn't have this problem in July.

"I have a towel," I offered, holding up the one that I'd been using as a makeshift blanket. She walked toward me and held out her hand for it, but instead I wrapped it around her shoulders like a cocoon and pulled her toward me. She fell onto my deck chair so we were looking right into each other's eyes, my hands still holding her towel in fists.

Reader, I kissed her.

136

It was a really short, small kiss. I wanted to give her the chance to get up and walk away if she wanted to—though if she had, I don't know how I would have let her go.

But she didn't. She kissed me back, and there was nothing short or small about it.

The next thing I knew, her towel was gone and my hands were on her skin, holding on to her as tight as I could, and her legs were threaded through mine, and I was tasting the chlorine on her everywhere.

We didn't say a word, as if someone would have heard the moment we spoke and come outside to investigate. I wanted to say *I can't believe this is happening* and *I have been wanting this since the moment we met*, but the only sound I made was breathing into her ear, and I trust that she knew everything I meant.

We went inside just as the sun was starting to hint at the sky. And I wrote this all down now. So I won't forget.

"Arden."

Arden's head snapped up in surprise, and she clicked off her phone.

"Are you ignoring me?" Lindsey crawled onto the bleacher next to her, knocking over a mother's purse as she went. The mom gave her a dirty look and moved up a row. Lindsey went on, "I've been calling your name since I walked in the door."

Arden rubbed her eyes with the heels of her hands. "Sorry, Linds. I was reading something and I just . . . got really caught up in it."

Lindsey swigged some water. Arden could tell from the sheen of sweat on Lindsey's face that she had run all the way here, which made Arden's sedate-walker cardiovascular system want to curl up into a ball and die.

"I was looking at some guy's blog," Arden explained, which felt like such an understatement of what Tonight the Streets Are Ours was, or what it meant to her—but she felt like she had to say *something* about it to Lindsey, because when things mattered, Lindsey needed to know.

"Some guy. Is he hot?" Lindsey asked.

"Please, Linds. I have no idea." Which was not to say that Arden hadn't tried to find out. She had searched for every relevant combination of words she could think of: *Peter and Bianca. Peter and Leo. Peter and art school. Peter and bookstore.* Whatever she tried, she didn't have enough information to find photos. She suspected he was probably hot, though.

"Yeah, right," Lindsey said. " 'No idea.' You are such a stalker. This is going to be like Ellzey's house all over again. What's this guy's last name?"

"I don't know. His first name is Peter."

"You're going to be like, 'Peter, I read your blog,' and his mom is going to say, 'Well, I'm *Mrs.* Peter.' "

They both cracked up. A few more parents moved away.

"It's a basketball game," Lindsey said loudly. "It's okay to get a little rowdy."

"Wooo!" Arden shouted toward the court, to support Lindsey's statement.

"Wooo!" Lindsey agreed. All the bleachers within a six-foot radius of them emptied.

Once the game had ended, Arden drove Roman and Lindsey home, despite Lindsey's protestations that she could run home the way she came. "Please don't," Arden said. "Just the thought of it makes me want to take a nap." In the car, Roman seemed subdued, even for a child whose basketball team had just been totally crushed for the hundredth time this season.

"You killed it out there, Huntley," Lindsey told him. "You wiped the court with those guys. I bet they're scared to come back next time."

Roman had been in the game for all of six minutes, and Lindsey was a terrible liar, but it was possible that a child might believe her.

Roman didn't seem to be paying attention to her, though. "I don't know where Mom went," he said.

"To New York, Roman," Arden said. "You do know."

He shook his too-big head. "I saw her in the stands, though. I saw her while I was playing. But she wasn't there afterward. Why wouldn't she come say hi? Because we lost?"

Arden and Lindsey exchanged a glance. "She wasn't there," Arden said. "I promise." But there was a tightness in her chest. If her mother *had* been there, she would have noticed—right?

"Yes, she was," Roman insisted. "She was sitting right under the exit sign."

Then Arden realized what had happened. Roman hadn't been wearing his glasses, so of course it made sense that he would have gotten confused, from a distance. "No, Roman," she explained, and she felt so bad for him, her baby brother, who had so much learning to do about the world and all of its disappointment. "That wasn't Mom. That was just me."

Arden's mother explains herself

It was funny that Roman thought their mother would come home for his basketball game, because the next day, she sort of did. Not in a literal, physical sense. But she sent a letter. It was addressed just to Arden, and her father hand-delivered it while she was sitting in her room doing homework on Monday after rehearsal.

"No," Arden said when he handed it to her. "What is this? No."

"Your mother asked me to make sure you got this."

"And what, you just do everything she tells you now?"

"I think doing this particular thing makes sense," Arden's father said. "You won't take her calls. You don't respond to her e-mails. I think you should hear her out."

"Do you know what she says in here?" Arden asked, weighing the unopened envelope.

"I have a pretty good idea."

Arden gave an impatient snort. "I don't have time for this.

There's a huge math test tomorrow that I've barely studied for, and I'm supposed to call Chris in twenty minutes, and Naomi is freaking out over some costuming thing, and I can't rearrange my entire life just because Mom has written a letter."

"Fine," her dad said. "I don't have time for this, either. It's pro day for a lot of big college teams, and I need to keep track of it all." He turned and left her room.

A minute too late, Arden said, "Oh, Dad, that's not what I . . ." She sighed. She hadn't wanted to fight with her father. But the person she wanted to fight with wasn't there.

A *letter*. Could there be a more one-sided form of communication? A letter was saying, *I'm going to state my thoughts, and you can't argue with them because I'm not even there to hear you. All you can do is listen to me.* A letter was not a conversation.

Arden threw it in the recycling bin. Then she fished it out and opened it. Her curiosity always got the best of her.

This is what her mother's letter said:

Dear Arden,

I know you're angry at me, and I don't blame you. I'm certain what I've done has been traumatic for you, and it pains me to think about how you might be suffering, or what you might think of me now. But this was something I had to do. I'm hoping that enough time has passed since I left that you might be willing to consider what I have to say, to try to understand why I felt like I didn't have any other options.

The first thing I need you to know is that I did not leave because of anything you or your brother did, or failed to do. I love you both with all my heart, and all my soul, and nothing that you ever *do, or fail to do, could change that. Please understand that.*

Things between your father and me have been difficult for a while, and in recent years, instead of improving, they've only gotten more challenging. As you're well aware, your grandparents fought constantly when your dad was growing up, and it affected him in a lot of negative ways. So it was important to him that you and Roman not be exposed to the same sort of parental conflict that he was, and I agreed with that. But the truth is that just because two people aren't yelling at each other doesn't mean that they're making each other happy.

To put it simply, your father and I have very different ideas of what it means to be a parent. And I reached a breaking point. I felt like I had done all the running of our household for seventeen years. I wasn't getting the sort of support from your father that I needed. And I couldn't take it anymore.

I felt like years of injustices and unequal distribution of responsibilities all caught up to me at the same time. It frustrated me to feel that your father prioritized his job over his home and, even when he was home, that he prioritized his fantasy sports over his real family in front of him. It's never seemed fair to me, and lately it's seemed less tolerable than ever.

It's not something you and I have talked much about, but I think you know that before you were born, I was working on getting my master's degree in social work. I had this idea that I could be a really great social worker. And maybe I couldn't have, maybe that was all in my mind, but that's what I imagined.

I was incredibly excited to have a baby. It was my dream come true. But I realized very quickly that I couldn't be the sort of mother I wanted to be—the sort of mother I thought you deserved—and also be going to classes and studying and doing field work. It didn't seem possible. Someone had to take care of you. And I didn't want to get a babysitter for you, or send you to day care where a bunch of babies would all be vying for attention. I thought you should be raised by a parent. And your father was not interested in being that parent. So I set aside my master's degree and figured I would come back to it once you were in school.

Once you were settled at school, we had Roman. And, again, this was my dream come true. *The problem wasn't that I got to be a mother again—that was a blessing. But your father didn't agree that, since I had done all the work of raising you, this time around maybe it was his turn. He felt like he was the breadwinner of the family, and he was doing pretty well for himself at that point, and he loved his career. And my idea of going back to school was a pipe dream, which might never turn into anything profitable. He was going to stay at his job, and if I wanted to go back to school, he said, then Roman could go into day care.*

But I'm sure you remember what a fussy baby your brother was. He needed his mother. He needed me. *I wasn't going to hand him over to some stranger who could never love him with the intensity that I did.*

And your father said, basically, that was my choice. I could choose grad school or I could choose spending all my time with my children, and I chose my children, I chose that freely, and so what reason did I have to be unhappy?

Making that choice made me feel like I mattered—I must *matter, if my family needed me so much. And then I kept making that choice every day, until eventually it became too late for me to unmake it.*

I kept thinking I would someday go back and finish my degree. But there was always something else to do. There was always a basketball practice or a parent-teacher conference or an upcoming Spanish test. I loved being so involved in the lives of my family, but at the same time I felt like I'd lost sight of myself. I only knew who I was in relation to somebody else. For years I was somebody's wife, somebody's mother, somebody's friend, somebody's daughter. And for once, I wanted to be somebody for myself.

I didn't know how to find that in Cumberland. I felt like as long as I was in that same house and that same situation, I would keep making those same choices. So, I left.

I don't know if this is anything you'll be able to sympathize with, or if it will give you any peace to know all of this. I'm telling you because I hope that it will help, and because I think you're old enough to hear what's going on.

Your father and I are trying to work things out. We're talking about all of these issues, and I'm hopeful that we can come to some sort of understanding, some way forward, so I can come home again. The bottom line is that I love you totally and completely, and I always have, and I always will. I would be happy to discuss all of this further with you. Or just to hear how you're doing. You can e-mail or call me at any time.

Love,
Mommy

Arden stared at the letter for a long time, the words blurring together until they became just meaningless shapes. Then she tore it up into as many tiny pieces as she could, and she threw every last one of them in the garbage.

Stalking people, take two

It wasn't fair of Arden's mother to blame her running away on Arden's dad. It was ridiculous and self-centered. Okay, so he didn't do the everyday parenting. He rarely took Roman to sports games, collected Arden from school, managed their schedules, oversaw their doctors' appointments and haircuts, set up playdates, or noticed when they outgrew clothes or finished a carton of milk. Yes, their mother did all that boring, mundane stuff. Give her a standing ovation.

But that didn't make their dad a bad parent. On the contrary, when there was a big thing in his kids' lives, their dad was first in line to document it with photos and video, or to cheer them on, or to coach them in the necessary skills.

He was the one who taught them to ride their bikes, for example. He was the one who taught them how to catch and throw a ball—really poorly, in both Roman's and Arden's cases, but he did try. When they went to the beach, he helped them build elaborate sand castles, and when they decided to get a dog (RIP,

Spot), he was the one who took them to the animal shelter so they could choose one. He had tried very hard to instill in them a love of pro football, his passion. While it never stuck, he was always delighted for his kids to sit on the couch to watch a game with him, and he would regularly e-mail them articles about the teams he followed, whether or not they'd expressed any interest in reading them.

When he taught Arden to drive last year, he left nothing to chance, telling her everything he knew about how to handle different road situations she might someday find herself in. Together they logged almost double the number of required practice driving hours, and when he took her to her driving test, she passed with flying colors. Even the officer administering the test commented that he'd rarely seen drivers her age who were so confident. Her dad took this as a personal compliment and printed out official-looking certificates on thick cardstock, one for Arden saying WORLD'S BEST TEEN DRIVER and one for himself saying WORLD'S BEST DRIVING COACH. They both still had them hanging over their respective desks. Once she had her license, he even helped her purchase the Heart of Gold, matching her dollar for dollar.

He was a good dad.

Thanks to the Heart of Gold, Arden spent every day last summer driving. She'd drive as far and as often as she could, usually with Lindsey in the passenger seat, since Lindsey was game to go anywhere at any time. Often they would drive forty-five minutes to a crumbling independent cinema called the Glockenspiel, which showed artsy films, some of which were in

French or Italian with subtitles, or which were old and in black and white. It's not like they were such huge cinephiles. It was simply that the Glockenspiel was far away, and seeing a movie there was *something to do*.

Plus, they were obsessed with the Glockenspiel's manager.

Her name was Veronica and she had bleached blond hair with an inch of obvious brunette roots. She always wore chunky platform shoes and her arms were covered in tattoos, and she cursed up a storm when she introduced any film ("Truffaut was an effing genius and *Jules et Jim* is one of his shittiest films, and yet for some effed reason it's the only one anyone effing talks about when they talk about Truffaut"). She embodied the mandate, handed down by one of their English teachers, of knowing something about everything and everything about something.

For a while, Arden wanted to grow up to be someone like Veronica. Lindsey wanted to grow up to marry someone like Veronica.

Arden came up with a plan. Every time they went to the Glockenspiel, they would ask Veronica a question. Just one. Just one question would seem perfectly natural and conversational, and maybe with time, they would befriend Veronica, or, barring that, at least they would know what she would say when asked various questions, and then they could mimic her responses in future conversations with other people.

Arden and Lindsey would spend the entire car ride to the cinema brainstorming what to ask. While they were buying their tickets, they would ask their one question. And then they would spend the entire car ride home analyzing Veronica's answer.

When Arden asked what the best song in the world was, and Veronica answered, "Smashing Pumpkins, '1979,'" the two girls found that song online and listened to it over and over as they drove back to Cumberland.

When Arden asked where she and Lindsey should apply to college, Veronica answered, "Don't bother. A college education will be irrelevant in ten years anyway. You can teach yourselves anything you really want to know." This prompted a vicious argument between Lindsey and Arden on the ride home, because Lindsey thought that was the best advice she'd ever been given about college applications, and Arden thought that you needed a college education if you ever wanted to do anything of substance with your life, and Lindsey's crowning piece of evidence was "Well, Veronica says you're wrong," and how was Arden supposed to argue with that?

When Arden asked Veronica what her dreams were for the future, Veronica answered, "Being the manager at a movie theater." Which wasn't exactly Arden's or Lindsey's dream, but after talking it through, they decided it was wisdom about appreciating what you have when you have it, rather than wishing your life away.

Arden always had to do the asking. Lindsey was too intimidated.

When Arden asked Veronica how you knew when you were in love with somebody—because this was when she was thinking of saying it to Chris, but she wasn't quite sure whether she meant it—Veronica leaned out of the ticket booth and said, "I have a question, too. Why do you guys always ask me such weird things when you come here?" When they didn't say anything, Veronica said, "Never mind," and she sold them their tickets.

The film that night was *Who's Afraid of Virginia Woolf?*, a classic from the sixties. It was depressing, about a long-married couple who just tore each other down and tore each other down, using everything they knew about the other to hurt them, just because they could.

After that movie, Arden and Lindsey didn't speak at all on the car ride home. And they never went back to the Glockenspiel again, either.

*Sometimes, people aren't who
you want them to be*

Chris was biding his time. He had confided in Arden that he felt high school plays were—no offense—beneath him. "I'm not saying that I have nothing left to learn," he'd explained. "You can always find something to learn from every experience, if you look for it. But let's be honest, Mr. Lansdowne is not a top-tier director, and the people I'm playing opposite . . . well, enough said." A sigh. "I'm worried that I've plateaued."

Chris had big dreams, dreams that could never be realized in Cumberland. He wanted to be a Hollywood star. He resented his parents for raising him in a small town so far away from the movie industry, and for their complete lack of interest in helping him find an agent, get professional headshots, or attend audition coaching. Chris's father's hardware store had previously been managed by Chris's grandfather, which meant he considered it basically written in stone that it would someday be managed by Chris.

Arden knew it was hard to make it in Hollywood. None of

her other drama club friends even imagined it. Kirsten thought maybe she would audition for some musicals in college, or maybe she wouldn't, but that was as far as her theatrical ambitions went. But Arden thought that if anyone from her town could manage a professional career as an actor, her boyfriend would definitely be the one. He had a deep voice, he could cry on command, he had a dimple, his arms were just the right amount of muscular, and he was tall—though she'd also read that most movie actors were surprisingly short, so maybe that wasn't actually a point in his favor.

Chris kept an eye out for auditions and open calls held anywhere remotely nearby and, now that he had his license, too, he drove to them whenever he could. That's why he was spending sixth period on Thursday, two weeks after that stupid letter came from Arden's mother, running lines for a film audition that he was going to on Saturday. The film was a very, very small-budget production about coal miners, which was going to be shooting some scenes on-site in nearby West Virginia.

"Gretchen," he said to Arden, squeezing up his eyes as he tried to remember the rest of the line. "I can't help but think that you and I—"

"Me and you," interrupted Arden, glancing at the audition script. "Not 'you and I.' Remember, the character left school when he was twelve to become a miner and support his family."

Chris sighed and took back the script to study it further.

Sixth period on Thursdays was when Arden and Chris had theater class, which they signed up for because they could take it together, and because it was an easy A. Since they both were heavily involved in theater after school, Mr. Lansdowne already adored them. So while he made the other fifteen students in the class play games where they mirrored one another's body movements or pretended to be animals, he let Arden and Chris do whatever they wanted. Today, this meant that Chris was brushing up on his backwoods accent, while Arden was ostensibly working on a history paper while actually finishing up her read-through of every single entry from last autumn on Tonight the Streets Are Ours. And here's what she had learned:

The rest of September had been confusing. After Peter and Bianca got together that night in the Hamptons, they saw each other seemingly constantly—for about two weeks. Leo was off at college, out of the picture, so they had almost unlimited access to each other. Peter's senior year started at the same time, so there were some posts about readjusting to school, deciding whether or not to stay on at the bookstore (yes, but only on Saturdays), and bemoaning how little writing he'd gotten done over the whole summer and how hard it was going to be to find time now that he had homework again.

But mostly he wrote about Bianca, just short bits and pieces, as he seemed to be too busy spending time with her to spend much time describing what they were doing. Still, these brief posts about Bianca (*This morning I brought her coffee on my way to school, just to see her smile*) resulted in dozens of reader comments.

But then there were eight days of silence.

And then that post about his brother running away.

And then that post about Bianca breaking up with him.

Both came completely without warning, and Arden's heart ached for him. When September began, Peter was the guy who had it all. He even had the girl of his dreams, at last. But less than a month later, it all came crashing down.

The illogic and injustice of life killed Arden. You have to walk through this world knowing that at any moment your brother might vanish, your mother might leave. No warning. How can you live staring that reality in the face? It didn't seem right that somebody else's carelessness or selfishness could have such a huge impact on your life. Could destroy you. It didn't seem fair that your happiness was constantly at the mercy of everybody else.

Arden found herself hating Bianca, a surprisingly intense feeling for a girl she did not know—indeed, a girl she'd admired with just as much intensity since she'd first read about her. Bianca, so beautiful. Bianca, the angel. Bianca, who was going to run the United Nations and travel the world someday. It all sounded so good.

But Bianca couldn't even be there for Peter in the moment that he needed her. When Peter's brother went missing, and Peter was in a tailspin, all Bianca did was break up with him. And tell him *Don't worry, you'll meet someone else.*

For the first time since she'd started reading about Peter's world, Arden felt superior to Bianca. Sure, maybe she was plain and dependable in comparison. Maybe she was a small-town girl who had to look up where "the Hamptons" were and bought most of her clothes from chain stores and thought a thrilling night out was a school semiformal. But that didn't matter, because she would have been there for Peter when he'd needed her. When the going got tough, Arden could tough it out.

She just wished she could tell him that.

From the comments, Arden saw she wasn't the only one to feel that way. His post about his breakup with Bianca had received more comments than anything else on Tonight the Streets Are Ours, with readers saying, *I can't believe she did this to you. What is her problem???* and, *It's going to be OK. You two are fated to be together. Just give it time,* and, *Now that your single, gimme a call* ☺—with a racy photo pasted below.

Peter spent the rest of the fall piecing himself together. Some days he sounded as carefree as ever, analyzing a novel he was reading, or relating a funny story from school that day, or describing something weird that a stranger did on the subway and ordering Future Peter, *Include this as a character in a story someday!* But other days he would write on and on about how much he missed Bianca and how much he missed his brother.

October 29

They're two different experiences of loss, so maybe I shouldn't compare them. Both didn't have to happen like this. Both simultaneously have *everything* to do with me and yet nothing to do with me. But the big difference is that I know where Bianca is. She's living in the same apartment and attending the same school as the last time I saw her. So it seems like there must be something I could do (some combination of words I could speak, some gift I could give, some change I could make to my mind or body) that would win her back. If I could just figure out what that is . . .

As for my brother, though, he could be anywhere in the world. Or nowhere. He could be dead by now.

With both of them, there's this feeling like *I should have done more*. I should have tried harder to hold on to them. My brother and I weren't so close when he left. We've always been very different people, and the older we got, the more obvious those differences became.

But that never really mattered, because we'd grown up together. We got head lice at the same time and had to stay home from school for two weeks. The one and only time we went to overnight camp, my brother decided that we were leaving after just one day and had us both pack our bags and try to walk out the front gate. (We didn't get far.) Stupid, childish memories, things that are way in the past—but aren't those the things that make up a life? Even as recently as June, we were going to parties together. And then of course there's the fact that we suffered through our parents together, which should bind two people together for life.

Should. But didn't.

Not a day goes by that I'm not seized with worry

157

about him. I want him to come home, but if that can't happen, then I just want to know that he is safe.

December 1

Kyla is always saying things like "Ugh, if only I were prettier, I would be all-around happier and more loved." Not in those exact words, but that's the sentiment. That's actually how she thinks.

I'd make fun of her for being so illogical, but that's how I feel, too, except about my writing. If only I were a better writer, everything would come easily to me, I would be happy all the time, and never ever lonely. If only I were a better writer, Bianca would want me back.

But creating art is supposed to be ITS OWN REWARD. EVERYONE KNOWS THIS.

Unfortunately, I am not much of an artist. I am a minstrel, I am a dilettante. I will work for adoration. I am pathetic.

"Babe," Chris said. *"Babe."*

Arden looked up, slowly coming back into the present day, the auditorium that they sat in the back of while the rest of their class was on stage, playing Machine. This was a theater game in which each one of them did a repetitive action to form a complete "machine." This particular machine would be really helpful if you needed your head patted insistently, or if you needed to hear Beth Page say the word *boop* a hundred times in a row. Otherwise, it wasn't a super-functional technology.

"Sorry," Arden said to Chris, subtly navigating away from Tonight the Streets Are Ours. "What's up?" For some reason that she couldn't pinpoint, she was sick of Chris calling her *babe*. She wished he'd just call her by her name. She used to love that anyone should think of her as a babe. Now it made her think of Babe the pig.

"Can you help me figure out a way to memorize these three lines here?" He indicated the place on the script. "I keep getting them confused."

Arden scrutinized the page, then said, "They go in alphabetical order."

"Genius!" Chris declared, grabbing it back from her.

She gave him a weak smile. Arden had recently developed a really bizarre, guilty, and specific fantasy. In this fantasy, she broke up with Chris. In this fantasy, Chris realized, suddenly, everything that would be missing from his life without her, and he tried desperately to win her back by showing up outside of her bedroom window holding a boom box aloft, or bringing her bouquets of flowers, or asking her to prom in an embarrassingly public and over-the-top manner (like on horseback, with a marching band). Eventually, he would wear down her defenses, and she would accept. He would have to really work for it, though.

She didn't know why she was fantasizing about this. She just knew she wasn't going to act on it. If Chris were a bad guy, then sure. She'd break up with him. If he were a criminal or a drug dealer, if he cheated on tests or if he cheated on her, if he were violent or racist. Then yeah, easy, decision made.

But he wasn't any of those things. He was smart and handsome and talented and ambitious. Teachers liked him, parents liked him. Pretty much everyone liked him except Lindsey. He was obviously, as Kirsten and Naomi put it, "a keeper." The only reason to break up with someone like Chris would be if she thought she could do better. And why would she think that?

"Chris," she said.

"Yeah, babe?" He glanced up from the page.

But now that she had his attention again, she didn't know what she'd wanted to say. She settled on saying, "I'm excited for our anniversary."

One year was a crazy length of time. That was one-seventeenth of her life. Arden already had their anniversary night all planned out, even though it was nearly a month away. She'd used most of what remained of her tutoring money to get a hotel room to surprise Chris. She would wear a sexy dress, one he'd never seen before—she'd already bought that, too, a lacy, shimmery thing—and he would arrive at the hotel not knowing what to expect, only to find her lounging provocatively on the king-size bed. There would be no little brother and no parents and no theater crowd and no Lindsey; just the two of them, in love. And then their relationship would go back to feeling the way it was supposed to. *She* would go back to feeling the way she was supposed to. That was the plan.

Chris rubbed her shoulder. "I'm excited, too. Can you give me even a tiny hint about what we're doing to celebrate?"

She grinned and shook her head. "Nope!"

He laughed. "I don't know any other couples at school who have been together for a *year*. And who knows—if we're lucky, maybe I'll have a role in a movie by then."

"It'll be a good anniversary either way," she told him, reaching up to squeeze his hand.

He went back to his script. She went back to Peter.

By the end of last year, Peter had all but stopped writing about his missing brother. Arden supposed that there was no news to report, and Peter had said on the matter all that there was to say. He was still trying to move on from Bianca, though. He'd made out with a couple other girls, even though he swore his heart wasn't in it. Arden thought back to Lindsey's question and decided Peter was *definitely* hot. If she and Chris ever really did break up, it would probably take her a number of *years* before she found a couple other people willing to make out with her, and Peter had managed it in less than three months.

Then the year changed from last year to this one, and something happened that Arden had never seen coming.

January 2

I should have written about this yesterday, but Bianca and I have not been apart for a single second

161

since New Year's Eve, so I haven't had a moment to breathe and record what happened.

"Bianca?" you're saying right now. ("You" being "my readers"—Happy New Year, folks!) "I thought she had cut your heart out of your chest and then thrown it to the floor and stomped on it in high heels."

That was true. But that was before my *grand geste.* (French again. Those French understand romance better than we ever will.)

It was December 31st. The end of a year. Out with the old, in with the new, *auld lang syne* and all that. But I didn't want to let go of the old. Julio and Raleigh had both invited me to their New Year's parties, but I didn't feel like partying. If I could have spent New Year's Eve alone somewhere with Bianca, I would have preferred that to the best soiree in New York City. (Soiree: *also French.*)

I asked Miranda, my amateur relationship coach, "How do you reach somebody who doesn't want to be reached?"

She replied, "Art!"

Not helpful, Miranda.

But it got me thinking. I'm a writer. I know how to say how I really feel. Just give me enough words and I can say how I really feel here in this journal, and if somebody reads it, maybe they would understand.

But I never told Bianca—or anyone I know in my real life—about Tonight the Streets Are Ours. I have no way to make Bianca read these words. I could write her a letter, but she would never open it.

I needed something that she couldn't ignore, a letter that she couldn't help but open. Art that's so in-your-face that there could be no misunderstanding.

And that's when I came up with my *grand geste*.

It took a day of phone calls. I started with my dad's Rolodex and I went from there. There may come a time when my dad finds out just how many of his clients and colleagues I called, and if that time comes, I will be in trouble. But it was worth it.

Apparently this thing that I was asking for can be done, but it costs money. It costs a lot of money. But I got it as a favor, from one of my dad's contacts who does something obscenely important with Dow Jones and happens to have a soft spot for me and my family, especially after what happened with my brother. This is a good thing, because at that point I would have paid the money, no matter how much it was, and I would have paid it with my dad's AmEx. And he would have legitimately disowned me. That's always the threat with my father: if you don't follow his rules, you won't get his money. It's how he keeps everyone in line.

I went to Julio's party, after all. I was antsy the whole time. I talked to people but don't remember what I said. I kept staring past them at Julio's giant flat-screen TV, which was showing the mayhem in Times Square as they prepared to drop the ball at midnight. A million people came to see it in person this year, and a billion watched on TV.

At 10:30, it happened. On the electronic ticker tape circling Times Square, these words appeared:

BIANCA—A NEW YEAR MEANS A NEW START. COME FIND ME AT THE PLACE WHERE WE FIRST MET, AND WE WILL START ANEW. I'LL BE THERE WAITING FOR YOU AT MIDNIGHT. LOVE, PETER.

The message circled around twice before it was replaced by the headline news of the day.

"Dude," Julio said, staring at the TV. *"Dude.* Is that you? Did you do that? How did you do that?"

"Now that is so sweet," the cold-looking news anchor said to her cohost. "Bianca, girl, wherever you are, you should take Peter back!"

"Don't you wish some man would send *you* such a romantic message?" asked the other host.

"You know it!"

"Man, you are such a *baller*!" Julio hooted, punching me on the shoulder. "How did you make that happen? Are you a magician now?"

"I have to go," I said. I grabbed my coat. "I have to go."

"Go where?" some girl asked. "It's not even midnight yet."

"To the bookstore," I tried to explain. "I said I'd be there, so I need to be there."

"What if she's not there?" Mark asked.

But I couldn't think about what I'd do if she wasn't there. I still don't know what I would have done.

It's impossible to get a taxi on New Year's Eve, so I took the subway from Julio's, and then I ran the remaining blocks to the bookstore. It was cold, of course, my breath coming out in crystalline gasps, but I couldn't slow down, because I couldn't miss her, I couldn't afford to miss her.

When I got to the bookstore, it was a bit past 11 pm, and no one was around. The store was closed, the iron grate pulled down over its windows. No Bianca.

I checked my phone. I checked my phone over and over. No Bianca. And when the clock struck midnight, my phone chimed with a hundred "Happy New Year!" text messages, and none of them were from Bianca. That glittery ball in Times Square must have fallen, but I was in no position to see it.

All I wanted was another chance. I didn't need her to feel about me the way I feel about her. I only wanted her to try.

Just as I was about to admit defeat and go home alone into a new year, she appeared under a streetlight in front of me.

"That message," she said. Her laugh formed a cloud of air in front of her mouth. "How did you do that?"

I shrugged. Tried to play it cool. "A magician never reveals his tricks."

"What even made you think I'd be watching?" she asked.

"You said you would be. That day, in the park . . ." Though it was so hard to reconcile that summer afternoon with us here, now, in the freezing cold dead of night.

"You remember that?" She sounded surprised.

"I . . . ? Of course I do." *I remember everything you've ever said to me,* I wanted to tell her.

"Well, I wasn't watching," she said. I blinked at her. "But lucky for you, my friend was. She freaked out when she saw my name. She was like, "It's you, it's you!" And I thought she was being ridiculous. But it was me, huh?"

"It was." Now that she was here, I didn't even really know what to say. "What took you so long?"

"It's really hard to get a taxi on New Year's," she said.

She stepped forward, and I pulled her toward me, I wrapped my arms around her, and we've been together ever since.

Arden broke away from the screen. *They were together again.* And they had been for three months now.

Of course she could have known this if she'd just read ahead in his blog. There'd been no rule that she had to read it in chronological order, even though that was how Peter experienced it. She could have learned his life in any order she'd wanted, and she didn't know why she hadn't skipped ahead, except that she hadn't wanted to miss anything.

Now Arden felt something really intensely, but she couldn't put her finger on what it was. She was happy for Peter that he and Bianca got back together, of course. That was the way it should be. It was like Beauty and the Beast making amends, Prince Charming giving Sleeping Beauty her kiss of life. Balance was once again restored, and what was halved was now whole.

But it also felt like Peter had been taken away from her. Like if he weren't now Bianca's, he could have somehow been Arden's.

But that didn't make any sense. With or without a girlfriend, he was never going to belong to Arden. After all, she didn't even know him. And he didn't know her. They didn't know each other at all.

And *that* was the thing that she was feeling so intensely. She just didn't know the word for it.

Anyway. She wasn't alone. Peter had Bianca again now, and Arden—Arden was fine. She had Chris.

She leaned over and kissed her boyfriend. He wasn't expecting it, and his mouth was a little slow to move against hers. When she tried to deepen the kiss, Chris pulled away. "Come on, babe," he said. "We're in public." He waved toward their classmates on stage, none of whom was paying them the slightest bit of attention in between their coordinated "beep beep beeps" and "weee-ooos."

"So?" Arden asked, suddenly feeling very small. "I'm your girlfriend. Don't you think they assume that we kiss sometimes?"

"Sure," Chris said, "but it's weird. We're in the middle of the school day. Let me just work on my audition for now, okay? If you're bored, you can help."

He held up the script, and, after a moment, Arden took it.

She knew she should be proud of her boyfriend. He was trying to achieve something. Okay, it wasn't a sign in Times Square. But it was his own attempt at grandeur. It mattered to him.

But *proud* was not how she felt.

Maybe Arden was just jealous of Chris and his ambition, the starry lights of Hollywood that always beckoned to him from afar. Because more and more these days, she wondered if the most exciting moment in her life was already in her past. If maybe the greatest thing about her had happened when she was nine years old, and it had all been downhill ever since then.

What happened on the best day of Peter's life

By the middle of April, Arden was reading Tonight the Streets Are Ours in real time, experiencing Peter's life alongside him basically as it happened. In real time, here's what was going on:

Less than two months remained in Peter's senior year. There was still no update on his brother, so Peter had little to say about him—just memories from their childhood, or occasional dreams about him.

Peter had recently gotten into NYU for college, so he would be staying in New York City next year, but moving into a dorm. He'd been accepted into a handful of other schools, too, but they were all "too artsy" for his father, who said that he wasn't going to pay for a degree in creative writing, which was hardly a "real degree" anyway, and would be just the start of a lifetime of Peter moving back home and blowing through his parents' money.

April 13

They say that tragedy changes you, and I guess I'd hoped that the positive side of his older son's disappearance would be my dad realizing that life is finite, and people don't stick around forever, and you should let them pursue their dreams now, before it's too late. But that is decidedly *not* what happened.

I've been trying to find a way to show my dad that being an artist or a writer *is* a real career, and you *can* make a living without donning a suit that's identical to every other guy's suit, and squashing onto the subway at 7:30 every morning along with a zillion other guys in matching suits, and going into an office where you have a boss and your boss has a boss and your boss's boss has a boss, and everybody tells everybody else what to do all day long, for the rest of your life.

I told Bianca that all I want to do once I'm an adult is work at the bookstore and see the world, and write about all the things I've seen. "You should do that," she agreed. "I want to make money, though. But I want to make it doing something interesting."

"You could make money and we could get married, and I could live off *your* money," I suggested.

She laughed. "We're still in high school."

"I didn't mean now. I meant someday."

I kind of did mean now, though. I mean, I was kidding. But I'm not a very patient person.

Peter and Bianca were properly together now, and had been ever since the first of the year. There was no mention of Leo, so Arden pieced together that Bianca and Leo had broken up by December, if not earlier, and that was why she had returned to Peter on New Year's Eve. Arden wondered if Peter had been a factor in Bianca and Leo's breakup. If Bianca had told Leo that she'd been cheating on him, or if Leo had somehow found out all on his own. Or maybe not—maybe Bianca had just grown tired of Leo's buffoonish behavior and told him she wanted to move on. Peter never said. It was as if he was so focused on their perfect relationship now that he didn't want to waste any time thinking about what a struggle it was to get here, the obstacles that had once stood in their way.

April 17

Last night was Raleigh's birthday party and the theme was "fifties sock hop," so all the girls got poodle skirts and I wore a bow tie. Bianca looked like Sandy from *Grease*. She had Sandy's pre-transformation outfit and post-transformation sexiness. Other guys at the party kept trying to talk to her, and I was like, "Gents, she is here with me. Hands to yourselves."

Nicola told me I looked like Buddy Holly, and somehow Bianca didn't know who Buddy Holly was, WHICH IS AN OUTRAGE, so I made Cormac play every Buddy Holly song he could think of on his guitar, and Bianca and I cha-cha-ed around the apartment. Raleigh said that she wanted to learn to cha-cha, too, so I taught her, but in the process she fell into the table with her birthday cake and knocked the whole thing onto the floor. (She was pretty wasted.) We ate it anyway.

I will regret growing up. I don't know if I'll make a good grown-up. I'm not sure adulthood really fits with my character. I do know that being 13 didn't fit with my character—though that's probably true of everybody's character. Being 13 sucked.

But I am awesome at being 18. Going to school in the daytime, going to parties on the weekends, making money at the bookstore and spending it however I see fit, dancing to Buddy Holly and eating cake off the floor . . . I look at my parents, and they don't get to do anything like that, not even close. They never did. The au pair basically raised us, and whenever my parents were in charge it was like we were going through some infinite checklist of accomplishments, always set to a kitchen timer. *Go do your homework.* Kitchen timer set for forty-five minutes. *Go practice the violin.* Kitchen timer set for half an hour. *Go help your father with his filing.* Kitchen timer set again. Do they even know what fun looks like? My dad's idea of happiness is a bottle of whiskey, and my mom's is a bottle of sleeping pills.

Last night reminded me how many positive things there are in my own life, and it frightens me to think that someday all that might disappear. How long do you get to live like this? During college? After that? How long do you have until everyone expects you to hang up some dreams as impossible and commit yourself to being responsible?

It infuriated Arden to read about Peter's parents. In their pursuit of "perfect" sons, they had managed to drive away the actually great sons that they already had. Why couldn't they see how talented Peter was? Why couldn't they love him the way he deserved to be loved, the way all parents should love their children?

She just wanted Peter to be happy.

Arden would say this about her mother: she might have walked out on them, for reasons that Arden found wholly unacceptable and indefensible, but at least she never tried to make her children into anybody they were not.

The next Tuesday, Arden was at her usual lunch table. Naomi, Kirsten, and the rest of the girls in her group were deep in conversation about some drama club gossip. Naomi reported that the teacher's aide who'd been working with Mr. Lansdowne wasn't coming to rehearsal all week, and so now they were trying to figure out whether a) he had quit, b) he had been fired for hooking up with a student—and, if so, which student—or c) he was just out sick.

Arden was reasonably interested in this debate, but not *that* interested, and about twenty percent of her brain was thinking about how she hadn't checked Tonight the Streets Are Ours since before school that morning. She subtly pulled her phone out of her bag and quickly refreshed it. And indeed Peter *had* written a new entry since seven a.m. And when Arden read it, all her interest in student-teacher made-up sex scandals vanished.

April 20

TODAY IS THE BEST DAY OF MY LIFE.

I hadn't mentioned it here because I didn't want to jinx it or anything, but I've been reaching out to various literary agents to see if they want to represent my writing. I just feel like I'm almost done with high school, I'm 18 years old, and what do I have to show for my life? If I could publish a book, that would be something real and tangible. Even my father would have to admit that's real.

So I've been sending out samples of my short stories and those 50 pages of the novel I wrote last year, because if somebody wanted to publish it, I would definitely get my shit together to finish writing the rest of it. And one of the agents that I queried was interested enough in my writing that she asked to see more. So I sent her this link, to Tonight the Streets Are Ours. And . . . SHE LOVED IT!!!

She wants to represent me. She wants to represent ME! We just got off the phone, and her vision is to turn Tonight the Streets Are Ours into a memoir. Not the novel, not the stories—she says THIS is where my unique voice shines. (She actually said that: my "unique voice"!!) I can use a lot of the material that I've written here, but obviously flesh it out and smooth it into a cohesive story. And once I do that, she'll pitch it to publishers to try to get them to publish it. AS A BOOK. THAT YOU COULD BUY. IN BOOKSTORES.

This is the happiest I have ever been.

The comments went on and on after that. More than fifty people commented to say *Congratulations!* and *I can't wait to read the book!* and *I always thought you deserved a wider audience.*

The chatter and laughter of the cafeteria swirled around Arden as she stared at Peter's news on her phone. She was thrilled for him. Obviously. He was happy, just as she'd hoped he would be. His dream was coming true. She'd watched him want this for months, forever.

But her happiness for Peter tasted bittersweet. Because with each new person who discovered his writing, he became a little less hers and a little more everyone else's. If this literary agent sold Tonight the Streets Are Ours to a publisher, and it became a book, and one day years in the future she went to a bookstore event for Peter, and she waited in line with all his other fans to get him to sign her book, how would he even know that she had been there *first*? That she wasn't just another fan, that she was special in all the world?

"Do you guys know anyone who's written a book?" Arden asked her tablemates loudly, looking up from her phone.

Their deliberations about who had or had not slept with the teacher's aide ground abruptly to a halt. Naomi's eyes immediately glazed over, and she stared off toward the football players' table across the room. Arden's question seemed to come out of nowhere, and it also seemed way less interesting than a conversation about people they knew making out with each other.

"No," each of the girls said, or, "I don't think so," or, "My aunt wrote a mystery novel, but it's not published or anything."

"Arden, *you* are the person I know who's closest to having written a book," Kirsten said, twisting her mermaid hair into an improvised upsweep, then dropping it to let it slowly cascade down her shoulders.

Arden blinked at Kirsten in confusion.

"Your Just Like Me Doll books," Kirsten reminded her.

"Oh. That's not the same, though. I didn't write those."

"Why do you want to know?" asked Lauri, idly peeling the cheese off her pizza in the way that one might peel a scab off one's skin.

"Because my . . . friend is writing a book." Arden frowned. *Friend* was not the right word. She was at a table with six girls. *These* were her friends. She didn't know what Peter was to her. But it was something else entirely.

"That's cool," said Naomi. "Which friend?"

"Lindsey?" asked Candace dubiously, because usually when Arden referred to a friend who was not at their lunch table, she did indeed mean Lindsey. But nobody really thought of Lindsey as a book-writer.

"No," said Arden. "Just some guy. You don't know him."

"Cool," Naomi reiterated, and then immediately redirected the conversation toward the likelihood of various classmates hooking up during the marching band's upcoming trip to Disney World. If Arden's author friend wasn't anyone they knew, then they weren't all that interested.

Arden hears her calling

If Tuesday was the best day of Peter's life, Arden was prepared for Saturday to be the best day of hers. She woke up and opened her window, and it was warm at last—after what had seemed like a never-ending winter, she could smell spring in the air. She texted Chris, HAPPY ANNIVERSARY!!!, and practically waltzed downstairs. She baked peanut butter brownies—Chris was wild about peanut butter—and somehow managed to maneuver them into a tin and out of the kitchen without losing more than two squares to Roman's gaping maw. For a skinny kid, Roman could lay waste to a surprising number of brownies.

Then she showered and blow-dried her hair and worked and worked on her makeup. There were like five layers of stuff on her face. There was the foundation and then there was the powder and then there was the blush and then there was the bronzer and then there was this spritz to keep it all in place. There were Internet videos for each step along the way, to make sure she was doing them right. There was even a video chat with Naomi, who oversaw makeup for their school plays and understood the necessity of getting her face exactly right for tonight, her anniversary.

"You are so lucky to have Chris," Naomi told her authoritatively as they ended their call.

"I know I am," Arden agreed. She did know. And tonight she would be good, she would be so good, she would be beautiful and charming and attentive and positive, she would listen to his every story and applaud his every choice, because she was so lucky to have him, and that was what he deserved.

She packed a small bag with bonus makeup supplies, a toothbrush, the brownies, pajamas, and the sexy dress. For now she just wore jeans and a T-shirt—normal, unsuspicious weekend clothes.

She knocked on the door to her dad's study.

"Come in," he called.

She did. He was sitting at his desk, wearing khakis, an old sweater, and slippers that Arden had given him last Christmas—*his* weekend clothes. He removed his computer glasses to smile at her.

"I'm going over to Lindsey's," she said.

Arden was certain he would look at her and say, *Obviously you're not. I know that today is your anniversary with Chris, so I'm sure you're going to a hotel with him in order to engage in uninterrupted adolescent sexual activity.*

But he didn't say anything like that. Probably he didn't even know it was her anniversary.

"I'm sleeping over there," Arden went on, holding up her bag as if that were proof.

He nodded.

"So you'll stay here and take care of Roman?"

"Of course," he said. "What else would I do?"

What else would he do? Go to the office. Get involved in some fantasy sports thing or work project and lose track of time. There were a lot of other things he might do.

Since receiving her mother's letter, Arden looked at her dad a little differently. She didn't want to. She kept telling herself that it wasn't his fault, it couldn't be his fault that he had been left behind. He had always done the best he could. But she was finding it hard to get her mother's words out of her head. *I felt like I had done all the running of our household for seventeen years. I wasn't getting the sort of support from your father that I needed.*

Arden shook herself out of that line of thinking. "I love you, Daddy," she said. "I'll be home around noon tomorrow."

She gave him a quick kiss and hightailed it.

Check-in time was at two, and it was 2:03 when Arden parked the Heart of Gold in the lot of the hotel on the other side of town. The receptionist asked to see her driver's license, and even though she'd prepared for this, Arden's chest tightened. She'd gotten a fake ID specifically for tonight but had no idea if it would pass muster. She'd paid Kirsten's stepbrother handsomely for it, as he was older and "knew a guy." She didn't have a clue what would happen if the hotel saw this ID for what it was: an overpriced square of plastic. Best-case scenario, they wouldn't let her into the room. Worst-case scenario maybe was jail?

But the receptionist had no visible reaction to Arden's fake ID. She barely glanced at it before handing Arden a card key and saying, "Take the elevator to the fourth floor."

So Arden did.

The room was clean and quiet and felt strangely immobile, like humans never disrupted it—even though of course they did; it's just that the hotel had a paid staff to dispose of any evidence of that fact. There was a king-size bed in the center of the room, dominating the space. There was almost nothing else to look at.

Chris was supposed to arrive at four, so Arden would have plenty of time to prepare the room and herself before going down to meet him in the lobby. Once he was here, she had a whole evening planned out for them: ordering in room service, watching as many old musicals as he wanted on the room's big TV screen, and, of course, lots of time in that king-size bed together.

Arden had told Chris the street address to come to but nothing else, and had begged him not to look it up. "It's a surprise," she'd told him weeks and weeks ago, when she first started planning this whole day. "So don't ruin it."

He'd sworn up and down that he wouldn't. "I'll like the surprise, right?"

"Of course. And tell your parents that you won't be home until the next day."

"I'm intrigued. Are you kidnapping me?"

"Maybe."

Planning this whole secret event had been fun: collaborating with Kirsten and Naomi to find the right outfit and practice her hair and makeup, getting the fake ID, saving up for this hotel room, and, especially, dangling the whole secret in front of Chris, a present he couldn't open yet. It had seemed like he was actually interested in finding out what this anniversary surprise would be. For once it had seemed like Arden knew something that he didn't, and he was interested to find what it was.

Now she set out the brownies on the dresser and changed into her dress. She studied herself in the mirror. The dress was made of slightly iridescent fabric that clung to her body, with thin shoulder straps and a cut-out diamond shape over her shoulder blades. She was pretty sure this was sexy, though it was hard to say. Kirsten had reassured her that guys were into it when girls revealed unexpected sections of skin, so Arden supposed she just had to trust her.

Her phone buzzed. Chris.

I GOT THE PART!

Arden's heart leaped. IN THE COAL MINING MOVIE?? she texted back.

YES!!!!

She responded with a series of exclamation points of her own. For all his auditions, this was the first movie Chris had ever been cast in. His first step out of the Allegany High theater and into the real world of professional acting.

What could be better than celebrating an anniversary with your boyfriend? Celebrating your anniversary with your boyfriend who was going to be a famous actor, that's what.

U R AMAZING! she wrote. SO PROUD OF U. NOW WE HAVE 2 THINGS TO CELEBRATE TONITE! CAN'T WAIT 4 U TO GET HERE.

A minute later her phone rang. She answered it immediately. "This is *awesome*!" she squealed into it, hopping up and down. "Chris, I can't wait to see you on the big screen!"

"Me, too!" he enthused. "But the lame part is that I'm not going to be able to come tonight."

"What?" Arden stopped hopping. She sat down on the bed. "You're not going to be able to come . . . where?"

"To wherever our anniversary surprise is," he explained.

"Why not?"

"Because we're doing an all-cast meet and greet this evening, and I have to be there by six."

"But that's such short notice."

"It's not my choice. They're on a tight schedule and they're going to start shooting next week. That's just how indie films work." He said this last sentence in a bit of a pompous tone, like he was an expert on how indie films work, like he hadn't just been cast in his first film all of five minutes ago.

"Why don't you just tell them that you can't go?" Arden asked, clutching the phone. She caught a glimpse of herself in the mirror next to the closet. She thought she might look pale, but with all that makeup, she couldn't even tell.

"Babe, I'm the youngest cast member. I'm the only one still in high school. I don't want to seem like I have all these special needs and restrictions."

"But it's our anniversary," Arden whispered, feeling so stupid, so *girly*, for caring.

"I know!" He groaned. "Trust me, I never, ever would have planned it like this. But it's not something I get any say over. Do you want to just tell me what the surprise was going to be, or do you want to try to do it next weekend instead? Or maybe I could come after I've done all the movie stuff tonight? I could probably get to you around midnight—would that be too late?"

Arden looked around the hotel room. She looked at the brownies, neatly arranged in the best tin she could find in the pantry. She looked down at her dress, at her freshly shaved legs, at her pedicured toenails. "I want you to come now," she said. "Please."

"Babe." Chris's voice grew slightly exasperated. "I told you. I can't. I was looking forward to this, too, I promise. But we can celebrate a little belatedly, and it will be just as special. This is my dream come true, remember?"

"Your dream is having a bit part in a low-budget movie about *coal mining*?" Arden asked. She knew this was a mean thing to say. But she felt mean.

"Getting a part in a movie, period," Chris retorted, sounding stung. "You know that. I've worked toward this for my entire life. Can you please just be a little supportive?"

"Can *I* be a little supportive?" Arden stood up, her knees locked, her left hand curled in a tight fist. "Can I be a *little* supportive? Are you kidding me? All I do, Chris, is be supportive. That's what I do. Do you feel like I don't honor my blank check to you *enough*? Do you really want to say that to my face?"

"I don't know what you mean," he said. "What blank check?"

"I just wanted us to do this *one thing* together!"

"Babe, we do like *every* thing together. And we will celebrate our anniversary together, too—just not right now. I'm sorry, I swear. Can you please not be so dramatic?"

She was silent. Because that was the first thing she'd promised him: no drama.

"In a few months, we're going to look back on this together and laugh," Chris promised. "We'll go to the movie premiere and this whole thing will be just a distant memory."

Arden swallowed hard. "Just go," she said. "I hope you have the best night of your life."

"Babe—"

"If you're not going to come here right now, then I want to get off the phone with you," she said. "Please."

There was silence. "Okay," he said at last. "Bye. I love you."

"Bye," she said.

They hung up, and she threw her phone onto the bed, hard. She threw herself down after it.

If she'd told Chris all of it, all the hard work that had to go into creating a seemingly magical night, would he have come after all? Or would it just have made her seem pathetic, to work so hard and to care so much?

Tonight was supposed to be *it*, the ultimate proof of their love for each other, their ability to be happy together. Because if they couldn't even get it together on their anniversary, when they had brownies and sexy dresses and hotel rooms and months of preparation on their side, then what hope did they have? How good could their relationship be, really, if this was as good as it got?

She stretched out her arm and dragged her phone back across

the bedspread toward her. She opened up Tonight the Streets Are Ours. She wanted to forget herself. She wanted to disappear into somebody else's life.

But what she read there made her realize that today, Peter's life wasn't any better than hers. His latest entry had been posted less than an hour ago, and this is what it said:

April 24

Bianca broke up with me on Wednesday.

Again.

For good, this time.

She said there's no *grand geste* that can win her back again. She said I shouldn't even try.

It's hard to believe that Tuesday I was so happy when today I am so miserable. For a brief moment, it felt like maybe I actually could have everything I wanted, and today that all seems like a ridiculous illusion.

How dare she take this happiness away from me? I was going to spend this weekend celebrating. Now I'm spending it crying. And in the future, when I think back on this time when one of my dreams came true, I will always be forced to remember that it's also the time when my other dream went up in flames.

It reminds me of the time when I was in sixth grade and we went to Paris and my mom's purse got stolen. She was so upset. And she tried to explain that it wasn't about the purse itself. "I can buy a new bag to carry my belongings," she said. "I can cancel my credit cards and get new ones. I can replace my cell phone and my lipstick. That's frustrating, and it takes time and money, but I *have* time and money. What makes me sad is that this was supposed to be our trip to Paris, and now I'll never again be able to look at photos of us outside of Notre Dame without remembering that on that very same day, a thief stole my purse."

This is how I feel about Bianca. A thief stole my happiness.

And now I have to go work at the bookstore for the next eight hours and pretend like my heart isn't in pieces.

Arden let the phone again fall from her hands. She rolled onto her back and stared at the cream-colored ceiling.

Peter. He seemed to have so much going for him. He was rich. He was probably hot—all signs pointed that way. He went to cool parties, constantly. He was a really talented writer. Maybe he'd even get a book deal. He had fans across the Internet, people he didn't even know.

And yet. The people who were supposed to be closest to him, who were supposed to be on his side . . . where were they? His brother was out of the picture. His parents, from everything he said about them, were cold, bossy, and judgmental. His girlfriend broke up with him—twice. His art-school friends always seemed to be right there when it was time to party, but when he needed support, their names never came up.

What Peter needed was someone like Arden.

No.

He didn't need someone *like* Arden. He needed *Arden*.

She sat up. Peter needed her—and why shouldn't he have her?

She grabbed her phone and called Lindsey.

"How goes the big anniversary?" Lindsey asked when she picked up.

"Miserable. Want to go with me to New York?"

"New York *City*?"

"Yeah."

"When?"

"Now."

"You're going to New York City, *now*. On your anniversary." Lindsey paused, calculating. "I take it Chris isn't with you?"

"Nope."

"Are you okay?"

Arden shrugged, knowing that Lindsey couldn't see her. "I need to get out of here."

"How the hell are you getting there?"

"I'm driving the Heart of Gold, obviously. How else?" She had not even considered the question until Lindsey asked, but now it seemed like the only logical answer.

"Okay," Lindsey said. "Yeah. I'm in. Can you come pick me up?"

"Wait, seriously?" If Lindsey hadn't said yes, Arden might

have concluded this whole plan was absurd, and not even a plan anyway, and New York was a six-hour drive away, and she'd never driven that far, and certainly not in the Heart of Gold, and she had no idea what she would even say to Peter, and maybe she should stay right here, like the good girl she was, have a sleepover at Lindsey's, like she'd told her dad all along.

But Lindsey said, "Seriously. My track meet's already over, so I'm just hanging out. You know I'll take any excuse to get out of here."

And Arden said, "Okay. Meet me down the block from your house in fifteen minutes."

She grabbed her overnight bag and her brownies, she left the card key on the nightstand, and she walked out of the hotel room, letting the door slam shut behind her. And as she did so she felt her heart expanding in her chest—because finally, *finally*, something was happening.

Part Two

On the road

"Hi, is Peter in today?" Lindsey said into her phone. She paused. Arden tightened her grip on the steering wheel. "Oh," she said, "you don't have a Peter there? That's cool. Don't worry about it." She hung up.

Arden cursed under her breath.

About thirty miles out of town, once Arden had finally started to wrap her mind around what she was doing, she'd realized that she didn't actually know what bookstore Peter worked at, just that it was somewhere in New York City accessible by subway. "No problem," Lindsey had reassured her. "How many bookstores could there be?"

A lot, apparently. Arden hadn't known. Cumberland had only one bookstore, which doubled as a cat adoption center and a tobacconist.

While Arden drove, she instructed Lindsey to pull up a list of NYC bookshops on her phone, and now Lindsey was systematically calling them all. But so far, none of them employed Peter.

"What if we *never* find him?" Arden asked, her eyes trained on the road. "What if the store where he works is unlisted or something?"

"Then we'll hang out in New York City for the evening," Lindsey said. "Get dinner in Little Italy. Take in a Broadway play. Go home with a good story."

"I'm not driving six hours for a good story."

The Heart of Gold shuddered a little, as it always did when Arden tried to edge the speed above fifty-eight miles an hour, as if it wanted to remind her that in this car, the trip was likely to take more than six hours. Arden glanced at the clock on her dashboard. It was now just past three. If all went well, they should reach Peter around eight forty-five. Nine at the latest.

Assuming, of course, they could figure out where he was.

Since stopping to pick up Lindsey on the way out of town, Arden had filled Lindsey in on the failed anniversary and the inconvenient start to her boyfriend's film career.

"Are you kidding me?" Lindsey had demanded when Arden told her what Chris had done. "What a jerk! It's like he doesn't even care."

It was one thing for Arden to think mean thoughts about her boyfriend, but another thing entirely for Lindsey to say them aloud. Lindsey didn't get where Chris was coming from, and she didn't love him like Arden did.

Or like Arden hoped she did.

"I'm sure he cares," Arden defended him, even though she wasn't actually sure that she was sure. "He just wants so badly to be a professional actor. And this is his chance. It's complicated. I should be happy for him."

"You don't have to be happy for him if you don't feel like it," said Lindsey.

Arden shrugged.

"So is this it? Are you guys breaking up over this?"

"What?" Arden started, taking her eyes off the road for a moment to stare at Lindsey. "Of course not. It's just a fight, Lindsey. People do way worse things than this all the time, and they stay together. I'm not going to break up with my boyfriend of one year just because we had a fight."

Anyway, what she felt toward Chris . . . it wasn't *anger*, not exactly. She was sad. And disappointed. In him, and in herself for somehow still managing to come in second place in his priorities, even when she was trying her hardest to be the girlfriend she desperately wanted to be.

She didn't want to talk about Chris anymore, especially not with Lindsey, who was biased against him anyway. Arden changed the topic to explain Tonight the Streets Are Ours as best she could. Lindsey listened, enraptured, as Arden told her about Peter's brother and his unexplained disappearance. About their parents, money-obsessed and status-conscious, who somehow refused to acknowledge the gifted artist living right under their own roof. About Bianca, beautiful and ambitious and perfect—who couldn't handle it when Peter experienced real tragedy or real success of his own. And about Peter himself, talented and wise and *heartbroken*, over and over again. And now Lindsey was calling bookstores, trying to track him down.

"Why didn't you tell me about Peter before?" Lindsey asked in a break between phone calls.

"I told you I was reading some guy's blog."

"But you didn't tell me how *interesting* it was."

Arden scrunched her eyebrows as she tried, and failed, to switch lanes. She didn't have much experience with highway driving, and the other cars out here were much less accommodating than cars on the streets of Cumberland. Finally, she swerved her way back over to the slow lane and said to Lindsey, "I didn't want you to think I was weird. You know, spending this much time following people we don't even know."

"Arden," Lindsey said, "at this point, it is way too late in the game for me to think you're weird. I *know* you're weird." Arden laughed, and Lindsey reflected for a moment. "Plus, it's not really any different from following characters on a TV show, is it?"

Arden nodded thoughtfully.

"Typical Arden," Lindsey said. "You can't stand to see anyone suffer, even for a second, even when you don't know the guy. It's like that time you saved that bird's life."

"What bird?" Arden asked.

"You remember! We were kids. You found a baby bird in a pool of oil in the woods between our houses. It couldn't get out. It must have fallen out of the nest or something. My dad wanted to wring its neck, to put it out of its pain. But you kept it in your room and nursed it back to health and set it free."

"No, I didn't."

"It was definitely you. It's not like I was playing in our woods with somebody else who rescued a bird."

"I mean, no, that never happened at all. That was the plot of one of the Arden Doll books."

Arden snuck a sideward glance to watch this realization slowly dawn on Lindsey. "Oh, yeah!" Lindsey said. "God, that's so wild."

Arden didn't know what she'd do if she encountered a drowning bird. Probably she would try to rescue it. But maybe she would just walk away in horror.

"Well, whatever. You're rescuing a brokenhearted boy today, which is basically the same as a broken bird."

"Only if we find him," Arden reminded her.

Lindsey got back on the phone. "Can I speak with Peter, please? He's supposed to be working there this afternoon . . . Oh, sorry, I must have the wrong number. My bad." After hanging up, she said to Arden, "Are you *sure* he never said the name of his bookstore?"

"Positive." Arden had read every entry—and there were hundreds of them. Some she'd read more than once. She knew everything he'd ever put in there. "Anyway, I have no clue what I'm going to say to him if we do find him," she went on. " 'Hey, I just drove a million miles to meet you' sounds kind of stalkery."

"Let's role-play," Lindsey suggested. "I'll be Peter, and you can be you."

"Sounds like a theater game," Arden cautioned, making a face.

"Not really, because you're pretending to be *yourself*."

"Okay, fine." Arden cleared her throat. "Hi, are you Peter?"

Lindsey put on a deep, fake-masculine voice. "Who's asking?"

"Uh, my name is Arden. And I just wanted to . . . meet you, I guess."

"Are you another one of those girls who heard Bianca and I broke up? And now you're trying to make your move as soon as Bianca's out of the picture? That's very exploitative, Arden—is that what you said your name was? I'm still in mourning. I'm not looking to just move on to the next available girl."

"You are a terrible role-player," Arden said. "Do you know that?"

"I just want you to be prepared for the worst," Lindsey said in her normal-pitched voice. "Actually, I just thought of an even worse scenario."

"Fabulous," Arden muttered.

"What if the whole thing is an elaborate ruse?" Lindsey went on. "Like 'Peter' is just a code name for a kidnapper or murderer who's created this artsy, sensitive online persona so he can lure unsuspecting young girls into his clutches. And then he keeps them locked up in a penthouse somewhere. Where he forces them into lives of servitude. And drinks their blood."

"You're conflating approximately a dozen distinct paranoias there," Arden told her. "Also, I think there has got to be a better way to kidnap girls than to create a fake online journal, update it every day for a year, and then wait for your readers to somehow piece together what bookstore you supposedly work at."

"It's not out of the question, though," Lindsey said. "Admit that it's not out of the question."

"Do you want me to let you out right here?" Arden asked. "I'll do it. You can hitchhike home."

They drove past the turnoff for Hancock. Lindsey snorted. "What a dumb name for a town."

"I assume it's named after John Hancock," Arden said. "You know? One of the signers of the Declaration of Independence? Famous old dude? Ring any bells?"

"It sounds like slang for something sexual. Like 'hand cock.'" Lindsey made a jerk-off motion with her hand.

Arden rolled her eyes, then cracked up. "You have a filthy mind, Lindsey."

Half an hour later, they stopped for gas. The Heart of Gold had been making a weird *whump-whump-whump* noise, so Arden walked around, inspecting it. She felt like a fraud, since she blatantly had *no* idea what she was looking for on her car, and she was still wearing her shimmery anniversary dress, which presumably was not what people wore when they were engaging in auto mechanics. She had considered changing back into her normal clothes while she was still at the hotel. But she had this dress. She had planned to wear it today, and she still wanted to wear it. And if Chris wasn't going to appreciate it, maybe Peter would.

She didn't even bother to ask Lindsey for her automotive insight, since Lindsey did not have her license, due to a combination of being young for her grade, never practicing, and knowing that she could rely on Arden to drive her everywhere.

Arden's one course of action about the *whump-whump-whumps* would have been to call her father, but she didn't know what *he* would have done about it, either, or how he would have reacted to the news that she'd gone sixty miles out of town without telling him. So she just got back into the driver's seat and drove on, turning up the volume on the Heart of Gold's crappy stereo to drown out the noises coming from under the hood. Arden watched the road and thought about Chris heading to his cool cast meeting, and she wanted to text him and say, *I'm heading somewhere right now, too.*

"I think I'm going to work on a farm this summer," Lindsey announced in a break between songs. For miles, all they'd been able to see out the windows was farmland.

"Which farm?" Arden asked.

"I don't know. I'm going to look at job postings and stuff online to see if anybody nearby needs extra farmhands. It'd be like when I was a kid, you know?"

"Then you're going to have to get your license fast," Arden advised her. "Because I am not driving you to a farm every morning. I *know* how early farmers have to wake up, and I want no part in that."

"Hopefully I can find a place where I can live for the summer," Lindsey said, resting her head against the window. "That way neither of us will have to worry about driving."

Arden snuck a sidelong look at her. "You'd really live at a farm?"

"Sure, if I can."

"Without me?"

"You could come, too, if you wanted."

Arden did *not* want—unless there were zebras there, and possibly not even then. Zebras had lost some of their appeal over the past eight years.

"It'll only be for the summer, anyway," Lindsey went on.

Arden felt a twinge in her stomach. She thought about how much trouble Lindsey could get into when left to her own devices for ten minutes, and she shuddered to think what could happen if the two of them were separated for ten whole weeks.

A couple years ago, when Arden's family went to Atlantic Beach for a grand total of eight days, Lindsey had decided it would be a good idea to dress up in a sheet and stand alongside the road in the nighttime, to make drivers think they'd seen a ghost. One driver panicked when he saw her, swerved, and crashed into a tree. Nobody got injured, but the car required thousands of dollars of repairs, which Lindsey was still paying off. This was the sort of thing that happened when Arden left Lindsey alone.

But Lindsey probably wouldn't go through with it, anyway, Arden reassured herself. The number of plans like this that Lindsey had made over the years, only to abandon because they took too much effort or were replaced by new, more exciting ideas—they were countless. If Arden took every one of them seriously, she would never have time to do anything else but worry.

"Hey," Arden said, pointing to a green road sign. "Shartlesville, Pennsylvania. The town you go to when you try to fart but you-know-what comes out instead."

Lindsey guffawed and held up her hand. Arden smacked her a high five, swerving the whole car to the right. The truck behind her blared a long honk. "Arden Huntley," said Lindsey, "you are a clever girl, you know that?" She picked up her phone again and dialed. "Hi, is Peter working tonight?"

She paused. Arden focused on the road before her.

"Teenage guy?" Lindsey said into the phone. "Goes to art school?" A moment of silence. "Cool, thanks. We'll be there by ten." She hung up.

"So," Arden said, her heart fluttering.

"So," Lindsey said. "I found him."

The heart of the Heart of Gold is called into question

At six o'clock, they drove past the first road sign for New York.

"New York City, one hundred thirty-five miles," Lindsey read aloud.

Arden felt suddenly gripped by the extraordinary potential of highway signs. They made the country seem deceptively small. The only thing that stood between her and New York City was the number 135. She could keep driving even farther and hit Connecticut, or Vermont—or Florida if she made a turn to the south—or she could turn around and drive through the night and the next day and the next night and the next day until she hit California and the Pacific Ocean. Highway signs made every place in America seem equally within reach, and even though Arden had been driving for hours now—even though her eyes were dry from watching the road continually unfurl before her like a never-ending ribbon—this first sign for New York City made her feel like she could keep going forever.

Twenty-five minutes later, her car broke down.

She was driving in the slow lane, as she had been for basically the entire trip, but then suddenly the Heart of Gold wouldn't even keep up with the pace of the slow lane, and its muted *whump-whump-whump*s turned into a full-on whirring noise, and it started to smell bad, and . . . something was clearly wrong.

Arden coasted into the breakdown lane, stopped, and turned off the engine. She and Lindsey looked at each other. The traffic whizzed by them.

"What happened?" Lindsey asked.

"I don't know." Arden examined the lights and dials on her dashboard. The "check engine" light was lit up, but that was always lit up, so she didn't put too much stock in it. She also noticed that the dial for the car's temperature had gone up really, really high. Into the red zone. "Maybe the engine overheated," she guessed.

"So what should we do?" Lindsey asked.

"I don't *know*, Lindsey," Arden snapped. "I am not a car expert. I have never driven farther than the Glockenspiel before. I don't have access to any vehicular insider information here, okay? What do *you* think we should do?"

Lindsey was silent for a moment, slouched in her seat like a kicked puppy. At last she said, "We could hitchhike."

"Great plan. Let's abandon my car here and get a ride from a total stranger for the next hundred and twenty miles. What a safe and wise course of action! And you thought *Peter* might be a murderer or a kidnapper?" Arden said. "Lindsey, you have no sense of self-preservation."

The two girls glared at each other across giant cups, left over from a Dairy Queen stop much earlier in the state of Pennsylvania.

"It's not my fault your car broke down," Lindsey said finally.

This was true. Arden was frustrated, and she knew she was taking it out on Lindsey. It was Arden's fault she'd bought a shitty car, Arden's fault she never bothered to figure out why that "check engine" light was always lit, Arden's fault she hadn't learned the first thing about car mechanics, Arden's fault they were on this highway on this wild goose chase in the first place.

But even though Lindsey wasn't to blame for this situation, that didn't stop Arden from wishing that Lindsey would at least try to help fix it.

"It doesn't matter whose fault it is," said Arden. "We can't sit on the side of the highway for the rest of our lives."

When there was a break in the traffic, she got out and popped open the hood of her car. This, at least, was something her dad had taught her how to do. She peered at the machinery inside, then dumped her water bottle onto what she thought was the engine, followed by the remnants of their Dairy Queen Blizzards for good measure. If the engine was overheated, then it stood to reason that it needed to be cooled down.

When Arden climbed back into the car, Lindsey had her phone out. Not making eye contact with Arden, Lindsey said, "I looked it up online, and apparently the closest train station is in Lancaster. It's not too far from here. We could take a taxi there."

"And then what?" Arden asked.

"Well, then there should be a train back to Cumberland at some point."

"What point is that, exactly?" Arden asked. "It's nearly seven o'clock. I doubt that any more trains are running from here to Cumberland tonight. And even if there are, what makes you think there would be seats left on them? And how much would those last-minute seats cost? And who exactly would be paying for those train tickets, not to mention this supposed taxi ride to get us there?"

Lindsey was silent, her hair hanging in front of her face like a curtain separating her from Arden.

"And what," Arden added, hearing her voice crack, "would happen to the Heart of Gold?"

Arden thought again of that baby bird, slick with oil, trying to climb its way to fresh air, to freedom. It was fictional, of course. It was entirely made up. But did that even matter? Couldn't it inspire her anyway?

One last time, Arden turned her key in the ignition. And the car came back to life.

Neither of the girls said a word, in case commenting on what was happening would jinx it. Arden just eased her way back into traffic, and they continued on toward New York.

Meeting Peter

The bookstore where Peter worked was called The Last Page. It was situated on a commercial street in Brooklyn, busier than almost every street in Cumberland, but calmer than most of the New York streets Arden had driven down to get there. She'd gotten honked at more times than she could count, and twice she had almost run over jaywalking pedestrians, one of whom was carrying a baby. Both times they yelled at her, which seemed unfair, since *they* were the ones walking against the traffic light, in the dark, wearing all black. Also, it was past nine o'clock, and she was no baby aficionado, but she thought that child should probably be in bed.

Once she'd found the store, she spent about ten minutes driving around, looking for a parking space she could pull into. When she realized no such parking spaces existed around here, she spent another five minutes trying to parallel park—a skill that she'd achieved competence at before her driving test and had not practiced once since then. For a while Lindsey offered up her opinions ("Maybe you should turn the wheel to the left. Maybe you should pull out and start over again") until Arden snapped, "Do *you* want to drive?" at which point Lindsey shut up.

Finally, the car was parked. Arden took a deep breath, grabbed her tin of peanut butter brownies, and marched into the store. She didn't know exactly what the brownies were for, but one thing her mother had taught her was that people tended to be nicer to you when you gave them baked goods.

The Last Page was surprisingly big, bigger than its storefront had led Arden to believe, and it was filled floor to ceiling with books: new titles displayed on the ground level and a basement jumbled with used ones. The girls started on the main level, walking through every aisle, sort of looking at the books, mostly staring at the people and trying to figure out whether they were customers or employees and, if the latter, whether they might be Peter. Arden didn't know if it was a New York City thing or just an annoying thing that no one in this store was wearing even a name tag, let alone a uniform.

"We could just ask someone," Lindsey suggested. "Like, 'Hey, where's Peter?'"

"Sure," Arden said. "Go for it."

Lindsey stuck closer to Arden and didn't ask anyone.

Fortunately, there weren't that many high school–age guys in the store. Saturday night was apparently not the most happening of times for their peers to be book shopping. On the first floor they saw one guy with a little girl who must have been his sister or babysitting charge or someone; either way, Peter wouldn't be working with a kid by his side. In the back Arden saw another one who was also probably her age, with long, unwashed hair, pants falling halfway down his ass, in the process of picking his nose.

"That could be him," Lindsey pointed out. "Do you think an employee would wipe his boogers on a book spine like that?"

Arden paused. "That seems like customer behavior to me. Let's come back to him."

She pushed back a niggling worry that maybe the Last Page wasn't even Peter's bookstore. Maybe there was some other adolescent bookshop employee with the same name. New York was a big city; it was possible. Or maybe this *was* Peter's store and he'd left already. There were so many reasons for him not to be here, and she didn't want to think about any of them.

Downstairs they saw a guy who definitely did work at the store, because he was helping an old woman find a book, and at first it seemed like he *could* have been in high school, but then Arden noticed the wedding band on his ring finger.

That left one teenage-looking guy in the store. The one behind the checkout counter downstairs. The one standing behind the computer, his elbows propped up on the counter in front of him, holding a copy of Dante's *Inferno*.

"That's him," Arden said to Lindsey. "That's him."

Arden pretended to be interested in the books on the nearest display table, but really she was just sneaking peeks at Peter. She hadn't consciously known what she'd expected him to look like, but seeing him now, she realized that she'd pictured him looking like . . . well, like Chris.

He didn't. For one thing, he was Asian. Arden had just assumed he would be white, like she was, like almost everyone in Cumberland was. She felt immediately guilty for expecting, however subconsciously, that everyone she met would look like her. Peter was shorter than she'd anticipated, too, and he was wearing glasses, which she hadn't pictured but which seemed just right on him. Yet he was still immediately, self-evidently Peter.

"He's hot," Arden whispered to Lindsey. "Right? He's so hot."

"I don't know," Lindsey whispered back. "Dudes aren't hot to me."

"Bullshit," Arden hissed. "Even though I don't want to make out with girls, I can still tell whether they're hot. You're gay, Lindsey, not *blind*."

"Okay, I think he's probably hot," she whispered.

Arden checked her watch. Almost ten. Peter was going to get off work at any minute. She needed to approach him *now*. While he was still working and she was a customer and he would be required to talk to her.

Her hands felt clammy, and she wished she and Lindsey had taken their role-playing of this scene a little more seriously.

Seeing the book in his hands gave her a flash of inspiration. Without saying a word to Lindsey, Arden ran back to the poetry section and scanned the shelf desperately.

There it was.

She grabbed a book, bypassed Lindsey, and headed straight for Peter.

Her heart was pounding.

She stood right in front of him.

She set the book down on the counter.

Peter put down his copy of the *Inferno* and gave Arden a polite smile. "Will that be all today?" he asked.

She nodded mutely.

He took her book and moved to scan it, but then—because he was Peter, and she knew he couldn't work cash registers without commenting on a customer's purchase, he never managed to stop that, no matter how many book buyers he offended— he smiled and blurted out, "*Sonnets from the Portuguese.* Good choice. I love Elizabeth Barrett Browning. 'How do I love thee? Let me count the ways—'"

"'I love thee to the depth and breadth and height my soul can reach,'" Arden finished.

They looked at each other. He raised an approving eyebrow. "You know it."

Only because of you, she thought.

He scanned the bar code and bagged the book. Arden watched him carefully, but he didn't write a note to her on the receipt, he didn't stick his phone number in there. She supposed that was a one-time trick, and it didn't end so well the last time.

"Enjoy," he said. Then he stretched. "And I'm done! You're my last customer of the day."

"I know," Arden said.

He cocked his head. "You know?"

She felt shaky and focused, like she was about to dive off the end of a very high diving board. Though she'd never done that before, actually. When she was a kid, every time her mom took her to the YMCA, she would climb all the way up, and she would walk to the edge of the board, and she would stand there and stand there, feeling this same feeling she had right now in her heart and her throat and all the way down to her fingers and toes. Then she would turn around and retreat back down the ladder, to the poolside. She did this dozens of times. Eventually she just stopped climbing up there. The outcome was the same either way, and at least when she stayed at ground level, she never felt like she was failing at anything.

Even now, though, years later, Arden identified that feeling. That moment between certainty and mystery, between safety and soaring.

"Yes," Arden said. "I know." She swallowed hard, then thrust the tin in front of him. "Do you want a brownie? I baked brownies."

Peter blinked a couple times when she pulled off the top to the tin. "Sure," he said at last. He took a brownie.

As he was about to bite into it, Arden blurted out, "I read your blog. I love your writing."

And that was all it took. Peter's face split into a huge, dorky, tooth-filled smile, and for what felt like the first time all day, she exhaled.

"What's your name?" he asked.

"Arden."

"Thank you, Arden." He stuck out his hand and shook hers, and she took all of this in, the smile on his face, the sensation of his palm against her own. "It's a pleasure to meet you," he said. "I'm Peter."

Dinner with Peter

Arden, Lindsey, and Peter went to a kitschy diner down the street from The Last Page. Arden knew she should be ravenous—other than that Dairy Queen Blizzard, she hadn't eaten since breakfast—but as it was, when the waiter brought over her basket of chicken fingers, she couldn't imagine being able to choke them down.

"So how did you find Tonight the Streets Are Ours?" Peter asked after he'd swallowed his first bite of veggie burger. He sat across from Arden and Lindsey, shifting his gaze between them.

"Arden found it," Lindsey explained. "Just Googling some stuff, right?"

"What exactly were you searching for?" Peter asked.

"Um." Arden felt herself blush. "The sentence 'Why doesn't anybody love me as much as I love them?'"

Peter looked impressed—maybe with her memory, or maybe with the poignancy of his own words. "Did I write that?"

"Yes. About Bianca."

"Oh. Of course." Peter's face slipped into a frown, but he shook it off. "So where did *you* get that phrase from?"

"I guess it's something I've wondered sometimes," Arden said quietly. This seemed like a lot to reveal to a stranger. But Peter didn't feel like a stranger.

"And have you ever found any good answers to that question?" he asked, leaning forward.

Because I don't deserve to be loved that much, Arden thought. But she didn't say it, because obviously Peter *did* deserve that—that and more—and she didn't want to let on that in this one regard, she wasn't like him at all.

"I think maybe I just love people too much," Arden answered aloud. "So if other people love me a normal amount, that doesn't come close to matching the way I feel about them."

She felt Lindsey shift beside her, but didn't look at her. She couldn't say these words to Lindsey. But she could say them to Peter, because he could understand.

"Maybe I do, too," Peter said. "Maybe we're like mutant superheroes. Part of some government experiment gone awry, and we were left with a preternatural capacity for love."

Arden broke into a smile.

"No way," Lindsey objected, as Arden had assumed she would. "That's not even true."

"You mean we're *not* superheroes?" Peter asked, raising his eyebrows in mock surprise.

"That nobody loves Arden as much as she loves them. Tons of people love you, you know that. Your parents, Chris, me, our other friends . . ."

Arden nodded at Lindsey's words, but she thought about their argument when the Heart of Gold stopped running, and how wide the gap was between her and Lindsey's definitions of love. Love meant taking care of someone else. It meant solving their problems for them, protecting them, supporting them even in times of crisis. In her heart Arden knew: *There must be more to love, more than this.*

"So what happened with Bianca?" Arden asked Peter softly, then quickly added, "You don't have to talk about it if you don't want to."

But he did want to.

"She broke up with me three days ago," he said, his long lashes fluttering as though he was blinking back tears. "She called before school, while I was still in bed. Usually I'd ignore a call while I was trying to sleep, but this was *Bianca*, and I never ignore calls from her. I used to silence my phone overnight, and now I leave it on just in case she needs something or wants to talk.

"Anyway, she called really early, and before I could say anything she told me that this was it, and it was over for real this time, and she never should have given me a second chance."

"I'm so sorry," Arden murmured. This wasn't any new information, but hearing it from his mouth made her heart ache.

"Did she say why?" Lindsey asked.

"Well, a literary agent offered to represent me on Tuesday," Peter began.

"Which is amazing, by the way," Arden interjected. "Can we

take a moment to discuss how amazing that is? I don't know anybody who has an *agent*. You're going to be a published author. *You* are! And then the whole world is going to know how talented you are."

She hoped that this speech did a little bit to make up for Bianca's demoralizing response. Peter was right: this should have been the happiest moment of his life. She wanted to give him that happiness.

"Thank you," he said. "I don't know if I will actually get published. It might never happen. But just knowing that an agent, a professional in the field, read my writing and thought it *might* be good enough to be published? It's unreal. It's the only thing I ever wanted."

He stared off into the distance of the diner for a moment, his gaze resting on the glittery portrait of a 1970s Elvis Presley hanging on the wall. Arden looked around, too. She felt overdressed for chicken fingers at a diner, but it didn't take her long to notice a girl wearing an even shorter dress than hers and a guy wearing even more makeup, so that helped her feel at ease.

"Bianca," Lindsey prompted Peter.

"Right." He refocused on the girls. "I told her the good news as soon as I found out. I thought she would be proud of me. At first, it seemed like she was. But the next time we talked, she said she didn't want Tonight the Streets Are Ours to be published. She didn't want people reading it."

"People *do* already read it, though," Arden pointed out. "Whether or not it becomes a book, it's out there."

"I know. And she freaked out at me about that, demanding that I take down the whole website. She'd never looked at it before, and once she took the time to read it, she immediately hated everything about it. She said I *had* to take down Tonight the Streets Are Ours, and I *had* to tell the agent that I didn't want representation, and I wasn't *allowed* to publish a book that mentioned her in any way . . ."

He started picking apart his veggie burger, not eating it, but separating out each onion ring, ripping up the lettuce leaves. "I offered to change her name if she was worried about privacy, but she said that wasn't good enough. And then I asked her to just *understand*. I've wanted to have success as a writer for my whole life. And if she really loves me, even a little bit, couldn't she just try to want for me the same thing I want for myself?"

"Couldn't she help you get the thing that would make you happy?" Arden supplied.

He nodded vigorously. "*Exactly.* But the answer was no. She couldn't. Or wouldn't. And I won't take down the blog, or give up my chance at becoming a published author. So she broke up with me." He paused, and swallowed hard. "I feel like a jerk saying this about her, but I wouldn't say it if I didn't believe it was true: I think she's jealous. I think she couldn't stand to see me achieve something that would fulfill me and that didn't involve her at all."

"It *did* involve her though, right?" Lindsey asked. "Since you talk about her in there and stuff?"

Peter stared at Lindsey blankly. Arden grimaced and gave her a little poke in the thigh.

"Are you going to eat the rest of your fries?" Lindsey tried.

He considered it for a moment, then said, "No. Too heart-broken." He shoved his plate across the table, and Lindsey dug in.

"Trust me, she *is* a jealous person," he went on, his words rushing out like they had been pent up inside of him for too long, like laying out the whole story for Arden was helping him fit together the pieces. "She's constantly jealous over other girls, for example. Which is ridiculous, since I've told her so many times that she's amazing and I'm crazy about her. But whenever someone else even remotely female is nearby, she gets all, 'Oh, I see you checking out that chick. Do you think she's hotter than me?'"

"You never mentioned that on the blog," Arden said, not sure how she felt about this sudden chink in Bianca's armor. Arden had been led to expect an angel. And what kind of angel felt threatened by mere mortals?

"It was such a small part of our relationship," Peter explained. "It never seemed important enough to write down. I never imagined it would *balloon* in this way. Anyway, I don't write down every single thing that happens on every single day. I write down the bits I want to think more about, or want to remember later. And Bianca making snide comments when I'm nice to the cashier at Starbucks?" He shrugged. "Not really something I want to think about.

"And isn't *that* a problem, that she can't trust her own boyfriend? I'm telling you, she could come in here right now and see us together and leap to conclusions about what's going on between us, even though there would be *no* reason for her to be concerned."

"That's crazy," Arden got out weakly.

Even though there would be no *reason for her to be concerned.*

Because, of course, who would look at Arden sitting in a diner with Peter and think there was something going on, something worth noticing? Only a crazy girl would think that.

She took a deep, calming breath and reminded herself, *You didn't come here to seduce Peter anyway. He just lost the love of his life. And you have a boyfriend.*

Thinking of Chris, Arden did a quick phone check. One new text.

HOPE YOU'RE HAVING A GOOD NIGHT. CAN'T WAIT FOR YOU TO MEET THE REST OF MY CAST! EVERYONE IS SO NICE.

Even though Chris didn't come right out and reference their fight, she knew that this was him trying to smooth over things between them with his customary pluck. Like if he could just get her to text back *Sounds great!* then all their problems would be solved.

Instead she stuck her phone back in her bag and leaned across the table to ask Peter, "Did you tell your parents about your breakup?" because she was curious to know more about them, too; she was curious to know about every last character on Tonight the Streets Are Ours.

"Yeah. They hadn't really wanted me to be dating Bianca in the first place, so it's not like they care that it's over."

"Why didn't they want you to date her?" Lindsey asked.

"Let's see." Peter tossed back a gulp of Diet Coke, and Arden watched his Adam's apple bob as he swallowed. "Oh, I know: because they don't want me to get the things that I want in life."

Arden was a little surprised that Peter would reveal this so openly and honestly to two girls he'd never met before. If their roles were reversed, she wouldn't lay it all out there, about her sad workaholic dad, her neurotic kid brother, her mom who got sick of them all. Not when she knew from Tonight the Streets Are Ours that Bianca had a perfect family with parents who were still together and loved each other and their daughter as much as they ever had.

But Peter must have realized that he had already told Arden all his secrets. In his year of writing Tonight the Streets Are Ours, he'd laid out everything—maybe not *for* Arden, but she was the one who'd gotten it. It would be silly to try to keep something from her now.

And isn't that such a freeing thing, to talk to somebody who already feels like your journal?

Perhaps Lindsey, too, felt that Peter's openness gave them permission to know everything, because the next thing she said was, "So what happened to your brother?"

Arden kicked her under the table because, *rude*, Lindsey.

"I don't know," Peter said, his voice soft. He stirred the ice in his glass around and around.

"I have a brother, too," Arden offered, "and I don't know what I'd do if I lost him. I'd do anything to protect him. So I can imagine how hard it must be."

Peter nodded, but it seemed like he was trapped inside his own memories, not listening.

"But what *happened*?" Lindsey pressed on, her blue eyes bright with curiosity, as if she were Nancy Drew in the Case of the Missing Sibling.

"When he disappeared? Well. He'd just started at Cornell."

"Wow," Lindsey said. "Your brother must be smart."

Arden nodded. She knew Cornell was an Ivy League college in upstate New York, but she couldn't name anyone who'd ever gone there. Even though Allegany was one of the better schools in Maryland, it was not turning out yearly droves of Ivy League–quality students.

But, of course, Peter's family lived in New York City. They were rich. Their children went to private schools and had an au pair. They probably took them to museums and the opera on weekends, sent them to summer enrichment camps, paid for SAT tutors. If Arden had all of that going for her, there would be no reason she couldn't go to an Ivy League college, too—no reason other than her record of suspension and drug possession, of course.

"He *is* smart," Peter agreed with Lindsey. "And stupid." Peter stared off at the jukebox in the corner, like he was trying to decide how much to say.

You can tell me anything, Arden willed. *I'm here for you.*

"He—" Peter began.

His phone rang.

"Hey, man," he answered it. "Yeah . . . Yeah . . . I know, I don't, either . . . Sure, yeah, sounds cool. Jigsaw Manor? . . . Okay, you got it. Later."

He clicked off his phone and gave Arden and Lindsey a broad grin, all traces of his missing brother gone from his face. Like it had never even happened. "Hey," he said. "Do you girls want to go to a party?"

An early spring night's dream

Arden drove to the party, which was in a different part of Brooklyn. She plugged the address into her phone and let the GPS direct her there, because, although the party venue was only a few miles away, Peter had no idea how to get there. Apparently he took the subway or taxis everywhere.

"But I *could* tell you how to take the G to the L to get there," he offered from the backseat. She'd been worried that the Heart of Gold wouldn't live up to whatever rich-person transit he was accustomed to, but instead he just seemed delighted that there was a car for him to ride in at all, no matter how busted it was.

"I'll G your L," Arden replied, having no idea what these letters stood for. "Do you even know how to drive?" It was funny, these gaping holes in her understanding of Peter. She knew everything and nothing; she knew his inside jokes and most profound anxieties, but not simple facts like his last name or whether he had a license. Which of those was more important? Which of those did you really need to know a person?

"It's okay if you can't drive," Lindsey said from her customary passenger seat up front. "Say it loud and proud. It's not really as important a life skill as people make it out to be."

"Only if you, like Lindsey, have a built-in chauffeur," Arden said.

"I can drive," Peter said. "We have a summer place out in the Hamptons—"

"I know you do," Arden interrupted.

He shook his head and laughed. "Of course you do. I keep forgetting how much you know. It's hard to believe. Anyway, sometimes I drive my parents' car when we're out there. There's just not much point to driving in the city. The subway runs twenty-four hours, and even if I did have a car here, it's almost impossible to find legal parking. I'm surprised *you* have a car, actually."

"Well, we don't live here," Lindsey said. "We're just in town for tonight."

"Where do you live?"

The topic hadn't come up at the diner, while they'd been busy discussing Peter's love life. "Maryland," Arden said. "Close to the happening states of both Pennsylvania *and* West Virginia. MaryVirgiPenn."

"Arden is trying to make 'MaryVirgiPenn' a thing," Lindsey explained. "It hasn't caught on yet, though."

"Except with you," Arden pointed out.

Lindsey tilted her head in accord. "I do say MaryVirgiPenn a lot."

Peter looked impressed. "That's a far drive. What brought you to the city this weekend?"

Arden shared a sidelong glance with Lindsey. She could be honest. But would that creep him out? She would be creeped out if a stranger drove hundreds of miles just to see her.

"Arden's mom lives in Manhattan," Lindsey said finally, which was a true statement, if not *the* truth.

"Where?" Peter asked.

"One thirty-three Eldridge Street," Arden said, reciting the address from memory. She'd intended to throw away that slip of paper her dad had given her. She'd just never quite done it.

"Ah, a Lower East Side lady," Peter said. "Cool."

"Not really," Arden said shortly. She didn't totally know what or where the Lower East Side was, but any place where her mother lived did not sound that cool to her.

Clearly Peter could tell that she didn't want to say anything more about it, because he changed the subject. "Why do you call your car the Heart of Gold?" he asked.

"It's after the spaceship in *The Hitchhiker's Guide to the Galaxy*," Arden explained.

"Oh, yeah, I never read that book, but my brother was into it."

Arden waited for him to volunteer more information about his brother here. When he didn't, she went on. "Well, that was the name of their spaceship, and it got them everywhere they needed to be, just like my baby here." Arden patted the dashboard.

"Plus, the Heart of Gold spaceship ran on the infinite improbability drive," Lindsey added. "And it is infinitely improbable that this car will ever start."

Arden smacked her shoulder. "Shh, you'll hurt its feelings."

After another fifteen minutes of harrowing New York City driving, Peter said, "Okay, you can park somewhere around here." They had reached a quiet, run-down part of town, all concrete and trash on the ground, with none of the boutiques or restaurants that had characterized the Last Page's neighborhood—but fortunately, lots of easy parking spaces. It seemed to Arden like the sort of place where your car would get stolen, your purse would get stolen, and you would be left for dead. If Chris were here, he would have locked all the doors and ordered her to keep driving. So instead, she parked and got out.

They joined a long line of people waiting outside a heavily graffitied door. Some were smoking cigarettes, drinking out of cans in paper bags, or sitting on the dirty sidewalk. Everyone was done up in some kind of costume, adorned with fairy wings or crowns of leaves or gobs of glitter.

"Your dress totally fits in here," Lindsey said to Arden in wonder.

"It's like I'd known we were coming," Arden agreed.

Peter spotted two guys whom he recognized and pulled Arden and Lindsey into line with them. The girl they cut right in front of sighed loudly and said, *"Really?"*

"Sorry," Arden said guiltily. She held out her tin. "Can I offer you a brownie?"

"I guess." The girl adjusted the enormous antlers sticking out of her head, then took two brownies. And said nothing more about their cutting.

Peter introduced the girls to his friends. "Arden, Lindsey, these guys are Trotsky and Hanson."

"Hey," Arden and Lindsey said. Arden didn't ask how they knew Peter, because she was worried they might ask the same of her in return. Fortunately, they didn't seem to care.

"What's the theme tonight?" Peter asked. He pulled a flask out of his pocket and took a quick sip, which seemed daring considering they were outside, and presumably public under-age drinking was as illegal here as it was in Maryland. Arden tensed—it was one thing to see strangers drinking on the street, and quite another to see Peter do the same—but nobody else seemed concerned.

"Enchanted forest," Trotsky said, sounding terribly uninterested.

"Like a *Midsummer Night's Dream* kind of thing," contributed Hanson.

"It's ironic," interjected Trotsky, "because it's only April."

"That's why I made this." Hanson put on a papier-mâché donkey's head and then said something else, but it came out as "Mumble mumble mumble."

"Ugh," said Trotsky, sounding somehow even more bored now. "Honey, I told you I can't hear you when you have that ass-head on."

"Hey, my . . . Chris was in *Midsummer's* once," Arden said. *My boyfriend.* She'd almost said *my boyfriend*, and she knew she *should* have said it, because that's still what Chris was.

But she didn't say it.

"Do you guys have any extra supplies?" Peter asked. "We didn't get our act together to make costumes. Clearly."

Hanson shook his head a number of times. Trotsky said, sounding both bored and doubtful, "You could smear dirt on your face. I guess."

"I have a couple colored Sharpies," Lindsey volunteered, pulling them out of her bag. Lindsey never, ever unpacked her bag. It was constantly filled with used tissues and empty Chapstick tubes and magazines that she'd already read. Clutter just didn't bother Lindsey very much. Generally this drove Arden crazy, but sometimes—like tonight—it paid off.

"Lindsey, my lady, you are resourceful," Peter said. "I like that in a girl." He gave her a winning smile. "Let me see them."

Lindsey handed over the markers, and Peter turned to Arden. He looked at her really intently, like he was surveying a blank canvas. She felt herself turning red, but forced herself to be still, to submit to his gaze, to take in the feeling of his eyes on her body. And suddenly she was glad she hadn't mentioned Chris.

"Okay, I have a vision," Peter declared. "Get your hair out of the way."

Arden swept it up in a ponytail, and he uncapped a marker and started to write on her. She shivered as the pen tip touched her chest bone.

"That is going to be a bitch to wash off," Lindsey said, sounding respectful.

"Lose the coat," Peter told Arden.

She pulled off the kelly green spring jacket and held it in her hand, stretching her arms out so he could reach her triceps, her clavicle, her shoulder blade. She felt cold in the nighttime air, but inside she felt like she was burning up. Lindsey was right that this was going to be a bitch to wash off. She didn't care.

When she looked at her extended arms, she saw that Peter had covered her in his words. The text wrapped around her wrists, across her shoulders, and down her back, at all different angles, so she couldn't read all of it, but she did make out *I miss you I miss you I miss you*, and *the only one*, and *to linger too late*, and, gigantic on her forearm, *loneliness*.

"I don't know what the hell to do with markers," Peter explained, handing the markers to Arden. "I'm not really an artist. The only thing I can draw are words."

"Words are enough," Arden said. And *Peter's* words were, as always, perfect. They made her feel less alone, more connected, and understood in a way that was giddily palpable. Having his words on her body made her feel like she was wearing armor.

By the time they reached the door, all three of them were covered in marker. They didn't look a thing like enchanted forest creatures. But they looked weird, Arden could say that for sure.

"Twenty dollars each," said the guy working the door, who looked to be a few years older than they were, and who was wearing a full-body chipmunk costume.

Hanson and Trotsky both vaguely patted at their pants, as though they couldn't quite figure out where they'd put their wallets, before Peter stepped forward and said, "Don't worry, I've got this." He handed the door guy a hundred dollar bill and waved off Arden's offer of cash.

Hanson opened the door, leading them into a basement that was designed to look like a—well, like an enchanted forest. Potted bushes lined the way, with silhouette cutouts of tree branches on the walls. Sculptures of fairies dotted the room, and giant colorful mesh butterflies hung from the ceiling. Eerie ambient music echoed around them.

"Whoa," breathed Lindsey. She squeezed Arden's hand, and Arden felt the remaining bit of the annoyance she'd felt at Lindsey, which had been hanging over her head like a dark cloud since their car ride, dissipate at last.

"It's an art," Arden said simply, and Peter burst out laughing.

"It's wild," he said. "It's like you're part of my brain."

"Have you never met one of your readers before?" Arden asked.

He shook his head. "Not like you."

"So what is the deal with this place?" Lindsey asked, stopping to study a blown-glass orb. "Is it like a nightclub, or . . . ?"

"It's an apartment, if you can believe that," Peter replied. "Well, it wasn't built to be an apartment. But it got converted a while back. And then a bunch of kids from Pratt—the art college, you know?—they rented it out. Every room in here has been passed down from Pratt student to Pratt student over the years."

"Like a fraternity," Arden said. "An art fraternity."

"A fart-ernity?" Lindsey suggested, and the girls giggled.

"Sure," Peter said. "It's called Jigsaw Manor."

"Jigsaw Manor?" Lindsey's giggles grew even louder. "That is *so* random. Why?"

Peter stopped to think about it. "Uh, I have no idea! That's just what it's called. There are probably a dozen people who live here now. They throw parties every few weeks to cover their rent. Every time somebody new moves in, they add their own work, so there are layers upon layers of art in this place."

"Also layers upon layers of dirt," Hanson called back. He was on his way up the flight of stairs in the back of the basement.

Arden tried to look at everything so she could commit every last bit of it to memory. This would probably be the only time she would ever go to an art fraternity with her best friend and the writer she was obsessed with and Sharpie marks all over their bodies. Already she felt nostalgic for tonight. Already she could imagine herself months from now, wishing that she had made more of this one night while she was still in it.

"Do you know anyone who lives here?" she asked Peter as they climbed the dark stairs, the roar of sound from the floor above them getting louder and louder.

"Yes. One of the girls is friends with my brother."

They opened the door to the next floor, and the dull roar burst into a cacophony. Jigsaw Manor was packed with party-goers in outrageous costumes, feathers and sparkles flying everywhere. At the front of the room, a ten-piece band was banging out something atonal and unrecognizable; each member seemed only dimly aware of the fact that a whole bunch of other instrumentalists were playing at the same time. A chandelier made mostly of duct tape and flashlights swayed dangerously overhead.

"Oh my God," Arden and Lindsey breathed at the same moment.

Trotsky looked around and blew out a long breath. "There's, like, *nobody* here tonight," he concluded.

"Do you want to explore?" Peter asked the girls.

"Of course!"

They ran all over the place. Jigsaw Manor seemed ever-expanding because they kept discovering new rooms, and Arden could not figure out how they all fit together. One room was barely the size of a twin bed, and a couple was making out in there. That room was pretty boring. But in the next space over, a girl was Hula-Hooping with a half dozen different hoops twirling around her body, each one flashing a rainbow display of light. A massive rope net hung suspended from the ceiling, and a dozen more partygoers lay atop it, their bodies swinging overhead. Behind a bookcase that turned out to be a door, Arden found a chest of drawers, each of which played a different rhythm when it was opened, so they could create a dozen different pieces of music just by opening and closing drawers.

On a balcony outside one of the rooms, they found an enormous cage housing a human-size rabbit that seemed to be made entirely out of moss, a mannequin head hanging from a noose, and three actual human beings, a girl and two guys. The girl said to Lindsey, "I dig your aura."

"Really?" said Lindsey. "What does that mean?" And the next thing Arden knew, Lindsey was all cozied up inside the cage with them, listening to a description of the colors that were supposedly emanating from her chakras or something.

"I'm going to keep exploring," Arden told her. "Text if you need me, okay?"

Lindsey shot Arden an exasperated look. "I'll be *fine*," she said. "God, *Mom*," she added, which made the three people in the human-size cage giggle.

Arden paused on the threshold, but then Peter grabbed her hand and pulled her away. They saw more rooms. One where everyone was dancing wildly, except for Trotsky and Hanson, who were hanging on the sidelines, snidely remarking on how boring and passé dancing was. Another with bins of soapy water and oversize bubble wands for them to play with. Eventually they wound up in front of a ladder propped against a wall in the back of the Hula-Hooping room. "Up," Peter said, pointing.

Arden craned her head back. "What's up there?"

"You'll never know if you don't climb, will you?"

She put her hands on the rungs, then turned back and said, "You're going to be able to see up my dress, though."

"I won't look," Peter promised, holding up a hand solemnly. "Scout's honor."

"I don't know many kids in the Scouts," Arden said. "We're more a 4-H sort of town."

"I don't know what 4-H is," Peter said.

"Exactly." Arden started to climb.

When she got to the top of the ladder, she found herself on the roof, looking down over the line of partygoers still on the street. It was windy up there, and her hair blew into her eyes and mouth. Peter pulled himself onto the roof a moment later and put his hands on his hips, surveying the night sky. "Nice view, right?"

"Sort of." There were too many lights from the city, and Arden couldn't see a single star in the sky. She thought that her dad would have nothing to look at with his telescope here, and then she felt a quick pang of guilt for being so far from home, in this starless city, when she had told her father she'd be only on the other side of the woods. He'd already had his wife run off. He didn't need for his daughter to do the same. He deserved better.

But that was different. Unlike her mom, Arden had her reasons. And unlike her mom, tomorrow she was going home.

"Did you get a glimpse of my underwear or what?" she asked Peter.

"I did not," Peter said.

"Good."

"But would it offend you if I told you that you have great legs?"

Arden stared at him. "Ha, ha."

"Oh, come on, I'm sure people tell you that all the time."

"Nobody's ever told me that," she said.

Although there were a number of other partygoers up on the roof, it was quieter than any of the rooms inside. No ten-piece band to contend with. Peter pulled his flask out of his pocket and took a long swig from it, tilting his head back. When he was done, he offered it to Arden.

She held the flask in her hands but didn't drink from it. It was heavy and sterling silver, engraved with the name LEONARD MATTHEW LAU. She looked up. "Is this Leo's? Bianca's Leo?"

He studied the engraving, as though he had forgotten what it said. "Yes."

She giggled. "So you took his girl *and* his flask."

Peter offered her a half smile. "Something like that."

Of course, it occurred to Arden, he'd managed to keep only one of those.

Peter turned, walked over to a giant rocking chair, and climbed onto it. There were a number of them scattered around the roof deck. Rocking chairs that could seat three or four people. Bicycles on rocking chairs. Seesaws on rocking chairs. Arden wondered what the emergency plan was if an underage drunk kid fell off a rocking chair seesaw on the roof of Jigsaw Manor.

She went over to Peter and gave his chair a little push.

"Look, Arden," Peter said, taking the flask back from her. "I just want you to understand. I've done some things I'm not proud of."

"So have I," Arden said. "So has everyone. I mean, Lindsey once stole a canoe, and she doesn't even know how to paddle a boat. She was pretty not-proud of that. I don't love her any less for it."

"That's sweet." Peter took another long swallow from Leo's flask. "I just want to be the person you thought I would be. The Peter you were promised."

She reached up to touch his arm, but the rocking chair put him slightly out of reach. "You already are," she told him.

"I worry about that, too," he said, staring off into the urban sprawl. "I worry that I'm not the person I seem to be on Tonight the Streets Are Ours. And then I worry that I'm *exactly* the person I seem to be."

"Just don't worry," said Arden. "Not about me."

He took his gaze off the skyline and smiled down at her. "Okay, friend," he said. "Climb on up here."

The chair was pretty high off the ground, and she wasn't sure how to get onto it.

"Just jump," he said.

She did. She didn't make it that high. She landed roughly on her waist and wriggled the rest of the way until she was finally sitting next to him. "That was like an Olympic sport," she said once she was settled.

"Then you just got a silver medal in climbing onto rocking chairs," he said.

"Why? Because you already took home the gold?"

"Well, yeah!" He grinned and again proffered Leo's flask. "Winners' toast?"

"Nah." She waved it off.

"You don't drink?"

"Is that a problem?" she asked, her words a challenge.

He shook his head. "Just wondering why."

"Well, I'm seventeen years old, so it's illegal. For a start."

"You don't know any seventeen-year-olds who drink?"

She rolled her eyes.

"Do you have a history of alcoholism in your family? Is that why?" he asked.

"I don't think so. Maybe I have a great-uncle or second cousin somewhere with a drinking problem, but no one I know of. I'm usually the designated driver, though," she explained. "I'm old for my grade, so I got my license before most of my friends— and I'd saved up enough money from tutoring to buy the Heart of Gold—so I just got in the habit of being the one to drive. Plus . . ." She shrugged. "Lindsey gets into a lot of trouble. Somebody has to stay sober."

Peter laughed. "She's that much of a handful? I wouldn't have guessed that from looking at her. She seemed pretty meek, actually. Out of the two of you, I would have pegged you as the troublemaker."

"Me?" Arden asked. "Why?"

He stared at her, like he was searching her face for the answer. "I don't know," he said at last. "You just seem like trouble."

They both leaned back against the chair, rocking back and forth. The party swirled on below them.

"You asked what happened to my brother," Peter said.

Arden gave a brief nod, not wanting to scare him off.

"I'll tell you the story. We assumed he was at Cornell, where he was supposed to be. We hadn't heard from him for a few days, but nobody thought anything about that except for my

237

mother. Dad and I were like, 'He's a freshman in college, he's not going to call home every couple hours.'

"Then we got a call from his resident adviser. His roommate had gone to her, saying that my brother hadn't been in the room for a few days and he was just wondering if anything was going on. They started looking into it, and it turned out *no one* had seen him for days. Not any of his professors or classmates. Not anyone at the frat he was pledging or the other guys on the football team. They sent out an all-campus e-mail, and heard back exactly nothing.

"So we started reaching out to everyone he knew in the city. High school friends, teachers, ex-girlfriends. Nobody had seen so much as a text message from him. That's when my parents got the cops involved."

"Maybe he was kidnapped?" Arden thought aloud.

"He's not a kid."

"You know what I mean. Abducted. Being held for ransom. No offense, but it sounds like your family has a lot of money."

"I'm not offended by that." The corners of Peter's mouth lifted slightly. "And that's good thinking, but it's not what happened. For one thing, if there were kidnappers, they would have told us their demands, right? And that didn't happen. For another thing, before he left, he sent us an e-mail."

"An e-mail?" Arden's eyes opened wider. "Saying what?"

"That he didn't want to stay with people who would treat him this poorly. That he was through with us. That he'd never really felt like he belonged in our family, and now he knew for sure that he didn't. That we should just let him live his own life and stop messing it up."

"Wow. That's intense. Did you have any idea that he felt that way?" Arden asked.

Peter scratched the back of his head and shifted uncomfortably. "We didn't grow up in the easiest of households. Our parents screwed us both. But that doesn't mean that the right answer would have been for them to never adopt him. Then he'd probably just be messed up in some different but equally delightful way."

"So where do you think he is? How do you think he's surviving?" Arden asked, trying to picture a brother of Peter's, fresh off the Cornell football team, living deep in the woods somewhere, off the grid.

"I can't really say." Peter buried his face in his hands. Arden resisted the urge to stroke his back, to hold him.

She considered saying she was sorry for Peter's loss, but that wasn't so much what she was thinking about. "It's so selfish," she said instead.

"What?" Peter looked up, and she realized that probably most people just said they were sorry, and that was the correct answer, and she should have stuck with that.

"I shouldn't have said that," she said. "I take it back."

"No. Tell me what you meant."

"Well," she said, "he just . . . left you. He was thinking about himself, and where he was going, but he obviously didn't give a damn thought to who he was leaving behind to worry about him and to pick up the pieces. Okay, so his life was hard. Big deal. Life is hard for you, too. And I'm sorry if he's out there begging on the street or dealing drugs somewhere, truly, I am. But he's not the only victim here. You are, too. And that's what makes him selfish." Arden shrugged. "That's what I think, anyway."

"I think you're right," Peter said. "And I don't want to feel sad tonight." Peter jumped off the rocking chair. "Screw that. I'm going to be a best-selling author, and you're only in New York City for one night. And if my girlfriend or my brother or anyone else isn't here to appreciate all that, then *screw them*. This is *our* celebration. From here on out, let's have no more talk of death and heartbreak. Tonight, let's have only happy things."

"Tonight, the streets are ours," Arden said, and she jumped to the ground.

Lindsey and Arden don't see eye to eye

Arden and Peter were playing on one of the rooftop seesaws, Arden shrieking with laughter every time her butt hit the ground, when she heard a voice call, "Peter!" She turned around to see a girl in an ethereal pink slip dress stumble-running toward them.

"Hey, cutie!" Peter climbed off the seesaw and kissed both the girl's cheeks. Without his weight to lift her, Arden thudded to the ground.

"I'm *so* glad you came," the girl said, her voice a little too loud, like she couldn't quite hear herself. She tilted to the side and balanced herself on Peter's shoulder. "Oh my *God* it's been forever! How *are* you, kiddo?"

He nodded. "I'm great. I'm doing great."

"Oh, that's so good. So where's Bianca tonight?" She looked all around without lowering her eyes the few inches it would take to notice Arden. Arden sighed and clambered to her feet, pulling her skirt around her.

The girl raised her eyebrows dramatically as she suddenly took in Arden's presence. "*Oh.* I see what's going on here. Peter, you are *such* a ladies' man. Like brother, like brother, am I right?"

"Oh, no," Arden protested, noticing Peter's hands clench. "It's not like that—"

"'Sokay," the girl said, leaning in close enough that Arden could smell the alcohol on her breath. "Your secret's safe with me. Just between us girls. What Bianca doesn't know won't hurt her, right?"

"Honestly," Arden said, "I'd never even met Peter before tonight—"

But the girl was squinting at her cell phone now and had already stopped paying attention. "Oh, yay, Leo's coming!" she squealed.

Peter startled, his whole body going rigid. "Here?" he asked, his voice strangled. "Leo's coming *here*?"

"That's what he says." The girl held up her phone as proof.

"Did you tell him I'm here?"

"Nuh-uh. I can tell him now . . ."

She started typing, but Peter said, "No, no, that's okay. We need to go anyway."

"We need to go," Arden echoed. She was curious, desperately curious, to see Bianca's ex-boyfriend in person. What did he look like? What had Bianca seen in him? Could he have ever really been a match for Peter? But she also understood why Peter wouldn't want to see him—maybe not at *any* point, but certainly not three days after losing Bianca.

"Do you want to do shots first?" the girl asked, but Peter was already rushing toward the ladder that led back into the building.

"Peter!" Arden shouted.

He turned back, wide-eyed. "I need to go," he said again.

"I know that. But give me one minute. We need to get Lindsey first."

"Okay," he said. "Fine. But be quick." He checked his watch and his phone and followed Arden back to the cage with the disembodied mannequin head.

Arden's adrenaline spiked as she realized that she hadn't even thought to worry about her friend in the whole time she'd been gone. Thank God, Lindsey was sitting right where she'd left her. She was deep in discussion with the pierced-nose girl who had complimented Lindsey's aura when they'd first arrived. But she was holding a joint in her hand.

"What the hell, Lindsey?" Arden said by way of greeting. "Whatever happened to you being scared straight and not trying any sort of drugs until college? Remember that?"

"Hey, look," muttered one of the guys in the cage. "*Mom* is back."

"I wasn't really smoking it," Lindsey said quickly. "This is Jamie's. Oh, right: Arden, meet Jamie."

The girl with the uncomfortable-looking nose ring stuck out her palm and said, without a trace of a smile, "Pleasure."

They shook, Jamie almost crushing Arden's hand in her own. Arden extracted her hand and pulled it into her chest for safety. She didn't give a shit who Jamie was, or who technically had ownership of that joint in Lindsey's hand, because none of that made up for Lindsey's complete inability to keep a promise, or to think about how her actions might affect anybody other than herself. "Peter needs to go," she said to Lindsey.

"Okay," said Lindsey. She didn't move.

"So, let's go," Arden said, exasperated.

"You can go ahead," Lindsey said. "I'll just stay here."

Arden's laugh came out as a loud snort. Jamie raised her eyebrow. "Don't be silly, Lindsey," Arden said. "We're going."

Lindsey shrugged. "I'm not ready yet."

"Why not?"

"Because. I'm having fun here."

"You girls can totally stay here if you want," Peter offered. "I'll just see you around, Arden, 'kay?"

He made a move toward the cage door, and Arden felt a desperate contraction in her chest. If they stayed here and Peter left, then this would be where it ended. She would have driven three hundred miles and called every bookstore in New York City for this, only what she'd gotten already and not one bit more, and it would be over. Peter would walk out of her life and on to his next adventure, and she would go home with nothing.

It reminded her of that party almost two months ago, at Matt Washington's house, the night she first discovered Peter. How she'd gone out expecting everything to change and come home exactly the same.

She wasn't going to let that happen again.

"No," she said to Peter, "we want to go with you." She grabbed Lindsey's hand and pulled. "Come on, Linds."

Lindsey leaned her weight back against the couch, her hand limp in Arden's. "I told you already," she said, "I'm not ready to leave yet. Just go without me, if it's so important to you to follow Peter."

Arden cast her eyes toward Peter and blushed. "I'm not *following* him . . ."

"You know what I mean. If you want to go, go. I'm staying here."

"That's not an option, Lindsey. I'm not leaving you alone with a bunch of strangers—no offense," she added to the cluster of onlookers.

"Why not?" Lindsey said. "I can take care of myself."

"Oh, please." The words were out before Arden had even considered them. But even if she *had* thought it through, she would have said the same thing—surely Lindsey must know that she was completely unfit to take care of herself. Surely this could not come as news to her. The joint in her hand, the physical proof of her failed promise, was just driving home this truth that they both already knew.

But Lindsey acted like this was all some big surprise. "What do you mean, 'oh, please'?" she demanded, standing up. "What makes you think I can't stay here by myself?"

"Because, what if something happens?"

"Something . . . like *what*?" Lindsey threw her arms out. "Like I talk to some nice people and make some friends and have a beer?"

"Lindsey, you're embarrassing yourself. Stop making this into a whole big deal, and just come with me."

"Stop telling me what to do," Lindsey said.

Arden's eyes widened.

"You always act like you know what's best for me. I'm sick of it. I told you I don't want to go. So how about *you* stop making this into a whole big deal and just let me do what I want."

"Oh, because things always go *so well* for you when you just do what you want?" Arden retorted.

"Sure," Lindsey said. "Things go fine."

"Right, I bet it does feel that way to *you*, because you just do whatever you want and you don't think about the consequences. Because *I* get all the consequences, Lindsey."

Arden was on a roll now. All of this had built up inside of her, because what she was getting from Lindsey now was basically the same thing she'd gotten from Chris twelve hours prior, and it was the same thing she got all the time, from everyone—people who didn't even realize how much she did for them, who didn't even appreciate her. She was sick of it.

So even though Arden had planned never to say this to Lindsey, she found herself demanding, "Do you *know* what happened that time they found your pot in my locker?"

"Yes, of course! You got suspended and—"

"And it's going on my permanent record," Arden interrupted. "It's going on the transcript they send to colleges. Not just that I was suspended once, but that I have a known history of drug use. My entire future will be different because of *your* dumb decision."

Lindsey was silent as Arden's words hit her. She slowly sank back onto the couch. One of the guys sitting with her gave a long, low whistle.

"You didn't tell me that," Lindsey said at last.

"Because I didn't want to worry you. I didn't want you to feel bad. *So why couldn't you just return the favor?* You claim you love me, and oh, that's so *sweet*, Lindsey, but I don't think you have any idea what it actually means. Love means sometimes sacrificing the things you want in order to make someone else happy. It means being there for someone, even when maybe you don't feel like it, because they need you." Arden's eyes felt hot as she added, "No wonder no girl wants to kiss you. You don't know the first thing about love."

She heard Peter suck in his breath.

"That's a low blow," Lindsey said, her voice catching in her throat. "That's really, despicably low, Arden. And as for the pot, you did not need to take the blame for that. Are you insane? I never asked you to do that for me."

"You didn't ask," Arden agreed, "but you let me do it."

"When you found out it was going to go on your transcript, you could have just told them the truth," Lindsey argued. "Let me take the blame. I would have been fine."

Arden imagined a Lindsey without the track team. She imagined how Mr. and Mrs. Matson would have reacted. She imagined Lindsey trying to apply to college or to jobs, trying to do *anything* with her life, with her terrible grades and a record of drug possession. Maybe this was Lindsey's real problem: a failure of the imagination.

Arden recalled her mother's old theory that some people are

flowers and some people are gardeners. Lindsey was the worst kind of flower: one who didn't even realize she needed a gardener to help her survive.

"You don't always have to jump to my rescue, Arden. I can handle things on my own." Lindsey gestured around the room. "I was handling this just great, until you showed up and started screaming at me."

"Oh, really?" Arden said.

"Yes, really!"

"So you don't even need me? When you were the first kid at our school to come out, you would have handled that without me? When your dad almost died, you didn't need me then, either? Do you honestly think you don't need *my* friends, *my* invitations to parties, rides in *my* car—you'd do just fine without any of that?"

Lindsey lifted her chin. "I didn't even need your stupid Disney vacation."

That struck Arden like a physical punch.

"You know what I think?" Lindsey went on, her eyes bright. "I think *you* need *me* to be the screwup. Because then you get to swoop in and save the day. 'La, la, la, I'm Arden! I'm important! Lindsey's going to absolutely fall to *pieces* without me!'"

"And you think I *like* that?" Arden asked, outraged.

"Oh, please. I know you do."

"You think I come to your rescue, when you're crying, or you're about to fail a class, or you're grounded, because it's *fun*. For *me*."

"I didn't say *fun*—"

"Lindsey, if that is how you feel, then I am done rescuing you."

Lindsey was silent, wary. She knotted her fingers in her lap and squinted up at Arden.

"I'm not going to force my unwanted support on you any longer," Arden said. "You can hang out here with your shiny new friends, and using all your awesome powers of self-reliance, you can find your own way home."

"Home . . . to Maryland?" Lindsey asked.

Arden hesitated. This did seem unrealistic. How, exactly, was Lindsey going to travel three hundred miles without her? On what bus? With what money?

"I mean, if you need my help . . ." Arden backtracked.

Lindsey scowled and shook her head

"Okay, then." Arden gave her a mirthless smile. "You're on your own. Just how you wanted it."

"What's her problem?" threw in Jamie, as Arden turned away.

Arden flinched. Of course a stranger thought this was all her fault. She didn't know anything about Arden or Lindsey or their years of friendship or how much had gone into this one moment. Arden didn't care what this girl thought of her. But she looked at Peter. Because if *he* thought she was in the wrong, she didn't think she'd have it in her to leave Lindsey now. Not if it meant losing his trust.

But Peter locked eyes with her, and he nodded. And that gave Arden the courage to say to Lindsey, "I'm over this. Good luck finding your way out of here."

She and Peter walked away.

"Arden, wait!" she thought she heard Lindsey call after her. But when she turned, Lindsey was laughing with Jamie, as if Arden had never even been there.

So Arden kept walking right back the way they'd come in two and a half hours earlier. Past the atonal ten-piece band, down the stairs lit only by a thousand glow-in-the-dark stickers, through the enchanted forest basement, all the way through Jigsaw Manor until she made it outside and into the fresh spring air, where she was, at last, free.

And that brings us up to the present day

Sucking air into her lungs, Arden keeps walking from Jigsaw Manor, step after step after step, like her legs have forgotten how to stand still.

"Where are you going?" Peter asks. He's almost jogging to keep up with her.

"Away."

She reaches the Heart of Gold and unlocks it, slamming herself into the driver's seat. Peter climbs into the passenger seat—Lindsey's seat—without a word.

She turns the key in the ignition. And . . . nothing happens.

She frowns and tries again. Still, the car does not start.

"Oh, come on," Arden mutters. She pulls the key out of the ignition and blows on it. She has no reason to believe that blowing on a key will do anything to it—a car key is not a too-hot spoonful of soup—but she doesn't know what else to do.

"Is something wrong?" Peter asks.

"My car won't start."

Peter looks baffled by this, and Arden realizes that even if she knows zero things about automobile maintenance, even if she did actually pour a Dairy Queen beverage under her car's hood earlier today, she is still doing better than this guy, who lives in New York City and doesn't drive outside of daddy's BMW at his beach house.

"It broke down on the highway earlier," Arden explains. "I let it sit for a few minutes to recover, and after that it seemed fine. The engine had overheated, I think, which made sense because I'd been driving it at top speed for hours. But now it's just been sitting here the whole time while we were in Jigsaw Manor, so I don't know why . . ." She trails off and tries the key one last time. *Please, please, please, I just need this to work,* she thinks as hard as she can.

Nothing.

"Aaurghhh!" Arden throws her key down, and it clatters onto the floor of the car. She flings open the door, launches herself onto the street, and starts kicking at the Heart of Gold, her feet thumping against the wheels as if they were punching bags.

She stops only when Peter grabs her from behind, wrapping his arms around her to stop her from hurling her fist through her window. "Shh," he whispers.

"Why won't it work?" she cries. "I take care of this car. I treat it right. So why—won't it—work!" She gets in one last good kick before Peter drags her away. He starts to laugh, and Arden whirls around, fists clenched. "Are you laughing at me?"

"No. It's just—you've only been here a few hours, and already you're acting like a true New Yorker."

"What are you talking about?" she demands.

"Picking fights with inanimate objects. Experiencing rage meltdowns."

"I am not a New Yorker."

"Fine, then you're just having a very New York response. Trust me, it comes with the territory when eight million people are trying to share limited resources. One time I saw a guy literally pick a fistfight with a mailbox because it was in his way."

This distracts Arden from her rage meltdown. "Who won?"

"The mailbox did, of course, but dude put up a good fight. I'm telling you, this sort of shit happens all the time in this city. People barely even register it."

Arden looks over to the crowd gathered outside Jigsaw Manor: the people waiting in line to get in (still, even though it's nearly two thirty in the morning), the winged fairies smoking a cigarette on the street. Peter is right. None of them seems to care that across the street, there's a girl physically fighting her car as if they're in a cage match. There's something unsettling about the fact that nobody is noticing her scene, nobody is coming over to ask what's wrong or if she needs help, but what's also unsettling is that this doesn't bother her, because it makes her feel like *she can do whatever the hell she wants.*

"What's the plan for your car?" Peter asks.

"I don't know. I just want to get out of here. I want to *go* somewhere."

"Me, too," Peter agrees. She sees him looking around, and she assumes he is keeping a watch out for Leo.

Now that her fury has passed, Arden feels drained. She sits down on the curb. Questions threaten the edges of her consciousness: *How am I going to get home, if my car doesn't work? How is Lindsey going to get home?* When *am I going to go home?*

As if sensing, somehow, that Arden is plagued by pragmatic concerns, and knowing that "pragmatic concerns" might as well be his middle name, Chris chooses this moment to call.

She answers automatically, not even bothering to consider whether or not she actually wants to speak to him at this moment. She feels like she doesn't have any fight left in her—she used it all up on Lindsey and the Heart of Gold, and now she's empty. "What?" she says, her voice weary.

"Oh, wow, you're still up! Okay, good. Well, I was just calling because, uh, Jaden wanted to know if we wanted to meet up for lunch at Piccino tomorrow. You in?"

This is weird, hearing Chris's voice and Jaden's name, these hallmarks of home, while she is sitting on a curb outside an enchanted forest party in Brooklyn, her skin covered in marker. She'd imagined that she'd entered into another dimension, but now it turns out that she hadn't.

"I can't do lunch. Sorry. Why are *you* still up?" she asks Chris distractedly. As soon as she answered the phone, Peter started wandering down the street. She's keeping an eye on him, wondering where he's going. It seems unlikely that he's going to just ditch her here—but if for some reason he did, she has no idea what she would do. She doesn't even know where she is.

"I was having trouble sleeping," Chris says. He clears his throat. "I guess I was worried . . . that you're still mad at me. Are you still mad at me?"

It feels like a million years have passed since her argument with Chris. It actually takes her a second to remember specifically what they were fighting about, and then it startles her to think of Chris, sitting in his bed alone and missing her, while she is hundreds of miles away, making giant soap bubbles in the air. The thought makes her feel powerful. Let him know what it's like, for once. Let him know how it feels to be the one who gets left behind.

"You seem like you're still mad," Chris says after a moment of silence from Arden.

She was, it's true, but now it seems absurd to be mad at him, when he is the reason she's here at all, in New York, with Peter. It seems absurd to be mad at him because no amount of her anger or arguing would ever convince him that what he really wants to do, most in all the world, is be by her side. She doesn't really know why she'd bother. She wants things between them to be right again. But being mad at him isn't going to make that happen.

"I'm not mad," she says. "I'm just disappointed." Peter has vanished from view and she stands up to try to figure out where he's gone.

"I'll make it up to you," Chris promises, and probably he could, and would, if her disappointment were only about him, and only about what happened today.

"How was the movie thing?" Arden asks. She is walking

down the street slowly, away from the party and her car, scanning for Peter.

"It was great," Chris replies. "Everyone there was super nice, and I really felt like they all treated me as an equal, you know? Not just some random high school student. This is going to be a great learning experience, I can already tell. The girl who's playing Gretchen seemed pretty interested in *American Fairy Tale*. She said she might check out one of our rehearsals some time, if it's okay with Mr. Lansdowne."

"That's good," Arden says vaguely.

Chris sighs. "Babe, why are you being so out of it?"

This snaps her attention back to her phone. "It's just really . . . late," she explains. "I wasn't expecting a call from you this late. But I'm glad you had a fun night."

"Okay," he says. "And you're good?"

"Yeah," she says. "I'm good. I'll talk to you tomorrow, all right?"

"Yup. Love you."

"I love you, too"—but the words feel like a lie, and she wonders if they did yesterday, too, and the day before that—if they were always a lie, or if she really meant it once upon a time, and if she could ever manage to mean it again.

She silences her phone, sticks it in her purse, and goes striding down the street in search of Peter. Once she gets past the crowd around Jigsaw Manor, the road is relatively quiet—relative to every place else she's seen in New York, that is—with just the occasional taxi rumbling past.

She sees Peter ahead, walking back toward her. "There you

are," she says. "I'm sorry, I had to answer that. I didn't mean to—"

He grabs her hand. "Come with me. I've found the solution to all our problems."

Arden scoffs, because they have so many problems between the two of them, she can't even imagine what a solution would look like.

They run down to the corner, and Arden looks in either direction, seeing nothing except a fast food joint and more taxis and more warehouses and a few piles of trash bags and a stretch limousine.

"Um," she says.

Peter opens the door to the limousine and gallantly gestures toward it. "My lady," he says.

"Peter," she says. "How did you suddenly get a *limousine*?"

"Oh, I just hailed it." He pantomimes sticking his arm in the air.

"You hailed it. Like a taxi. Only you hailed a *limousine*."

"Yeeeah." He drags out the word thoughtfully. "Sometimes people book a limo for a whole night. They want it there to drop them off and take them home again at the end of the night, you know? In the middle, the driver might cruise around, in case he can pick up some additional passengers and earn a little extra cash."

"So you hailed it," Arden says again, trying to wrap her head around this.

"Correct."

"How much does a limousine ride cost?" Arden peers inside

the open door. She's never ridden in one before, though she and Chris are going in with eight other theater kids to rent a limo for prom, which is only five weeks away. Yesterday's Arden was excited for Future Arden's first ride in a limo to be when she has her hair professionally done and the boy she loves all tall and handsome and debonair in a tux beside her. But today's Arden doesn't want to wait.

"I'm paying," Peter says. "And it's cheap."

Arden's eyes flicker back down the road, toward her car.

"You said you just wanted to get out of here," Peter reminds her.

"I do," Arden agrees, and she climbs in.

Peter gets in after her and shuts the door. Inside the limo is quiet, with long black leather seats around all the sides, a rich rosewood-colored table in the middle, and small lights glowing on the roof. There's a complicated audiovisual system with a TV and an iPod dock, and a panel with countless buttons that control everything from the temperature to the moon roof to the intercom with the driver. Arden presses them all.

"Where you going?" the driver asks over the intercom. He has a foreign accent that Arden can't place, and she feels a little like she's in the James Bond flick she watched at the Glockenspiel last summer. "I must to be in Williamsburg before four, so not too far," the driver cautions.

"Do you need to get home at some point?" Peter asks Arden.

She blinks at him.

"I mean, is your mom expecting you?"

Of course. He thinks she's staying with her mom for the weekend. Because that would make sense.

"At some point," Arden says. "Are *your* parents expecting you home?"

Peter raises his eyebrows and grins. "At some point." To the driver he says, "Take us into Manhattan. Over the Brooklyn Bridge, please."

He turns off the intercom, and the limo pulls away.

Arden and Peter sit on opposite sides, and they look across the table at each other.

"Well," Peter says, and Arden starts to laugh.

"You were right," she tells him. "You did find the solution to all our problems."

Arden is a catch

So who was calling you this late at night?" Peter asks as the limousine glides through the streets of Brooklyn. "Was that Lindsey asking you to come back already?"

Arden's stomach turns at the sound of Lindsey's name. "It was my boyfriend," she admits.

Peter perks up at the word *boyfriend*. He's immediately interested, and Arden wonders, not for the first time, if the most interesting thing about her is that she is somebody's girlfriend. "What's his name?"

"Chris."

"How long have you two lovebirds been dating?"

"A year." She swallows hard. "One year today."

Peter whistles. "What's his deal?"

This is easy; Chris has a very straightforward deal. "He's a junior, like me. He's a super-talented actor. He wants to go to college for theater, and after that he plans to go to Hollywood.

He's a good student, though. It's not like he slacks off in his other classes, even though he doesn't need *great* grades to get into a theater program, if his audition is strong enough."

"He's popular?"

Arden shrugs. "Not in, like, a *cool* way. But he's well-liked."

"Good-looking?"

Arden nods.

"Athletic?"

"I mean, he can run a mile, so by my standards, yes."

"Does he recycle?"

Arden laughs. "Yeah."

"He sounds perfect," Peter concludes. He rests his elbows on his knees and leans forward, looking at her. He doesn't ask the follow-up question, but Arden can sense it in the air between them: *If Chris is so talented and so ambitious and so smart and so well-liked and so good-looking, then why aren't you with him right now? If Chris is so perfect, then* why are you here?

Peter doesn't ask, but Arden wants to tell him anyway. He's revealed to her all his secrets. There's no reason she can't do the same.

"I'm just not sure that he's perfect *for me*," Arden says.

She's never admitted this. Not even to herself. Everyone else knows Chris, and knows her as part of a Chris-and-Arden pair, and they wouldn't understand. In Chris she'd gotten everything she wanted, but still she doesn't feel happy. So maybe it's that there is something wrong with her. A deep-seated discontentment.

Peter says, "If for some reason it doesn't work out between you two, I'm sure you will find somebody else."

Arden snorts. "Me? At Allegany High? Not likely."

"Well, I don't know what the dating pool is like at Allegany High. But maybe. If not there, then somewhere else, you'll find somebody else."

"Why?" she asks.

"Why what?"

She shakes her head, because she doesn't want to put into words what she means, which is: *why would anybody else want to be with me?*

But it's like he understands her unspoken question, because he answers, "Because. You're a catch."

He searches under his leather seat, and his eyes light up when he finds what he was looking for: a liquor cabinet, which he opens and triumphantly pulls out a glass bottle of dark brown liquid.

Arden asks, "But what if I *don't* find anybody else? Or what if anyone else who I like . . . doesn't like me back?" She doesn't want to admit that she'd never found anyone prior to Chris, because Peter seems so much more experienced in love and dating than she is.

"Well, then, you'll be alone." Peter pours himself a tumbler of the liquor. "It's not the end of the world, is it?"

"Don't *you* think it is?" Arden counters.

He smiles and takes a sip and says nothing.

"Is it even legal to drink in a moving vehicle in New York?" Arden asks.

"Tinted windows," Peter says, swirling around the liquid in his glass.

"Why is there just a bottle of alcohol hanging out in here, anyway?" Arden wants to know.

"I would guess that whoever rented the limo for the night *also* wanted to drink in a moving vehicle."

"Is it really okay for you to drink their stuff?"

Peter rolls his eyes. "They're rich enough to rent a limo for a night, even though there are hours in there when they're not even using it. I think they're rich enough that they can stand to lose a shot of Jameson."

Arden accepts that there are some things about this city that she just does not understand, and moves on. "Hey, Peter, I wanted to say that I'm sorry about what happened back there," she says. "That fight with Lindsey, and my freak-out at the car. You must think I'm crazy, just showing up here and screaming all over the place, when you've never even met me before."

Peter shrugs this off. "I don't mind a little crazy. And anyway, like I said, we've all done things we're not proud of."

And Arden feels like this links them together. Their shared guilt.

"Do you think there's any truth to what she was saying about me?" she asks. "That I need her to be the screwup so I can be the savior? All that stuff?" She doesn't know how Peter would be able to answer this question when he doesn't know *her*—but she feels as if he knows everything.

"No way," Peter says. "She was just pissed off."

Arden leans her head against the window. "When I woke up this morning, this isn't where I thought my day would take me," she tells him.

"Me, neither. But nothing ever seems to go the way I expect it will. I don't know why I keep expecting anything."

"Where are we even going?" Arden asks. Right now, she feels like she could go anywhere.

"I don't know," Peter says. "But hey, look out the window. I don't want you to miss this."

She looks. They are driving on a bridge across a river. It's a suspension bridge, constructed of stone and thick wires. The bridge towers before them arch up and toward the sky, calling to mind the photos of European Gothic cathedrals that Arden has seen in her history textbook. Beyond the towers, she sees the Manhattan skyline laid out for her, lit up in the night, its glittering high-rises and spires packed together so closely that they resemble one mighty monolith.

Arden remembers the abrasive neon signs of her childhood trip to New York with her mother. This view of the city has a similar glow. But it feels different, because she's on the outside, taking it all in. This reminds her more of the lush Maryland mountains that she drove through this afternoon: something so expansive that it's impossible to fathom.

"I never get tired of this view," Peter says, but his words are sluggish. He lies down. After a moment, Arden does the same on the seat across from him. She points her toes and stretches her arms over her head, and still there's room beyond her reach.

She has the unfamiliar sensation of the world moving around her while she is lying motionless.

The limo exits the bridge and descends into the city below. Arden and Peter lie across from each other, and they listen to the sounds of traffic beyond their tinted windows. And for them, all the red lights turn to green.

Arden feels like she's flying

After they've been driving through the streets of Manhattan for about twenty minutes, the limousine stops. Through the intercom, the driver says, "I must to go now. I say I will be in Williamsburg soon."

Peter and Arden thank him and get out of the car. As promised, Peter pays, and now they are standing on some random block in Manhattan. The street sign says MERCER, which to Arden could mean just about anything. There are more cars driving by than there were in Brooklyn. More lights. Roughly as many garbage bags. The fact that it's past three in the morning does not seem to have resonated with the people who are carousing in a bar across the street, or the open convenience store next door, with a cat sitting in its window, licking her paw.

"Where to?" Arden asks.

"Let's walk," Peter says.

They walk.

"So what are you going to do about Bianca?" Arden asks after a block or two.

Peter makes a face. "Tonight we're only going to discuss happy things, remember?"

"But tonight is the only time that you'll have me here to talk to in person. And I'm a lot more useful in person than I am reading your journal over the Internet. So, talk."

"I don't know," Peter says.

"Peter, even if you can't win her back, you'll find another girl. Somebody who *can* be happy for you when your dreams come true."

Peter grins. "Because I'm a catch?"

"Exactly."

The smile fades off his face as he says, "I don't understand how she can do this to me. I don't understand how anyone is capable of just leaving someone they love. Unless they didn't really love them in the first place."

Arden opens her mouth to agree with him, but then she doesn't. "I don't know," she says instead. "I just left Lindsey. And that's not because I never loved her in the first place."

"Oh, I didn't mean *you*," Peter reassures her.

But maybe he should mean her. Maybe she has just done something that Peter can't understand, because even she can't quite understand it. She's never done anything like that before. All she knows is that she doesn't regret it.

She wonders if this is how her mother felt when she walked away. This terrifying freedom. She has no one to report to.

Nobody needs her. Nobody knows where she is. She can do whatever she wants right now.

And she realizes that she doesn't even know what she wants to do.

She thinks again of her mother's letter, those words that clutter her brain against her will. *I only knew who I was in relation to somebody else. For years I was somebody's wife, somebody's mother, somebody's friend, somebody's daughter. And for once, I wanted to be somebody for myself.* Arden has a flash of understanding this because tonight, for the first time in her memory, she is being somebody for herself.

They come to a complicated intersection, with a half dozen different streets converging around a small patch of land that has an enormous cube-shaped metal sculpture in its center. "What's that?" Arden asks, pointing at the cube, which is balancing on one of its eight corners.

"It's a sculpture," Peter explains. "It's been here my whole life. Come on, let me show you something cool."

She nods, and he leads the way across all the lanes of traffic. Cars swerve around them, every one of them honking, but somehow they make it to the traffic island still alive.

Up close, the cube looks even bigger than it did from across the street. Arden's head barely reaches the lower corners. There's a man who looks to be homeless lying down under a gray blanket on one side of the cube's base, and on the other side three punk kids with green Mohawks and safety pins through their lips are sitting and sharing a bag of French fries.

"Excuse me," Peter loudly addresses the crowd. Arden reflects on how much he's had to drink and wonders whether he declaims at strangers when he's *not* full of whiskey.

The three punks look at him with evident hostility. The homeless man doesn't even muster up that much of a response. Arden wonders if the cool thing she is about to witness is Peter getting punched in the face. She hopes not. His is a face that deserves better than a punch.

"Arden here has never been to our city before," Peter goes on. He pauses, as if waiting for the strangers to say *Welcome, Arden!* They do not. He continues. "So, since this is her first time, she's never seen what this cube can do. Would you mind standing up, all of you, so that I can show her?"

For a moment nobody moves.

"I really don't want to step on you," Peter adds.

The girl punk shrugs. "What the hell." She gets up, moves away from the cube, and stands there with her arms crossed, ready to return to her post the instant she's granted permission. Once she's up, her two friends join her, and, observing that he is the only holdout, the homeless man heaves a weary sigh and also moves aside.

Now the area directly under the cube is clear, and Peter shoots Arden a dazzling smile. "Ready?" he asks. "Go put your hands on that corner." She does. He puts his hands on the next corner over. "Now push!" he shouts.

She does. At first she feels like an idiot, standing and pushing all her weight against an immobile steel slab, with her not-amused audience. But a minute later, with her pushing at her corner and Peter pushing the corner in front of her, the cube starts to rotate on its axis. Slowly at first, like it's been stationary for a long time and forgotten that it knows how to spin. But then it shakes off the inertia and picks up speed, spinning so quickly that Arden nearly has to run to keep up with it. She notices that two of the punks have joined in, each of them grabbing a corner of their own and running. They whoop and holler. They are going so fast that Arden's feet lift off the ground, just a little bit, and she holds on to her corner as tight as she can, because for a moment, she feels like she's flying.

After a few minutes, they slow down, and the cube grinds to a halt. The punks sit back down and resume eating their fries. The homeless man returns to bed. And Arden and Peter walk off into the night. Peter seems a little unbalanced, from some combination of the alcohol and the spinning, she suspects.

"What did you think?" he asks.

"I loved it," she says. "Now it's my turn. Do *you* want to see something cool?"

"Sure." He looks around. "What is it?"

"Come with me," she says, "and I'll show you."

Arden goes back to the start

After forty-five minutes of walking, they reach Arden's destination. It shouldn't have taken quite that long, but Arden was navigating by the map on her phone and made a few wrong turns at the beginning. By the time they get close, her phone has died completely.

"It's a grid," Peter has said loudly, multiple times. "You know the streets are laid out in a grid, right? Do you want to just tell me where we're going and I'll find it?"

"Shh," Arden keeps responding. She's concluded that Peter is, in fact, drunk. Most likely *quite* drunk, when she thinks about how much she's seen him imbibe over the course of the night versus how little he ate at dinner. He's holding it together better than anyone she saw drunk at Matt Washington's party, though.

At one point along their walk, Arden saw a small dark shape dart across the road before her, emerging from one of the piles of trash bags and then disappearing into a crack in a building facade. Even before she consciously realized what it was, she let out a shriek and grabbed hold of Peter's arm.

"What?" he asked.

"That was a rat!" Still holding on to Peter, Arden hurried him forward down the road to get away from the pile of trash that seems to have been the rat's lair—but ahead there is another pile of garbage bags, and beyond that still *another* pile, and Arden can't run forever—she can barely run at all—and there seemed to be no place on the street that was safe from rats.

"Did it touch you?" Peter asked, confused.

"Thank God, no."

He shrugged. "Then don't worry about it. Did you know there are as many rats in this city as there are people?"

"Are you *kidding* me?"

Peter still looked unfazed. "Nope."

Arden shook her head. "This place is horrifying," she said. "I am horrified." She kept hold of his arm as they walked on. Just in case.

And now here they are.

It's a big stone building on Fifth Avenue, in among the department stores and steak houses, not too far from Times Square. The walls to the first four floors of the building are covered in windows, so passersby can see the displays.

"Here we are," Arden says.

Peter reads the sign aloud. "The Just Like Me Dolls Store. Oh, yeah, I remember Just Like Me Dolls. All the girls in my elementary school had them. I even wanted one for a while, but my dad said boys don't play with dolls. My dad is inappropriately tied to gender norms."

Arden hasn't been here since she was nine years old. It looks startlingly familiar, and she realizes that her one visit here has been lodged in her brain all these years. In science class earlier this year, they'd learned about something called flashbulb memories—incredibly vivid and precise memories of monumental moments in one's life. Arden's mind had formed a flashbulb memory of her trip to the Just Like Me Dolls Store, and she didn't even know it until she saw it again.

"My mom took me here when I was a little girl," Arden reminisces. "It was our first trip without my father and brother. Our last trip without them, too. Mom said the Just Like Me Dolls Store was not going to hold any interest to a little boy and a grown man." She shoots Peter a smile. "Maybe she's too invested in gender norms, too."

Arden looks through the front window, which is floor-to-ceiling Jessalynn, the Just Like Me Girl of the Year, who is "patriotic and athletic, always bringing a ray of sunshine to everybody's day." Jessalynn is blond and brown-eyed and tan, and Arden can tell from her accoutrements that she is in her school's color guard. The Jessalynn Doll is surrounded by an absurd number of flags.

Arden wonders what will become of Jessalynn when she grows up. What if she learns new information about America, about its role in wars or corruption in its government, and she doesn't feel so patriotic anymore? What if she gives up flag-spinning and athletics in order to spend more time with a boyfriend or a girlfriend, or to join a gang, or to study for the SATs? What if she no longer wants to bring a ray of sunshine to everybody's day? What if that becomes just too much responsibility, or she simply loses the knack for it?

"Do you want to buy one?" Peter asks. "They're not going to be open for a few hours, you know. That's okay, though. We can wait. And when they open up, I will buy you a doll, Arden. I will buy you whatever doll you want. I'll buy myself one, too, just to piss off the old man."

She doesn't pay attention to him. She walks around the store, peering in all its windows. And there, in the farthest window around the corner, she finds herself.

This window sports a banner saying JUST LIKE ME GIRLS OF THE PAST, and its risers bear all the dolls of the past fifteen years. There's Tabitha, *her* Tabitha, "graceful and inspiring." There's "brave and committed" Jenny, "quick-witted and fun-loving" Katelyn, and dolls who were created after them, girls whom Arden does not recognize because she was already too old by the time they came about.

And there's Arden.

Brown hair, hazel eyes, overalls perfect for playing in the woods. She looks the same as the Arden Doll in the glass case in Arden's bedroom, but it's different seeing her here, among her doll brethren.

"That's me," Arden tells Peter, pointing at her doll, sandwiched in between Tabitha and Lucy.

"I know," he says.

274

She turns to him, shocked. *How* would he know such a thing? Could he have figured it out on his own? Nobody has ever discovered this fact about Arden without her telling them—but maybe it would make sense, for Peter to know something hidden about her when she knows so many hidden things about him.

"That's me, too," he goes on, and he waves at the store window and makes a funny face.

She turns back around, trying to understand what he's talking about or if he's just so drunk that he's not talking sense. Then she exhales as she understands what's going on. The two of them are reflected in the window, ghostly outlines of themselves visible in the streetlights. That's all he means.

She can see her sexy dress and her windblown hair and the words written in marker all over her torso. She sees herself so faint in the window, right next to the Arden Doll behind the glass, and for a moment it's hard to tell which one of them is real.

"No," she says to Peter. "I mean, *that's* me." She points to the doll. "Do you see where it says 'Arden is recklessly loyal'?" He leans forward to read it, then nods. "That's me," she repeats. "The Just Like Me Dolls Company based that doll on me."

He looks at her, not quite comprehending.

"Do you see?" she asks. "See how her hair is brown, like how my hair is brown? And her eyes are hazel, just like mine? *That's me.*"

He just shakes his head, unwilling to engage the mental

energy to decipher her meaning. "Don't be silly," he says. "You're not a doll."

It feels like the entire night grows still: the cars stop rumbling past, the streetlights cease their buzzing, the spring breeze calms.

"How do you know?" she whispers.

"Because," he says, looking impatient. "It doesn't make any sense. People can't be dolls."

He sits down on the sidewalk. Arden stays standing, staring at the dolls without seeing any of them. A long time passes.

"What does it mean, anyway?" he mumbles from behind her.

"What?"

"Loyalessly wreckful, or whatever it says."

"It means being there for someone you love, no matter what," Arden explains. Her voice grows bitter when she adds, "Even when you don't want to be."

"If you don't want to do something, then you don't have to do it," Peter says. "No one can *make* you do anything. It's a free country."

Arden at last turns away from the window display of dolls. "But if I wasn't recklessly loyal," she asks, "then who would I be?"

Peter takes off his glasses, as if to see her better, and in the glow of the streetlights his face looks so naked and so pure. "You'd be Arden, of course."

She sits down beside him on the curb and holds her knees in tight to her chest. She pictures her own pristine Arden Doll safe at home, looking exactly like this one, and she feels like Peter has swung a wrecking ball right through her case, shattering glass everywhere. She will never be able to piece it together again. Not even if she wants to. And what she found on the other side of that glass pane is just a doll. Not a mandate, not a future, not herself. Just an inanimate object for children to play with and then outgrow. Nothing more.

Sleeping with Peter

By the time Arden and Peter head to Peter's home in Gramercy, it's past five in the morning. Peter gives the taxi driver his address and spends the ride there with his head propped against the window, his eyes closed. He doesn't say anything, and neither does Arden. She's trying to figure out what's about to happen. She's going to sleep over at Peter's house, right? Why else would she be in a taxi with him? Where else would she sleep?

But sleeping over at Peter's . . . what does *that* mean?

She doesn't ask. Because if she asks, Peter might realize exactly what it is that they're doing.

They get out of the taxi and Peter hands the driver a wad of cash—too much, it looks like, but the driver doesn't protest, so neither does Arden. Peter's building is one of a dozen or so that encircle a small park. The park has a wrought-iron fence around it, and the gates to enter it are locked. "You can only go in there if you're rich," Peter says. "Normal people can't go into that park.

But if you're rich, you get a key. We have a key. Not on me, though."

"All rich people get to go into that park?" Arden asks, perplexed.

He blinks at her, as if she is the confusing one. "No. Just the ones who live here."

Okay.

They approach Peter's building, and he mutters at her, "Just act natural."

An instant later, she sees why. A fully uniformed doorman, with a cap and everything, holds open the door for them. "Good evening, Peter," the doorman says. He tips his head at Arden. "Miss."

"What's up, Kareem," Peter replies. Arden smiles meekly.

Kareem calls the elevator for them, and Arden keeps smiling meekly until she and Peter get inside. As soon as the doors close, she starts squealing. "I didn't know you were going to have a professional *door opener*! Is he going to tell your parents? Are we going to get in trouble?"

"For what?" Peter asks.

Where to start. "For coming home at five thirty a.m., when you've clearly been drinking and you have some random girl in tow for God knows what purpose?" She blushes at the last part, but she didn't say it because *she* thinks he has designs on her. She just knows that's what parents would assume. Look at Mrs. Ellzey.

"Kareem won't tell," Peter says. "He never tells. He's cool."

Arden wonders what else Kareem has never told. About Peter,

about Peter's brother when he lived here, about Peter's parents. Kareem must keep so many secrets under that flat-topped doorman cap of his.

The elevator stops on the eighth floor, and Peter says, "My parents should be asleep. My mom takes sleeping pills. She almost never wakes up. But—be quiet, okay?"

Arden shivers and nods. She wonders what Peter's parents would say if they saw her here. She could try to explain, of course. But what exactly would her explanation *be*? And she has no idea how she will leave here later without attracting parental attention, but she pushes that off as a problem for another time. For now she focuses on only one goal: making it to Peter's bedroom.

The elevator doors open, and they are deposited into Peter's apartment. Even in the dark and shadows, Arden can make out the art hanging in heavy frames on the walls, the wispy drapery covering the broad windows overlooking the rich-people park, the mahogany credenza in the front hall. Everything in here is quiet and climate-controlled. It seems like the sort of place where nothing bad could ever happen, which is confusing because Arden knows for a fact that bad things happen in this family all the time.

The two of them creep down the hall, which is, fortunately for their purposes, covered in a cream-colored carpet. It seems like sound is incapable of permeating this thick carpet and the even thicker windows, so the only things Arden hears are the rhythmic tick-tock of the art deco clock on the side table and her quick, anxious breathing.

They reach Peter's room.

He closes the door behind them and locks it.

They both breathe a deep exhale.

"I'm going to use the bathroom," he says. "I've had to pee since Thirtieth Street."

He disappears into the bathroom attached to his room, and Arden takes this moment to look around. This room has the same wall-to-wall carpeting as the rest of the apartment, and his bed is sleek and modern, with a low headboard and shimmery gray sheets. Arden's bedsheets are white and patterned with faded flowers, and this is the first time in her life that it occurs to her that looking at somebody's *sheets* could actually tell you something about them.

Peter's hung a few quotes and prints around his room, like Arden's mother's embroidered *You become responsible forever for what you've tamed* and *Practice random kindness and senseless acts of beauty.* None of that is what Peter's wall art says, though. His say things like *A writer is someone who has written today* and *There is no friend as loyal as a book.—Ernest Hemingway.*

A long bookshelf runs along one entire wall of his room, and under it is a desk sporting a brand-new laptop computer. That's the computer he writes Tonight the Streets Are Ours on. That's where the words come from. Arden cannot believe that she's in the same room as that computer. She cannot believe this is happening.

Peter opens the bathroom door, comes out, and flops down on his bed, clothes and all. "What a night," he mumbles.

Arden agrees. She stands there.

"You're not going to sleep in that, are you?" Peter asks her.

"What else am I going to sleep in?" Her heart is thudding so loudly, he must be able to hear it. She wishes she'd thought to bring her overnight bag with her, but it's still in the backseat of the dead Heart of Gold.

"I have some clean gym clothes in the top drawer there." He points lazily across the room at his wardrobe. "Take whatever you want. Get comfortable."

She opens the drawer and sees his neatly folded athletic wear. She wonders if he folds his clothes or if their maid does it. She grabs the first articles of clothing that she sees and takes them to change in the bathroom.

Arden locks the door and looks at herself in the mirror. "What are you doing," she says aloud.

Mirror Arden has no response.

"Who even *are* you right now," she goes on.

Mirror Arden remains silent.

She pulls on Peter's elastic-waist shorts, which reach down to her knees, and an equally oversize T-shirt. She finds herself hoping that the shirt will smell like Peter, but it just smells like clean laundry. It's from a Broadway musical—*The Lion King*—which amuses Arden, to think that Peter not only went to see a live staging of a Disney cartoon, but that he liked it enough to invest in a souvenir shirt. She wonders if one of his parents took him, even though neither of them sounds like they'd be big musical theater fans. Maybe they'd taken him just because buying Broadway tickets is a thing that rich people do.

Thinking about Peter's parents at *The Lion King* makes her think of her own parents' coming to her first play, two years ago. That's probably the last time her dad stepped foot in a theater. She recalls his comment that with any luck, next time she'd make it *on* stage. Standing in front of the mirror in Peter's private bathroom, she thinks that maybe her father was right. Not that she should be in the spotlight in a play—that has never interested her before and it doesn't interest her now—but that she could be in the spotlight in her real life. That maybe Chris isn't the only one who can handle a leading role.

She leaves the bathroom and sees that Peter has not moved from his rag-doll position on his bed. She stands there, holding her dress balled up in her hands, and still she does not know what to do. She knows what Bianca would do. Bianca would get right into that bed like she owned it. And Arden knows what she *should* do. She should lie down on Peter's thick carpet, on the floor, and go to sleep, and not think anymore.

But she doesn't do either of those things. She stands still.

"Hey," Peter says after a while, his voice low and heavy. "Come here."

She does.

He flaps his arm, haphazardly patting the mattress beside him. She sits. And then, because it is very late and she is very tired, she lies down, facing him.

"You don't have to be so far away," Peter says.

"I'm not."

He rolls over to her side of the bed and flings an arm over her.

"Peter . . ." she says.

"It's okay," he murmurs. "We're just cuddling."

They lie there, him in his jeans, her in his gym shorts. This is the latest Arden has ever stayed up. She can hear birds waking up in the rich-person park across the street. The darkness coming through the slats in Peter's blinds is no longer quite so dark. It is almost morning.

He is drunk and hardly awake, and Arden doesn't want to take advantage of that—but at the same time, she does want to, more than anything she's ever wanted. It knocks the air right out of her, how much she wants to.

She leans in just a little and kisses him.

His eyelids flutter, and he kisses her back. It's a slow, languorous kiss, and she is lost in it.

Then Peter pulls away. He rolls onto his back and presses his forearm to his eyes. "I can't do this," he mumbles.

"What's wrong?" she asks, still reaching out for him, and what she means to say is *What's wrong with me?* but the end of the question is trapped in her throat.

Peter doesn't respond. Within moments, his breathing grows calm and regular. He's asleep.

Arden wants to wake him up and make him kiss her again and again. But she doesn't.

She lies there on her sliver of bed. Between the birds chirping outside and Peter's breathing and her own pounding heart,

Arden can't imagine ever falling asleep. But somehow, she does. She sleeps long and hard and without dreaming.

The next time Arden opens her eyes, sunlight is streaming in through the windows, and she is alone in the bed.

But there is somebody else in the room.

A girl, probably close to Arden's age, with wavy red hair and big green eyes and a navy-and-white striped strapless dress. She is standing at the foot of the bed, and she is staring right at Arden. She needs no introduction; Arden recognizes this girl instantly.

"Who are you?" says Bianca.

The morning after

Ihis isn't what it looks like," Arden tells Bianca as she sits up in Peter's bed, pulling the sheets around her. This feels like the ultimate in clichéd things to say, but it is, quite frankly, true.

"Really?" Bianca asks. "So you're *not* some random girl sleeping in my boyfriend's clothes in my boyfriend's bed?"

Arden has no idea why Bianca is here or where Peter is or what's going on, but Bianca's assessment here seems needlessly harsh. "I thought you broke up with him?"

"Yeah, four days ago! Why don't you at least give someone a full *week* before you make your move? Just *try* to show a little class."

"I didn't make a move. It's really not like that," Arden says. She feels like she would wield more power in this conversation if she were to stand, but she also feels like she doesn't want to pit her boy-size gym clothes against Bianca's Anthropologie sundress.

"How long has this been going on for?" Bianca demands, looming over Arden.

"How long has what been going on for?"

"You and Peter."

Arden doesn't know what to say. She and Peter have been going on for nearly two months. Or, she and Peter have never gone on at all.

"I'm not hooking up with Peter," Arden insists.

"I would like to believe you," Bianca says. "Unfortunately, I can think of approximately one reason for you to be here right now. Who *are* you, even?"

"I'm Arden," says Arden. "And you're Bianca."

Arden's knowledge of her name momentarily silences Bianca.

"Look," Arden says. "Can I get dressed before we continue this conversation?"

Bianca gives Arden a look that somehow conveys both pity and disgust. "Fine. I'll wait."

Arden crawls out of bed, feeling like a chimney sweep in comparison to Bianca, with her crisp face and put-together outfit. She checks her phone to see the time, then remembers that it lost its charge on the way to the Just Like Me Dolls Store.

She grabs her clothes from the floor and closes herself in the bathroom to change. Unfortunately, her skimpy dress looks exactly like it spent the night in a ball on the floor, meaning that she probably resembles a particularly disheveled sex worker. She leaves the bathroom without glancing in the mirror.

Bianca is standing right where Arden left her. She watches

Arden emerge from the bathroom and asks, "What's on your arms?"

Arden looks down. There's *loneliness*, still, and there's *miss you miss you miss you*, winding all the way up to her shoulder. "We went to a costume party," she tries to explain. "At Jigsaw Manor."

"A-*ha*," Bianca exclaims. "So that's where you met Peter? Jigsaw Manor?"

"No," Arden says firmly. "I'm a fan of Peter's writing. I read his blog. Tonight the Streets Are Ours."

Bianca's eyes widen. "That's even worse," she says. "You're like a *groupie*. A groupie for some sad-sack, self-absorbed eighteen-year-old who has delusions that he's famous."

"That's not what he's like," Arden says, shocked and offended on Peter's behalf. *This* is the love of his life? This is how she talks about him?

"I think I would be the judge of that," Bianca shoots back. "Better than you, anyway. And where is he?"

"I don't know. I just woke up when you came in the room. He didn't let you in?"

Bianca blinks a few times. "No. The doorman did. I didn't see Peter anywhere else in the apartment, so I came in. I assumed he was holed up in here."

"So he just . . . left me here?" Arden asks, glancing around the room for a note from Peter. He might have texted her to say where he'd gone. Only no, he didn't, because even if her phone weren't dead, they'd never exchanged numbers.

Bianca sneers. "Get used to it."

Arden takes a step toward her. "Why are you being like this? Peter always made you sound like a really *nice* person."

This seems to give Bianca pause. "He told you about me?" she asks, her voice quieter.

"Bianca. He talks about you *constantly*." It occurs to Arden that perhaps *she* could help Peter win back Bianca's heart. She could convey how obsessed with Bianca Peter is, how much Bianca means to him. And maybe just by being here now, Arden seems like enough of a threat that Bianca will want to take him back, to get him away from other girls. This actually would not be a bad plan. Peter would be grateful to her forever.

Unfortunately, she doesn't want to win over Bianca. What she *wants* is for Peter to come back. To her. To whatever it is that they started here in his bed a few hours ago. She wants him to come back with a reasonable explanation for why he left her here. She wants to be the girl that people come back for.

"Let me be clear with you," Arden says. "I have been reading Peter's writing online, and I think he's incredibly talented. I live hundreds of miles away, and I have never met him in person before last night. I didn't have a place to sleep, because my best friend and I got in a huge fight and my car broke down and everything went to hell, and Peter gave me a place to crash because he's a *good guy*. So please stop acting like I'm swooping in here to steal your man, when A, I didn't steal him, and B, as far as I can tell, he is not even your man anymore, since you dumped him."

Bianca is silent for a moment as she seems to weigh Arden's

words. "So you definitely didn't hook up with him?" she asks at last.

Arden thinks about that one kiss with Peter last night—this morning, rather—how good it felt, how wrong it was.

It was only one kiss, though. And it wasn't even Peter's choice.

"I'm just a fan," Arden says. "That's all."

Bianca sighs noisily.

"What's your problem with that?" Arden demands. "He's a great writer."

"He has a way with words," Bianca concedes, "but personally I'm not a big fan of the bit where he makes it sound like I randomly broke up with him a week after his brother disappeared. You know, just to make him suffer. And then he heroically won me back, because we're 'soul mates.' And then I broke up with him again, right after he achieved his lifelong dream, because I am *so selfish* that I'm incapable of supporting anyone else's happiness."

Arden raises her eyebrows. "Well, *didn't* you do all of that?"

Bianca smiles grimly. "Look, Arden, you read one version of the story. Peter's. If you asked me, I'd tell you a different version. But nobody does ask me. Yes, I broke up with him—yes, twice. I have done things in the interest of self-preservation. And I have done some things that were stupid—really, really stupid—because I really, really wanted to. But I've never set out to hurt anybody, including Peter. *Especially* Peter."

"But you *did* hurt him," Arden points out. "You have to take responsibility for that. You have to *try* to hurt people as little as possible."

"No, I don't," Bianca says. "Why would I have to try to do that? If not hurting people was my number-one goal in life, I would never do *anything*."

Arden opens her mouth to protest, then closes it. Because after walking out on Lindsey, leaving her brother and father three states away, trying to cheat on Chris—maybe, no matter what she used to believe, trying not to hurt people isn't her top priority anymore, either.

Bianca goes on. "That stupid blog of his, that story that you love so much—it isn't true. And he's found some agent to represent it, and I bet he will find some book publisher to publish it as a memoir, and it will be this story about some poor lovelorn literary hero, constantly victimized by his bullheaded parents and his runaway brother and his meanie girlfriend, and that *isn't true*."

Arden doesn't understand what Bianca is driving at. "You might not like it, but that doesn't make it all fake. He didn't invent an imaginary online identity for himself." She thinks about Lindsey's idea, of Peter as some sociopathic vampire, and shakes her head. "Even just since meeting Peter last night, I have seen for a *fact* that the things he wrote about are true. He *does* work at a bookstore. I saw him there. His parents *are* loaded. Look at this apartment. He *does* go to ridiculous parties. He *does* love you."

Bianca looks suddenly exhausted. "Do you want to get brunch?" she asks Arden. "I can tell you what I mean, but this would all go down a lot more smoothly with a cup of coffee."

"What time is it?" Arden asks.

"A little past one."

Arden feels a sick knot in the pit of her stomach as her mind tries to come to grips with the passage of time: all the things she needs to do, how little time she has before she's due at school tomorrow morning, all the people she is surely supposed to report to, the number of text messages that must be waiting, the distance she has to travel, the impossibility of it all, how little she wants to do any of it. Even though she cannot see the demands on her darkened cell phone, she senses them there, tugging at her hands and clothes like beggar children. She wishes she had not asked Bianca for the time. She wishes it could have stayed last night forever.

"Yeah," Arden says, tossing her dead phone into her purse. "Let's get brunch."

They leave Peter's room and head back down the hallway. It's still dark in this corridor, as dark as it was in the dead of night. They're almost at the front door when a quiet woman's voice says, "Bianca?"

The girls turn. Arden sees three strangers sitting in the hypermodern, stainless steel kitchen. They are eating lunch and staring back at her.

Two of them Arden knows immediately to be Peter's mother and father. They're Asian and look older than she expects parents to be. She'd place the mom around sixty, and the dad maybe even seventy. He—Peter's dad—is wearing jeans and slippers, while Peter's mother is in yoga pants and a zip-up. They have the newspaper and a spread of fresh fruits and vegetables out on the glass countertop in front of them.

The third person she's not so sure of. He looks to be a couple years older than she is, with a muscular build and curly reddish-brown hair. He's wearing a T-shirt, track pants, and flip-flops, and he has a plate full of food in front of him. Arden feels a little bit like she did that night at the Ellzeys' house: like she's seeing something behind the scenes, something she is not supposed to witness.

"Oh, hello, Mrs. Lau," Bianca says to Peter's mother, her voice going high-pitched. She and Arden step into the kitchen. "Sorry, I was just dropping off a book Peter had lent me. The doorman let me in. I hope that's okay."

"Not a problem," says Peter's mother, though the chill in her tone belies her words. "We just got back from running a few errands. How nice that we caught you before you left. And who is this?" She stands and comes forward to shake Arden's hand.

"I'm Arden," she introduces herself, and she searches her brain for a normal explanation as to how and when she entered their house, who she is, why she is wearing this ridiculous dress. She could kill Peter for leaving her to handle this alone. If she had any idea where he was, she could kill him.

"Arden is a friend of mine," Bianca says firmly, and miraculously this prevents any further questions about the weird stranger with permanent marker on her arms. The attention redirects to Bianca entirely.

"Is Peter still in his room?" the dad asks. Like his wife, Peter's father has a foreign accent—Chinese, Arden thinks, though she hasn't known enough people born in China to be certain.

Bianca shakes her head. "He must have gone out somewhere."

Peter's dad sighs impatiently and says to his wife, "Mei, can you call him? He is supposed to be here. Tell him that he can't just run off to do whatever he wants whenever he wants."

This is exactly the sort of thing Arden would expect Peter's father to say: ordering people around, pooh-poohing Peter's activities. She looks away so she won't glare at him, glaring instead at the wall decoration hanging in the kitchen next to her: an ornately framed certificate heralding Peter K. Lau as the winner of a Scholastic Writing Award, three years ago.

"We have an appointment shortly," Peter's mother explains to the girls apologetically, picking up a phone. "We just want to be sure that Peter doesn't miss it."

She takes the phone into the other room to call him, and now the boy at the table speaks. He stares straight at Bianca and says, "Is it true that you two broke up?" His voice is higher than Arden would expect from someone with his build. It sounds funny coming out of him, but Arden does not feel like laughing, because there is something weird going on in Peter's home.

Bianca's cheeks turn pink, but she lifts her chin and says to the boy, "Yes."

"Well." He nods slowly. "I'm sorry, I guess. I hope you're doing okay."

"Thank you," she says softly. "I didn't know you were going to be here today. I thought you'd be up at Cornell."

Arden knows exactly who is supposed to be at Cornell. But this can't be him, because that doesn't make any sense.

"I came home for the weekend," he explains. "We have family therapy."

"Son," his dad says in a warning tone.

And everything feels shaky, like the floor is tilting right under her, and there's a buzzing in Arden's ears, because none of this makes sense, none of this makes any sense at all.

"It's okay if Bianca knows that we're in therapy, Dad," he says. "It's not a big, shameful secret. And I don't think she's judging us."

"I'm not judging you," Bianca confirms, her voice hoarse.

"Every family has its issues," the dad explains to the girls, as if they really *are* judges and to them he must provide a defense. "They're unavoidable. You just have to work together to get through them."

Arden and Bianca nod silently, their heads bobbing like birds on a wire.

"Now, may I offer you anything for lunch? Some fruit, perhaps?"

Arden prays with all her heart that Bianca will refuse, and fortunately, she does. "Thanks, but we already have lunch plans," Bianca says, staring at the boy. "It was good to see you, though."

"It was good to see you, too, Bianca," the boy says, and he returns to his food.

"If you hear from Peter," the dad says, "please remind him that we need him home."

"Of course," Bianca says, and she leads the way to the elevator.

As soon as they get in and the doors close, Bianca slumps against the elevator wall and lets out a long breath.

Arden knows the answer—how could she not?—but it's so unbelievable that she needs to ask, and she needs to hear Bianca say it. "That guy," she says. "The one sitting with Peter's parents." She rubs her temples. "Who is he?"

Bianca blinks up at her. "Oh, sorry, I should have introduced you. That's Leo."

"Leo?" Arden repeats, because that *isn't* the answer she'd expected, not at all. What the hell is Bianca's ex-boyfriend doing here?

"Yes, Leo," Bianca says. "Peter's brother."

Brunch with Bianca

"My treat," Bianca says once they're seated at the café a few blocks from Peter's apartment. "The least I can do to make up for yelling at you is feed you."

Arden agrees. When the waiter comes over, she orders a strawberry banana smoothie, whole grain toast, hash browns, scrambled eggs, and a croissant. The past twenty-four hours have caught up to her, and she is, suddenly, ravenous.

She expects Bianca-the-angel to be one of those girls who subsists off of watermelon and Diet Coke, so she's surprised when Bianca orders a burger and tears into it with decidedly non-angelic vigor.

"I don't understand what's going on," Arden says.

"What do you mean?"

Where to start. "I thought Peter's brother ran away."

"He did. Last fall. It was incredibly scary. It was like he'd disappeared off the face of the earth."

"But he's there right now," Arden says. "We just saw him."

"Well, yeah. He came home after a couple months. He came back in plenty of time for his second semester at Cornell."

"Peter never mentioned that on Tonight the Streets Are Ours." Arden thinks back, and she realizes that Peter hasn't explicitly written about the loss of his brother since November, December at the latest. He's written some fond memories of him, but that's it.

Still, shouldn't he have said, *By the way, my brother came home*? Rather than letting readers just assume that he was still gone? She wonders where Leo was all that time, and what finally brought him back.

"Are you kidding? That is so messed up," Bianca says. "So you thought he was still missing, all these months later?" Arden nods silently, and Bianca shakes her head in disgust. "I'd assumed Peter announced his return on his blog at the time, and I just missed seeing that particular entry. But yeah. That's what happened, Arden. I cheated on my boyfriend with his younger brother. And Leo found out. He was devastated. And he ran away."

It knocks the breath out of Arden. No *wonder* Bianca was acting so weird around Peter's brother today. Because he is her ex-boyfriend.

And no *wonder* Peter panicked when he heard Leo was coming to Jigsaw Manor last night. Because he didn't want to be there when Arden put two and two together.

"I can't believe it," Arden says—but she *can* believe it. It makes too much sense. She recalls the inscription on Peter's flask last night. *Leonard Matthew Lau.* The same last name that Bianca used to refer to Peter's parents. Of course.

The more this sinks in for Arden, the madder she gets. "Peter acted like his brother left for some inexplicable reason. Last night he blamed it on his parents. For months, I've felt so sorry for him. But actually it was *his* fault!"

"And my fault," Bianca volunteers.

Of course, Arden realizes. Bianca betrayed Leo, too.

Bianca goes on. "When Leo left, he e-mailed me and Peter to say that he knew what we had done, and he hoped we'd be happy now that he wasn't around to stand in our way."

Arden recalls Peter's version of this story, on the roof of Jigsaw Manor last night. *He didn't want to stay with people who would treat him this poorly. He was through with us. He'd never really felt like he belonged in our family, and now he knew for sure that he didn't.*

Bianca pulls her hair out of her face. "My therapist says that there must have been other factors at play—depression, a chemical imbalance, problems fitting in at college, maybe unresolved feelings about his adoption. Lots of people have issues with their girlfriends. Lots of people get into fights with their brothers. They don't all disappear for three months. The vast majority of them get upset and go on. Maybe what Peter and I did was the straw that broke the camel's back, but it can't have been the only thing at play. So my therapist tells me."

"So *that's* why you broke up with Peter right after Leo took off," Arden realizes. "Because you felt guilty."

"I couldn't stand to be around Peter. I couldn't see him

without thinking about what we had done to Leo, and to his whole family. His parents were crazy with worry. I felt terribly guilty."

"But Peter wanted you to stick around and be his girlfriend?" Arden asks.

"Oh, God, he clung to me. I think he felt like if he and I just stayed together, then there would be a point to Leo's disappearance and all that misery. It would be 'worth it' because it would prove we were 'meant to be.'" Bianca takes a bite of burger, swallows, then goes on. "He was a wreck the whole fall. Maybe he wrote about this on Tonight the Streets Are Ours, I don't know, but he went out and got wasted every night of the week. Mostly alcohol, but, I mean, he'd do whatever he could get his hands on."

Arden thinks about Peter's autumn-time posts, all the parties he flitted around, all the girls he supposedly made out with. Those things probably did happen. He just didn't mention that he was trashed for all of it.

"How did you know all that?" Arden asks. "I thought you didn't speak to Peter the whole time."

"I didn't. I just wanted to separate myself from the whole thing. I just wanted Leo to come *home*. But it's a small world. We know people in common—friends of Leo's and mine, mostly. They reported back on what was happening with Peter. They weren't aware that we'd been sneaking around together. They thought I'd be interested just because he was my boyfriend's kid brother."

"But you must have missed Peter."

"Of course I did. I was wild about him. And it killed me to hear how he was treating himself."

"So that's why you went to him on New Year's Eve?" Arden says.

Bianca sighs. "In hindsight, I can see I shouldn't have gone back to Peter. But yeah. Leo came home right after Thanksgiving, and he and I finally got to have a proper break-up conversation. I said, 'I'm sorry I cheated on you, I'm sorry I hurt you, and when there was someone else I wanted to date, I should have just ended things with you.' It was civil. He'd gotten a lot of perspective on it just from being gone. He'd hitchhiked west, camped out, lived on the street for a while, worked in the kitchen of some sketchy restaurant—anything where he wouldn't have to touch his parents' money. And when he was ready, he just pulled out their credit card and bought a plane ticket home. He told me that once he'd seen how hard the world could be, dealing with me and Peter seemed easy."

"Wow," Arden says softly.

"So then when Peter pulled that stunt on New Year's—which was *crazy*-romantic, by the way—I thought, well, maybe our time had come. Leo was safe. I was single. Let's see where this goes." Bianca shrugs. "And here's where it went."

It's extraordinary to Arden that this story that has captivated and inspired her for months is just that: a story. Even Peter's take on his parents was twisted for maximum sympathy. While they seemed uptight, especially when compared to Arden's own parents, they also seemed like they're trying to work things out, if they're going to family therapy together.

She can no longer accept that they don't even care about Peter's talent. Not when she's seen that writing contest certificate so carefully framed, so prominently displayed. Not when she considers that they spend the money to send him to a specialized art school where he can study writing. Shouldn't that have been a red flag all along? How many other warning signs did Arden miss in pursuit of believing Peter's fantasy?

Bianca signals the waiter for the check, and Arden feels the time pressure of needing to find out all the truth, now, while she can.

"Can I just ask you one more question?" Arden says.

Bianca waves her hand as if to say *Go for it*.

Arden clears her throat and asks what she's been wondering about ever since she first read this story, weeks and weeks ago. "Why did you do it? Why did you stay with Leo and see Peter on the side? Why not just break up with Leo? Or just *not* hook up with Peter?"

Bianca looks wrecked. "Knowing what I know now, seeing how it tore their family apart, I wouldn't do it. Obviously. But at the time . . . I cared about them both, in very different ways. I'd known Leo for much longer, because we went to school together. We had a lot in common. He was on the football team, and I'm a cheerleader, you know, so we already shared a whole friend group, anyway. And he's just honestly, truly, *nice*. The sort of guy who will accompany you to the hair salon, wait around for your whole appointment, and then take you home again, or who will make chicken noodle soup when you're sick and spoon-feed it to you no matter how germy you are. A sweet person, you know what I mean?

"And then I met Peter, and he . . . he was different. He wasn't like anyone else I knew. He was sexy, and romantic, and artistic, and I wanted him. And he wanted me, too, which was . . . very flattering. I didn't know if I should give up on somebody who I had this strong relationship with for somebody who seemed appealing from a distance. I didn't know what to choose. So I just *didn't* choose, which turned out to be the stupidest choice of all."

Arden has always trusted that Bianca and Peter are soul mates, just the way Peter said. But seeing the way Bianca's face softens when she talks about Leo, she's not sure anymore.

The waiter brings the check, and Arden senses that wherever Bianca is going from here, it does not include her. Which is rational, of course. They are not friends. Bianca knows nothing about her. And, as it turns out, she doesn't know very much about Bianca, either.

Bianca puts some cash on the table and stands up. The conversation is over.

"Thanks for brunch," Arden says.

"Thanks for listening to me," says Bianca.

And they go their separate ways.

Going home for the first time

Arden walks slowly down a crowded street, trying to figure out what to do from here. She is surrounded by more people than she'd find at an Allegany High sporting event, yet she is completely, irrevocably alone. Bianca has gone, she doesn't ever want to see Peter again, her phone is dead, her car is dead, and for all she knows, Lindsey is dead, too. She feels so *lost*.

When Arden was a little girl, her mother instructed her that if they ever got separated—in the supermarket or at a fair—she should tell an official but otherwise just sit there and wait, because her mother would come find her.

Arden doesn't think that this plan would work now that she's seventeen and lost in New York City. And anyway, she's done enough sitting and waiting to last her a lifetime. So she does something that she had vowed never to do. She stops walking, sticks out her arm—just like she saw Peter do at five o'clock this morning—and hails a taxi.

"Where you going?" the driver asks.

"One thirty-three Eldridge Street," she tells him.

The whole ride there, Arden feels like she's going to throw up—and not just because of the way the cabbie swerves back and forth across lanes of traffic and whips through yellow lights right when it seems he ought to be slowing down.

The driver drops her off at the address she gave him. It's a five-story building with a bodega on the first floor, and unlike at Peter's, there's no doorman, just eight buzzers. One of them is labeled HUNTLEY, and suddenly this all feels too real.

Arden has never envisioned her mother living anywhere in particular in New York City. When she thought about her mom's life now—which she tried really, really hard not to do— she pictured it taking place mostly in a vacuum, or maybe in the high-rise hotel where they'd stayed on their Just Like Me Doll trip.

But this is it. This is a plain brick building on a busy street with a fire escape outside the windows and her own last name on the buzzer.

Arden presses the button, and a moment later she hears her mother's voice through the intercom. "Hello?"

"Mommy?" Arden says, the word coming out squeaky, as though through disuse. "It's me."

A long minute passes. Then Arden hears the *slap-slap-slap* of feet running down stairs, and her mother opens the door. And she looks exactly the same as she did the day she left, with the same pointy nose, hazel eyes, and brown hair as Arden's own.

"Arden," she says.

"I'm sorry," Arden says. "I don't know what I'm doing here." And she starts to cry. Her mother holds out her arms, and Arden falls into them. "I don't even know why I'm crying," she blubbers into her mother's shoulder.

Her mother rubs her back and holds her close. "I think we need pancakes," she says after a while. "Can I make you some pancakes?"

And even though she just ate her weight in eggs and hash browns, Arden nods. "Yes," she tells her mother. "Pancakes sound perfect."

Arden finds out what love isn't

"Did Dad tell you I was missing?" Arden asks once she's settled on her mother's couch, sipping a glass of juice, her phone plugged into a charger. She keeps staring at her mother. Three months is a long time.

"No." Her mother stands at the counter, spooning pancake batter onto a frying pan. Her apartment is small. Much smaller than Peter's, which had felt almost like a house—albeit a one-story house. It's not hard for Arden and her mother to carry on a conversation even though one of them is technically in the kitchen and one is technically in the living room. "*Are* you missing?" her mother asks.

"Well, I haven't spoken to Dad in more than twenty-four hours, so as far as he's concerned, yes."

Her mother checks her phone to make sure, then says, "He didn't say anything to me."

There's a sour taste in Arden's throat. "I guess he didn't notice." What does she have to do to get him to pay attention?

"I'm sure he noticed," her mother says. She flips a pancake, and the batter sizzles and crackles. "I would guess that he didn't tell me because he doesn't want me to know that he lost you. But you need to call him, Arden. He's got to be worried."

Arden isn't sure she believes this. "He's not very good at taking care of us," she says.

"He's learning," her mother says.

"I don't want to call Dad," Arden says. She feels her eyes fill with tears again and all she can manage to say through the tightness of her throat is, "I just want you to come home."

Her mother looks up from the frying pan, her eyes glistening as well. "Part of me wants that, too."

"So do it," Arden says. "Come back with me."

"Sweetheart, it's not so simple." Arden's mother brings over a plate of pancakes, but neither of them takes a bite. She sits on the armchair across from Arden, curling her feet up under her. Arden does not recognize any of the furniture in this apartment—which makes sense, since her mother is just subletting it. Nothing in here is her mother's style; Arden sees no flowers, no inspirational quotes, no eyelets, no gingham—just a lot of black-and-white photos and boxy furniture. It feels like a stranger lives here, not her mother at all.

"I read your letter," Arden says.

"Thank you." Her mother blinks. "I wasn't sure, since you didn't say anything . . . I thought maybe you just threw it away."

"I did," Arden says. "But I read it, too."

"And what did you think?" her mother asks.

"It made me wish you hadn't felt like you needed to do all

that stuff for us. You *didn't* need to. The night you left—I didn't need you to make that dress from scratch, Mom. I never asked you to do that. You didn't need to make Roman some fancy mac and cheese. You know he'd just eat a bowl of cereal and be every bit as happy. I wish you'd done less for us and stuck around. We don't need you to be a perfect mom sometimes if it means you're a nonexistent mom the rest of the time. We just need you *there*."

"I understand that," her mother says. "I'm trying to figure out how I can learn to be a just-okay mom. I really am."

"I didn't get it at first," Arden says. "Your letter didn't make any sense, why you'd do all these things for us that we didn't need, and then complain about having to do so much. But there's something you said in there, about feeling like if people need you, then that must mean that you really matter. And I guess . . . that makes sense to me now."

Arden thinks about Lindsey's cold words last night, claiming that she didn't need anything from Arden, not even the Disney vacation. And maybe that's true. Maybe Lindsey could have gotten through her whole life without Arden ever lifting a finger to help her, without ever even running into Arden that day in the woods when they were little girls. But Arden believes with a deep certainty that it doesn't matter whether Lindsey ever *needed* her, because having Arden has made Lindsey's life better. And it works both ways, because having Lindsey has made Arden's life better, too.

"Here's what I want to know," Arden says. "All that stuff you always told me—about how some people are gardeners, and how kindness is my power, and how charity will do more for you than selfishness—was that all wrong?"

"No," her mother says. "Not wrong. All of that *does* matter. Other people matter hugely. But you have to matter to yourself, too. There has to be a balance. I'm still figuring out that balance, myself. But I know this one thing: sacrificing everything that you care about in order to make another person happy *is not love*. It's not really that some people are gardeners and some people are flowers, Arden. It's that we both must be both, each in our own time."

Arden considers this and at last takes a bite of pancake. It tastes exactly the way it's supposed to.

"Has moving here helped?" Arden asks after she's swallowed. "I mean, are you happy now?"

"I think it's given me some perspective," her mother replies. "It's been good for me. But I miss you so much. You know I had never been apart from you for longer than one night since you were born. So being away for months has been . . . well, it's been really hard."

Arden had never measured these things before, but she realizes now that her mother is right—the only times she'd been away from her mom for longer than the length of a school day was when she started having sleepovers at friends' houses. Roman can't even claim that: he still refuses to sleep over anywhere. Even more now, Arden sees the similarity to her situation with Lindsey. She *did* need to leave Lindsey. But now she needs to find her again. And hope that they can rebuild from here.

"Are you ever going to come home?" Arden asks her mother.

Her mother takes a deep breath. "Do you want to know honestly?"

"Yes." After her night with Peter, Arden has decided that she prefers hard truths over pretty lies.

"I don't know. Your father and I are in communication, as you're aware. We're working through things, together and individually. I may come home. We may separate on a more permanent basis. But *if* that happens, we will work out a joint custody agreement that's as fair as possible to everyone. You and Roman will always be my children and I'll always be your mother. Like it or not, kid, you're stuck with me."

"Joint custody," Arden repeats. "So would we, like, come to New York every weekend?" She looks around the apartment. "Where would we even sleep? And we should get a say in this. What if we don't *want* to come to New York that often? Would you move back closer to us?"

"Arden. You're getting ahead of yourself. Like I said, that might not even happen. What you need to do right now is tell your dad where you are, before he calls the police. Which maybe he already has."

Arden sighs and goes to get her phone from the charger. On her way across the room, her mother stops her and envelops her in a hug.

"I didn't know if you would ever be willing to talk to me," Arden's mother says quietly. "Thank you for coming here."

That is not why Arden came to New York, but she doesn't tell her mother that, because the reason she came here is not relevant anymore.

Arden turns her phone on and it goes crazy registering all the messages and phone calls she's missed over the past twelve hours. Four texts from Chris asking, with increasing degrees of annoyance, when she is going to be free to hang out. A text from Roman asking if she can pick him up from his hockey game. A text from her father also asking if she can pick up Roman, followed by a text from her father asking her to please call him, followed by a text in all caps saying WHERE ARE YOU?, followed by three missed calls and voice mails. Nothing from Lindsey, which could mean she is still mad and waiting for Arden to call her first, or could mean her phone died in the night, or could mean she is unconscious in an alley somewhere.

Arden skips over the texts and just telephones her father. He answers immediately. "Arden! Where have you been? Are you okay?" The panic in his voice is evident, and amazing because it sounds exactly like *he cares.*

Arden can't help the smile spreading across her face, or the laughter in her voice as she says, "I'm fine, Daddy."

"Don't you laugh, young lady. It is not a joking matter for you to run off like this. Where are you? And don't say you're at the Matsons', because I already spoke with them, and I *know* you and Lindsey aren't there."

"I'm with Mom," Arden says. "In New York."

"You went to *New York* without telling me?" he shouts.

"Please don't yell at me."

"I have every right to yell at you, Arden, because you scared the *hell* out of me. What would I do if anything had happened to you? What made you think you could run off to a different *state* without checking with me first? I don't know what's gotten into you lately, I really don't. You used to be a good kid. And now you're sneaking around, using drugs, going hundreds of miles away and lying about it—I feel like I don't even know who you are anymore."

"You don't," Arden says.

"What was that?"

Arden pauses. She could just let it go. It would be easier for her not to ask for what she wants.

But she has come this far.

"You don't know what's gotten into me because you're never around," she says.

"That's ridiculous. Of course I am. You're sounding like your mother."

"No," she says. "You're at the office all the time—"

"I have a job."

"—and when you're home you're always holed up in your study or watching TV or doing your fantasy football. You're always too busy for us."

"This isn't about me," he says. "This is about you, disappearing without so much as a text message."

"This is about both of us," she says. "If you want me to act more like your daughter, then you can start by acting like more of a father."

"Arden," he says, and his voice is brittle. "Do not get on your teenage high horse and try to lecture me. I need you to come home, and we are going to talk about consequences."

"I'm coming home," she tells him, "but we need to talk about a lot more than consequences."

It's not that her mom was the bad guy and her dad was the victim, she realizes. They were both bad guys. They were both victims.

"I love you, Dad," Arden adds. "I love you so much. This was something I needed to do. But I'm sorry I made you worry."

Her mother taps her on the shoulder. "May I speak with him for a moment?"

Arden passes over her phone. Her mother takes it and closes herself in the small bedroom, so Arden can't hear her parents' conversation. She stares out the window while she waits. There's an ambulance trying to drive down the one-way street, its siren wailing, but a moving van is parked in front of it, blocking its passage, so the wailing just goes on and on, and presumably someone is dying right this moment while the EMTs try to figure out a way forward. None of the pedestrians seem at all disturbed as they continue walking absurdly quickly and texting on their phones. Watching this scene, Arden feels very, very glad that she does not have to live in this city.

A few minutes later, her mother emerges from the bedroom and hands back Arden's phone.

"He's mad," Arden says.

"He was scared, Arden. We need to get you home. Not least because you have to be at school in about eighteen hours," her mother says.

Arden grimaces. "One problem. The Heart of Gold is dead. I left it parked on the street somewhere in Brooklyn."

"Where?"

"Outside of Jigsaw Manor?"

Her mother sighs. "Do I even want to know?"

Arden shakes her head.

"To be honest, I don't want you driving that hunk of junk all the way to Cumberland, anyway. It's dangerous. I can't even believe your car made it here in the first place. I can book you a train ticket now, and your father can pick you up from the station."

"No. I want to get the Heart of Gold repaired. I'll pay for it; you won't have to worry about it, I promise. Mom, I'm not leaving my car."

Her mother relents a little. "Let's go look at it. We'll see how bad it is, and we can work on getting it fixed, but there might not be time to do that today and still get you home at a reasonable hour. Does that sound fair?"

Arden nods. "We need to find Lindsey, too," she says. She calls her now, but it immediately goes to voice mail. She texts her, as well, though if Lindsey's phone is off, then she doesn't expect a text message will help with matters. She wonders where Lindsey slept last night. She wonders if she's okay. And she thinks that there is a big difference between sacrificing everything for another person and just doing your best to keep that other person safe.

"Where is Lindsey?" asks her mother.

"I have no idea."

Her mother rubs her eyes. "This is getting complicated. Okay. Let's start with the car, and then go from there."

Arden picks up her purse, and they head out together.

"By the way," her mother says as she locks the door behind her, "what are all these marks on your arms?"

Arden glances again at the words on her arms. *I miss you I miss you I miss you* and *the only one.* "They're lies," she says simply. "But don't worry. They'll wash off."

They walk down the four flights of stairs and out into the late afternoon sun. And there, standing on the sidewalk right outside her mother's apartment building, is a person Arden recognizes.

"Hey," says Peter. "I've been looking for you."

A garden of gardeners and flowers

Where did you go this morning?" Arden asks Peter. They have left behind her very surprised mother. "Who is this?" she asked when they emerged from her apartment building, looking back and forth between Arden and Peter with confusion, maybe suspicion, and a hint of amusement.

"No one," said Arden.

"Peter," said Peter, and he shook Arden's mother's hand firmly. He gave her a broad smile while simultaneously adjusting his glasses, a move clearly designed to set a mother at ease, communicating *I'm charming* and *I'm a studious boy who would never take your daughter to bed with me* all at the same time. Arden wasn't having it for a second. Maybe her mother was, though. Today Peter is wearing fitted jeans and a black-and-white-checked button-down. He looks just like someone you would trust with your daughter. He's a good-looking guy. Arden doesn't think she'll ever be able to unsee that, no matter how much she learns about him.

"Peter and I need to talk," she told her mother. "Just wait here for a few minutes. I'll be back in a little bit."

Her mother didn't ask questions. She just sat down on her stoop, pulled out her phone, and reminded Arden, "Not too long. We have to figure out how to get you home."

Peter and Arden walked in silence for a number of blocks. She had thought it likely that she was never going to see him again. She hadn't really *wanted* to see him again. Funny that she could spend so long searching for him, and it's only once she's not looking anymore that he turns right up.

Now that he's here, though, she wants an explanation. She wants him to explain *everything*. And when he doesn't answer her question right away, she repeats, louder, "Where did you *go* this morning?"

"To the library," he says.

"Why?"

"I needed to return a couple books. And I really like it there. Have you ever been to the main branch of the New York Public Library? It's massive. If you have time today, we should totally go."

"That's not what I'm asking. I meant, *why did you leave me?*"

He adjusts his glasses again and doesn't reply for a moment. Then he says, "Let's go in here."

She follows him into a little garden crammed between buildings. The sign on the gate identifies it as the Elizabeth Street Garden. She realizes that it's the first time her feet have touched grass since she arrived in this city. The space is filled with marble statues, human busts and cherubs and Grecian columns, that sort of thing. It's not big, but it's substantial enough for the city sounds to fade to a low rumble in the background.

They find a gray stone bench and sit down.

"How did you find me?" Arden asks when she realizes that he's not about to tell her why he left her earlier. The thought that Peter would track her down, as she did him, is flattering. But confusing. What does he want from her? Why abandon her, only to come back?

"You said your mom's address last night," he reminds her.

"You have a good memory for details."

He shrugs. "I'm a writer."

"But how did you even know I'd be there?"

"I didn't know for sure. I just figured you'd wind up there eventually."

"Why?"

He blinks at her. "Because she's your mother?"

Arden doesn't argue with that. After all, he's correct.

"I was waiting out there for a while," he offers. "If you hadn't shown up soon, I was going to take off."

"Okay," she says. "So you found me. Why did you want to?"

"I heard from Bianca," Peter explains. "She said she talked to you. So I . . . yeah. Just wanted to see what you two talked about."

A slight breeze ruffles the tree leaves. Arden opens her mouth, but then Peter barges on.

"Did it sound like she might want to get back together? Did she say anything like that? Do you think she misses me—could you tell?"

"What?" Arden asks.

"This afternoon was the first time she's texted me since we broke up. Did you say something to her, maybe, that made her change her mind? Did she talk about changing her mind?"

"No, Peter." Arden shakes her head. "No. That's not what we talked about, and no, I don't think she's changing her mind."

"Oh." He deflates. "I thought . . . you know, sometimes girls talk about those things. Never mind." He pulls Leo's flask out of his back pocket and takes a long swig.

"You know it's the middle of the afternoon," Arden says, watching him drink. "On a Sunday." She pauses before adding, "And we're in a park."

"What's your point?" He doesn't look at her. "Just because *you* don't drink, you're going to judge everybody who does?"

"I'm not judging you!" she retorts. "You don't know me, so please don't assume that you know what I'm thinking."

Now he looks at her. "Sorry."

"You want to know what Bianca and I discussed?" Arden asks. "She told me about Leo. She told me what the two of you did to him. She told me why he left."

"Really?" Peter raises his eyebrows. "I didn't know she talked about that with anyone. Well. Congratulations, Arden. Bianca trusts you. That's a big responsibility, but I guess you're the girl for the job." He flashes her another winning smile.

"Is this all some big joke to you?" Arden snaps. "Other people's lives are just here for your amusement? This person—your *brother*—he ran away because of what you did. Oh, and he's home now, by the way. So, thanks for mentioning that."

Peter's eyes widen; he's surprised that Arden knows all of this. And she thinks, *I'm smarter than you gave me credit for.*

Peter isn't smiling anymore. He takes another sip from the flask. "I know I screwed up. I know I hurt my family in ways that we can't just get over. I face that guilt every day."

No, you don't, Arden thinks. *You get drunk. You make a joke. You tell a story. You run away.*

Then again, what else could he do? If he looked in the mirror and saw himself for what he is and what he's done, how would he be able to stand himself?

"You *lied* to me," she says.

"Did I?"

"You know you did! You purposefully acted like Leo was just some dumb jock who you were casually friends with. You said you didn't know the reason he left, except that probably it was your parents' fault. You said that you and Bianca were soul mates, you were meant to be. You purposefully let me believe that your brother was still missing, that he might be *dead*, for God's sake. You said—"

"Arden, I never lied to you." He pauses. "Maybe I just lied to myself." She starts to speak, but before she has time to respond, he goes on. "It had nothing to do with *you*. I didn't know who you were before yesterday. I didn't even know you were reading Tonight the Streets Are Ours."

"But you knew that *people* were reading. And you led all of them to believe that you're someone you're not."

"It's my life," he argues. "It's *my* story about *my* life. And this is who I say I am. This is what I say happened. If Bianca wants her story about my life to be different, then good for her. Let her write her own version." His hands curl into fists.

Arden snorts. "You just loved getting all those comments from girls fawning over you, strangers sympathizing with you, telling you how *unfair* your life is."

"So what if I did?" He jumps to his feet, too agitated to sit still. "So what if I wanted that? And furthermore, what I wrote online basically *is* what happened. I said that I fell in love with a girl who had a boyfriend, which I did. I said that she cheated on him with me, which she did. Have you stopped to ask yourself why you were okay with that when Bianca's boyfriend was just *some guy*? Why is it, now that you know he's some guy who is my brother—now that you know he freaked out over it—suddenly it's not okay anymore? Suddenly I'm a *monster*?"

She stands as well to look him in the eyes. "I don't think you're a monster. But why do you do these things? And seriously this time, why did you take off this morning, when I had no idea where I was or how to reach you? That was an asshole thing to do, Peter."

And all of this is making her know even more that she really, really needs to find Lindsey, like, right now. She shouldn't even be wasting her time on this guy, trying to find answers that don't exist to questions she can't even express, when she should be out scouring every block and every building for Lindsey.

"You got me," he says, holding out his hands. "I'm an asshole. I do asshole things. You're right, Arden. You see right through me. That's exactly what I am.

"I woke up this morning and I looked over, and you were lying there, and I felt terrible—I mean, stomachache, headache, everything-ache. And I remember a *lot* about last night, but just the very end of it is fuzzy. I remember visiting that doll store on Fifth Ave. I just don't remember how we got home from there, or if we . . . you know, if anything happened after that."

"You don't remember if we had sex," she says flatly.

His cheeks flush a little. "And I know you have a boyfriend, and I opened my eyes and there you were, fast asleep, and I felt so terrible and everything just seemed so terrible, and all I could think was *Not this again, I can't believe you did this again, what is wrong with you, what is wrong with you?*"

"So you left," she supplies.

"So I left. I know I shouldn't have. But I do a lot of things I shouldn't do. I don't know why. I can't help myself. I just hope I didn't do anything to mess up things with . . . What's his name again?"

"Chris."

"Right. I don't want to be the grenade in your relationship."

You already were, she thinks. Aloud, she says, "Don't worry about it. You and I didn't have sex. Nothing happened."

"Oh." He clears his throat. "That's good." His hands drop by his sides awkwardly, like he's not sure what to do with them now.

"Are you honestly going to publish Tonight the Streets Are Ours as a memoir?" she asks.

He blinks rapidly a few times. "I'm going to try. If any publisher will have it, then yeah."

She takes a deep breath. "Don't do it, Peter. It's not fair
to Leo. It's not fair to Bianca, or to your parents. It's not fair to
anyone who reads it, who might feel like . . . like maybe you
understand what they're going through. You're taking advantage of all of them."

He turns his face away from her. "Stop. Just stop. Look, I
don't know what your life goals are. But I'm not going to stand
here and tell *you* that you shouldn't try to make them come
true."

She stares at him. "You're really going to do this."

He bends down to fuss with some flowers in a planter. "Some
of the greatest art in history is born from tragedy. Literature,
music, paintings. If I can create something beautiful and meaningful out of everything rotten that happened with me and
Bianca and Leo, then maybe . . . maybe there's a point to all of
this."

To Arden this seems like a ridiculous justification. The right
answer would have been to leave Bianca alone. Even if Leo had
been unhappy with his life anyway, even if he had wound up
leaving anyway, at least something else would have been the last
straw for him. At least Peter and Bianca would be innocent.

But it's too late for the right answer now. What's done is done.
And she supposes that Peter is only trying to work with what
he's got.

"Just do one thing for me," Arden says. "Don't write about

last night. Don't write about meeting me. Not on your blog, not in a book, not anywhere. I am not your story to tell."

"Fine," Peter says. "I can do that." He rubs his neck and looks at her through lowered lashes. "It's too bad, though. I would have a lot to say about last night. I would have a lot to say about you."

And she's curious to know what he would say about her—of course she is. But she's not going to ask.

"I need to go home," she says.

"Now?"

"Yeah."

"Are you mad at me?"

She thinks about this. *Mad* isn't the word. She had just wanted Peter to be someone different from the person he is. But whose fault is that?

She shakes her head. "I feel sorry for you," she says. "I feel sorry for all of you."

Peter nods, like this is the best response he could hope to get. "Can I walk you back to your mom's?"

"No, thanks. I've got it covered."

"Okay, then. I guess . . . I'll see you around. Maybe on my first book tour!" He laughs to show that he's joking, sort of. She pictures Cumberland's one fading bookstore, with its rack of cigarettes, and she thinks it's unlikely that Peter will ever have a book tour that brings him anywhere close to her.

He extends his arms, and she steps forward into them. They hold each other for a long moment, and Arden wonders about all the people who must have hugged in this garden over the years and whether any of them could have had a relationship like hers and Peter's. She thinks she hears Peter sniffle a few times while her face is pressed into his shoulder, but she doesn't look, and she doesn't ask him if he's okay.

"Are you walking out, too?" she asks when they pull apart.

"Not yet. I'm going to hang out here for a little while longer, read my book, you know. I just got to the good part."

She nods. "Bye, Peter."

"Bye."

She turns and heads back toward the street, toward her mother. Once she's outside, she glances behind her and she sees Peter sitting back on the bench, his book unopened in his hands, staring at a marble statue of a little boy, all alone.

Lindsey's big night

$\mathcal{U}$sing the directions stored in Arden's phone from last night, she and her mother navigate to Jigsaw Manor. "Why on earth did you think this would be a good place to leave your car?" her mother asks as they walk fifteen minutes from the nearest subway stop.

"I didn't have to parallel park," Arden replies. This gets a laugh from her mother.

When they reach the car, Arden's heart somersaults, because there is a person lying on its hood. A girl.

"Lindsey!" Arden cries, running toward her.

Lindsey sits up and slides off the car. She gives a laugh of surprise as Arden flings her arms around her and hugs her, hard. "I'm so sorry," Arden whispers. "I shouldn't have run off last night. I'm so glad you're okay."

"I'm sorry," Lindsey says. "I shouldn't have picked a fight with you. And I shouldn't have let you go."

"Well, *I'm* Mrs. Ellzey," Arden says. And the two of them

lose it, laughing so hard they have to hold on to each other just to stay upright.

"Lindsey, honey, it's so good to see you!" says Arden's mother as she reaches the girls.

Lindsey shoots Arden an inquiring look. Like, *What is your mom doing here, is this okay, do I have permission to show that I'm happy to see her?* Arden gives her the slightest of nods, and Lindsey squeals, "Mrs. Huntley, oh my God! How are you doing? I can't believe you're actually living in New York. Do you love it?"

Arden's mom laughs. Her cheeks are glowing. "It's different from Cumberland, that's for sure! It's an adventure."

"I'm so jealous," Lindsey tells her. "I would kill to live here."

Arden wonders what exactly Lindsey has seen of the city in the past sixteen hours to make her feel this way, but she doesn't want to ask in front of her mother. She says, "I thought you wanted to work on a farm."

"I do," Lindsey says.

"That's, like, the opposite of living in New York City," Arden points out.

Lindsey shrugs. "I can do both, someday."

Arden reflects on how ironic it is, Lindsey's blithe confidence in the longevity of her life, even though she seems to be constantly risking everything for something shiny dangling right in front of her.

"I want to go to college here," Lindsey tells Arden's mom. "I've decided."

"Maybe you girls can come back and we can all visit some

colleges in the city together," Arden's mother says. She hesitates and looks at her daughter. "If you want to, that is. And if I'm still here."

Arden thinks for a moment about letting her mother back into her life, even if it's just in this way. "Yeah," she says at last. "I do want to."

Her mother nods, her eyes soft. Then she clears her throat and focuses on the car. "Let's see what we have here. Good God, Arden, this car looks even worse than I remember it. No wonder it broke down." She shakes her head. "Key, please."

Arden hands over the key and watches as her mother gets into the driver's seat, puts the key in the ignition, and turns it.

The Heart of Gold roars to life.

"It's working!" Arden cries.

"Oh, I fixed it," Lindsey says, looking up from her bag.

"You did what?" Arden and her mother both stare at Lindsey. "I've really missed a lot since last night. You're an auto mechanic now?" Arden asks.

"No. I got someone to look at it this morning. They said there was something wrong with the car . . ." Lindsey trailed off.

"Well, clearly," Arden said.

"No, the *carburetor*. I just forgot the word. Anyway, they did some stuff, and it should be fine now." Lindsey shrugs. "So are we going to drive home?"

Arden's mother answers for her. "If you're going to be driving in this contraption, then yes, starting as soon as possible is a good idea. You have a long trip ahead of you, and I do not want you speeding. Keep to the slow lane, and don't go over sixty miles an hour, Arden, do you hear me? And take a break if you start to feel tired."

Arden does hear her, and she knows this is all wise advice, so she will follow it—but there's something sad, too, in hearing these words from her mother, because it's clear to them both that her mother has given up her right to tell Arden what to do. At least for now. You can leave, of course—you can always leave—but then you have to deal with the consequences.

Arden and her mother exchange a long hug. "I'll see you soon," her mother says. "I love you."

And Arden believes her.

The two girls get in the car, set up the GPS, and drive away. "You will reach your destination in six hours, two minutes," says the GPS.

"Man, school tomorrow is going to be *rough*," Lindsey comments.

"So tell me what happened to you last night!" Arden bursts out. "And why didn't you respond to any of my texts?"

"My phone died, obviously. Speaking of, do you have a charger in your car? I need to call my parents. I missed church. They're probably freaking out."

"They are," Arden says. "I know they talked to my dad."

Lindsey shrugs, unperturbed.

"Aren't you worried?" Arden presses her. "I mean, they could . . ." They could do anything. Ground Lindsey forever. Put her into some sort of boarding school for juvenile delinquents. Forbid the two girls from ever seeing each other. They were parents; the choice was theirs.

Lindsey sighs. "This is who I am. This is what I did. And, Arden, what you said last night made me think . . . like, okay, I should take responsibility for the things I do.

"So yeah, I'm sure they'll be furious. And yeah, I'm worried. But these are the choices I made, and this is where I am now. So whatever the punishment is for that, I'll take it. Because you know what? I wouldn't trade in last night for anything."

"Wow," Arden says. "Why do you say that?"

"*Well.* You remember that girl I was talking to? Jamie?"

"The one with the piercing that made her nose look like a door knocker?"

"It's called a septum piercing. I thought it looked really cool on her. I'm going to get one. She said it didn't hurt that much."

"Your parents will love that, too."

"Who cares? They're not my owners. Anyway, Jamie turned out to be really cool. She's a sophomore at Pratt and she actually *lives* at Jigsaw Manor. She showed me her room—it's hidden behind a curtain by the room where the band was playing when we came in. You'd never know it was there. And the walls are covered floor to ceiling with her work. She's good. She does mixed-media collages, like really politicized stuff, about gender and race and . . ." Lindsey trails off, as she seems to run out of politicized issues to list. "Anyway," she goes on after a pause, sounding unusually shy now, "she kissed me. I mean, we kissed."

"Linds! That's fantastic!" Arden takes her eyes off the road for a moment to look at her friend, who's blushing but grinning hugely. "And how was it?"

"It was everything I'd hoped it would be," Lindsey replies simply.

Arden feels a pang. She wants to feel that way about someone.

"She actually apologized for being rude to you," Lindsey goes on. "She thought we were dating and we were having, like, a lovers' quarrel. That's why she was being kind of nasty when you met her. Once she realized you weren't trying to get inside my pants, she was totally cool."

Arden snorts a laugh. "Us, a couple?"

"Well, when you take a moment to think about it, you can see exactly why she'd assume that."

Arden takes a moment to think about it. "Good point," she agrees.

"But she wants to see me again. She said next time I'm in New York, I should get in touch, and she'll take me out on a proper date."

Arden immediately thinks of all the ways this could go wrong, *will*, most likely, go wrong. This girl could break Lindsey's heart. She could leave her for someone older, someone who doesn't live three states away. She could stand in the way of Arden and Lindsey's friendship. Lindsey could try to go to college in New York City just to be close to Jamie, only to find that she and Jamie don't even really like each other that much.

But Arden sweeps these thoughts out of her mind. Because right now, Lindsey is happy. And there will be time enough to deal with the unhappiness when it comes.

"What happened after you kissed?"

"Not much. I mean, we made out a lot. She let me sleep in her room."

Arden waggles her eyebrows up and down.

"Not like *that*. I mean, I *would* like that, someday, don't get me wrong—I just thought having my first kiss was enough for one night. I want to have something to look forward to."

"So you just slept? I'm not missing anything here?"

"We just slept. And then this morning she made me a tofu scramble and a kale smoothie for breakfast, and I told her that the Heart of Gold broke down on the highway yesterday so she called over her friend who's a mechanic to work on it."

"Her friend did a good job." Arden rubs the car's steering wheel appreciatively. They're still on city streets, so it's easy to stay well under her mother's sixty-mile-an-hour edict. "Thank you," Arden adds. "You're a miracle worker."

"I know I don't always know the right thing to do or say," Lindsey says. "Sometimes it takes me a while to figure it out. Sometimes I do the wrong thing first. But if you give me enough time, Arden"—she shrugs—"eventually I'll figure it out."

Arden never imagined that she would like having the day saved by somebody else. But today, she is surprisingly grateful.

She merges onto the highway, which is, as she's come to expect from New York City streets, filled with traffic. "Something tells me this is going to take more than six hours and two minutes."

"I hope your night was okay," Lindsey says. "I'm sorry I didn't want to leave with you. I just really wanted to see if anything was going to happen with Jamie. And honestly? I wasn't that into Peter. Don't be mad. I know he's smart and funny and talented and everything. But there was something about him . . . Like, he never even asked how we managed to track him down. He just seemed to take it for granted that he's such a big deal that random girls *would* follow him around. You know? It just seemed a little self-absorbed to me."

"Funny you should say that."

"Why?" Lindsey asks. "What happened after you guys left?"

Arden takes a deep breath, then lets it out with a laugh. "Are you ready for a long story?"

Lindsey gestures at the packed road before them. "We've got nothing but time."

All stories must come to an end

My name is Arden Huntley, and this is my journal. I'm not posting it online. I'm not showing it to anyone. I'm writing it for myself and no one else, just so that I can know what happened. And this is what happened:

The day after I came home from New York, I broke up with Chris. It was hard and it was sad, but Bianca was right: you can't get through life without hurting people, sometimes even the people you love.

"Is this just because I missed our anniversary?" he asked, confused, and when I said no, he asked, "Is there someone else, then?"

But while I broke up with Chris in part *because* of Peter, I didn't break up with him *for* Peter, and there is a difference. I could have told Chris about that one forgotten kiss on Saturday night, led him to believe it was something much more significant than it actually was, and let him blame Peter. Let there be a bad guy other than me.

"No," I told Chris. "There's nobody else."

The truth is that Chris is a great guy, and a good person. He has everything going for him. And I bet that someday I'll see him starring in a Hollywood movie, and I'll tell everyone that I knew him when. And I'm not sure that I ever *will* find someone else, or at least not anyone who makes me any happier than I was with him. Maybe that is exactly as happy as I'm capable of being. But I don't want to mistake something good for something better. And I'm going to trust that the best parts of my life haven't happened yet.

I think that movie Lindsey and I watched the last time we went to the Glockenspiel was bullshit. Hurting people, really, deeply hurting them—that isn't something you do on purpose, not unless you're some kind of sociopath. It's just a by-product of living.

In the end, my fantasy of breaking up with Chris came half-true: although we indeed broke up, he never went to extreme lengths to win me back—or any lengths, actually. I guess that's the thing about fantasies: if you're lucky, they come partway true. And usually only the part that you have control over.

I kept reading Tonight the Streets Are Ours. Not every day, but sometimes, when I was up past my bedtime and everything was too quiet, I would look at it, even though I don't know what I expected to find there. I did it even though there's something shameful in it, in consciously trying to be fooled again by Peter's stories, now that I know better.

Shortly after the start of my senior year, Peter posted that his memoir, *Tonight the Streets Are Ours*, would be released by a major publishing company, one that has published best sellers and award winners. The post in which he announced this accumulated more comments than anything else he'd ever written in his journal. It seemed as if every girl on the Internet visited Tonight the Streets Are Ours just to express her personal excitement.

Not too long after that, Peter removed every last post and replaced them with a single message saying, *My debut book will be coming out next year—click here to preorder your copy!* And I clicked there. And I preordered my copy.

The disappearance of Tonight the Streets Are Ours left me with an odd sense of loss. I'd believed that maybe I had some impact on Peter's actions, even though he didn't act like it at the time. I'd hoped maybe he would think it over and realize that I was right: this book was exploitative of Leo and Bianca, the people he claimed to love, and it was wrong to publish it.

But really I think I had no impact on Peter. Our time together was just one in a string of nights, and when your life brings you luxury and adventure every day, one more adventure makes no difference to you. And if you do not write it down—as I asked him not to—then, once enough time passes, it will be as if that night never happened at all.

When I graduated from high school, I went to a good college in a small, quiet town about two hours north of New York City. I got in partially thanks to Lindsey, who voluntarily went to Mr. Vanderpool and took responsibility for the marijuana in my locker, striking it from my transcript; and thanks to Mr. Lansdowne, who wrote an absurdly complimentary letter of recommendation on my behalf.

By the time Peter's book finally came out, I was in my second year at college. I got my copy and sat with it under a tree in the quad, and I started to read. Reading Peter's words again felt like reuniting with an old friend. But I was surprised to see that the book was written and branded as a novel, not a memoir. Fiction, not reality. All the characters' names had been changed: Bianca's not called Bianca, and even the protagonist wasn't named Peter. Leo was split into two characters: the main character's inexplicably missing big brother, and Bianca's undeserving boyfriend—no relation.

I wondered if Bianca somehow convinced Peter not to use real names or brand this story as nonfiction. I wondered if perhaps his literary agent or publishing company found out the truth about Peter's stories. I wondered whose choice this was and whether I had any impact on it. I still don't know these answers.

Despite what he said in the garden near my mom's apartment that day, Peter did no book tour, and as much as I scoured the Internet, I found very little discussion about his novel: a handful of middling reviews, a couple of interviews with him on poorly trafficked blogs. Maybe if the book were presented as nonfiction, then people would have cared, in the way that I had cared. Maybe it's only in fiction that Peter's story seems— as *Kirkus Reviews* put it—"self-congratulatory, navel-gazing, and aimless." His book was published to a nearly universal lack of interest and then it disappeared, leaving behind almost no trace, like a rock sinking to the bottom of a very deep pond, or a single individual living high up in some big building in some very big city.

My friends and I visit New York City periodically to go to shows and museums, always by train or bus—I never try to drive the Heart of Gold as far as I did that time. My mom is no longer there; she moved home eventually, and she and my father are working things out, or trying to, anyway. Roman reports that Mom lets him eat school lunches now, even though they're less nutritious, and Dad hasn't missed one of his games yet this year, even though he is once again on a last-place team. Whenever I go to New York, I walk around outside, I ride the subways, and I look at the face of every person I pass, because any one of them could be Peter or Bianca. But none of them ever has been. As Peter himself once wrote: there are a million different New Yorks, all layered on top of one another yet never intersecting.

After successfully graduating from high school, Lindsey got an internship at an organic farm in Pennsylvania. As so often happens with her, Lindsey forgot all about her New York City dream. She did at last learn to drive—not just a car, but a trac-tor, too. And Jamie did break Lindsey's heart, and it was indeed sad, but now Lindsey is madly in love with a stable hand at her farm, and Jamie and her stupid nose ring are just distant memories.

I miss Lindsey every day. We don't always make time to talk, we don't have the same friends, and when Lindsey needs saving—which she has many times, and certainly will again—I'm not there to catch her. But when we do find each other, at home in Cumberland on holidays, or on the phone in those rare moments when Lindsey is resting and I'm awake, it's as if nothing between us has changed.

I used to think that loving somebody meant sacrificing anything for them. I thought it meant writing a blank check. I thought it meant that you would die without each other. But it turns out that Peter was right about that, too: death and a broken heart are not the same.

These days I think that love is not so dramatic as all that. Maybe loving somebody means simply they bring out the best in you, and you bring out the best in them—so that together, you are always the best possible versions of yourselves.

You were promised a love story. And this is mine.

Acknowledgments

I am tremendously grateful to all who have supported my writing career and helped make *Tonight the Streets Are Ours* a reality. To name some of them:

Thank you to Joy Peskin, who has always believed in me. To Molly Brouillette, for her creativity and enthusiasm. And to the rest of the extraordinary team at Macmillan Children's Publishing Group, including but not limited to Lauren Burniac, Angie Chen, Beth Clark, Liz Fithian, Angus Killick, Kathryn Little, Karla Reganold, Holly Ruck, and Mary Van Akin. You know how to treat an author right.

To Stephen Barbara: every day I feel lucky to have you on my side.

To everyone at Foundry Literary + Media—especially Jess Regel and Yfat Reiss Gendel—and to Michelle Weiner and her team at CAA.

To Venetia Gosling and the rest of the group at Macmillan UK for bringing my work to a whole other continent of readers.

To Kate Hurley, a ray of sunshine and my defender against inconsistencies.

To my writing partner, Rebecca Serle, for her unwavering love and support. And to the entire crew: Emily Heddleson, Lexa Hillyer, Lauren Oliver, Jess Rothenberg, and Courtney Sheinmel. Please let's never stop being Type A and talking about ourselves.

To all my friends and colleagues—especially Kendra Levin, Brian Pennington, and Allison Smith—who have celebrated with me the good times, helped me through the rough times, and understood when I just have to stay home and write.

To the alternative spaces and parties throughout New York City, both past and present, that inspired Jigsaw Manor, especially Rubulad and Death By Audio. And to the bloggers whose work I've loved over the years, especially Brendan Jay Sullivan.

To one of my favorite authors, Anne Spencer Lindbergh, for introducing me to the concept of reckless loyalty.

Thanks to all who have taken the time to read my books, and who have told me the ways in which my writing has affected them. I could never find the words to express how much your support means to me.

And thank you to my parents, Amy and Michael Sales. I love you totally and completely.